The Fault

Alden Studebaker

Anne & David —

Enjoy The story!

Alden Studebaker

October 21, 2020

For information, https://aldenstudebaker.com

ISBN: 9798696226514

Cover: Photo by the author, San Andreas Fault, Palmdale

This novel is fictional. Any references to actual events, businesses, organizations, government agencies and locations are only intended to give the story a sense of genuineness. Any resemblance to actual persons living or dead is entirely coincidental.

First Edition: Copyright © 2011 by Alden Studebaker.
Printed by Author House, Bloomington, Indiana
www.authorhouse.com
First published, 08/05/2011
ISBN: 978-1-4634-4002-2 (sc)
ISBN: 978-1-4634-4001-5 (hc)
ISBN: 978-1-4634-4000-8 (ebk)
Library of Congress Control Number: 2011912971

Other books by Alden Studebaker

Wisdom for a Lifetime in the 21st Century
How to Get the Bible Off the Shelf and Into Your Hands

Hoosieritis – The Contagious Condition That Is Indiana

The Grid

Not Just Any Bag of Bones
(editor & publisher)

For more information:
https://aldenstudebaker.com

Dedication

To my dear, departed friend, Joseph Della Sorte, who exemplified the creative spirit.

Acknowledgements

Donna Studebaker, my wife, and chief editor, for her expert advice and loving inspiration.

Public Television's travel hosts, Rick Steves and Rudy Maxa, for the Istanbul segments of their popular shows.

Nobel Prize Literature recipient, Orhan Pamuk, and his books, especially, *Istanbul: Memories of a City*, which acquainted me with both his beautiful writing and hometown.

California State University, Northridge and the California Institute of Technology, where I spent two afternoons walking around taking photos and pondering possible scenes.

U.S. and California Geological Surveys.

Kandilli Rasathanesi ve Deprem Araştırma Enstitüsü Sismoloji Laboratuvarı (Kandilli Observatory and Earthquake Research Institute), upon which I based the fictional Istanbul Seismological Institute.

National Park Service, Manzanar National Historic Site.

Chapter 1

THE SUN'S RAYS peeked out over the horizon and streamed across the desert setting both rabbitbrush and sagebrush ablaze with the fire of Mount Sinai, as another day began in the Antelope Valley. The calm coolness of the early morning air belied the wind and heat that would soon pervade the atmosphere. Now was the ideal time to be outside for a walk. With his heart pounding from the first hundred yards, and his left rotator cuff strained by the tenacious but tethered Molly, Jose Martinez quickened his steps in an attempt to keep pace with his overeager canine.

"Get back here you stupid mutt!"

Molly turned toward Jose, then ignored her master's insulting command and galloped up the northern face of the escarpment, a hill pushed up by the enormous geophysical forces of the underlying San Andreas Fault. Jose stopped, caught his breath, and firmly reeled her in from the pursuit of a bounding jackrabbit.

"Hey you, sit down, damn it, I'm in charge here!"

Staring back at him in defiance of his corrective measures, Molly nonetheless parked her hindquarters on the dusty trail.

Jose had reluctantly accepted the Irish Setter from relatives who could no longer handle her rambunctious personality within the confines of their LA apartment. The Martinez family's four-bedroom Palmdale tract home seemed to be the logical solution to Molly's extensive need for space, as well as Jose's exercise routine. Now he questioned the wisdom of accommodating this crazy, red dog. But, Jose could hear his doctor's words nagging at him, "You walk that dog every day, cut back on the rich food, and you can avoid having open heart surgery and type 2 diabetes like your brother." That thought alone helped Jose make peace with his new pet, but he often wondered who was really walking whom.

Without warning, Molly was off to the races after a second jackrabbit, dragging her master further up the hill in hot pursuit. Having seen the movie *Funny Farm* featuring Chevy Chase and an Irish Setter who always ran away, Jose knew better than to let go of the rope. He would spend hours searching the neighborhood for her when she got loose. Once found, Molly would glance up, twitch her eyebrows as she weighed her options, and then take off running. Usually, Jose would have to sneak up from behind and tackle her like a football linebacker. Then, with the choke chain firmly around her neck, he would lecture her all the way home about her flaky Irish Setter ways. This conversation was mostly in vain, but it gave Jose the illusion of control.

As they were nearing the crest of the hill, and in anticipation of his mountain climbing victory, Jose slowed his pace while his lungs strained for a few more molecules of oxygen. From the summit, a good three hundred feet above the valley floor, an expansive panorama unfolded revealing the patchwork quilt of subdivisions that made up the cities of Palmdale, Lancaster and Quartz Hill. Jose always took a moment to locate his house among the dozens in his neighborhood. However, this morning, Molly would not permit even a moment of sightseeing. She fervently kept tugging in a westerly direction with single-minded intent. Jose shook his head and muttered, "What's that idiot dog up to now?"

The Molly-Jose tag team lurched sharply toward a manzanita bush off to the left of the crest trail. Molly abruptly stopped and began sniffing something lying on the ground. As Jose approached he was startled to see a man lying face down, a light blue UCLA baseball cap on his head.

"Hey man, are you okay?" Jose bent down and nudged him with the back of his hand.

Molly began barking with an ear-piercing staccato cadence.

"Shut up!"

The sharp angle and intense brightness of the morning sun blinded his vision. Jose shaded his eyes with one hand while he tapped the man on the shoulder with his other hand. A lack of response triggered queasiness in the pit of his stomach. Unbeknownst to him, the man's bright red sweatshirt concealed the blood from a gunshot wound on his left side. Jose pulled out his cell phone and called home.

"Honey, there's this guy up here on the hill. Molly found him. He doesn't look so good. I think he might be dead!"

"What did you say, Joe? A dead man?"

Rosa couldn't believe her husband's words.

"Yeah, he's not moving even after I touched him a little. Maybe I should call the police."

"You better call the office and tell them you'll be late for your shift. I can't believe it, Joe. You really think he's dead?"

"I told you, he's not moving. It's kind of spooky. Don't tell the kids, please. It'll freak 'em out. Gotta go. Bye."

Jose clicked off his phone, punched in 9-1-1, reported the situation to the duty operator, then sat down on a rock and began praying over the unknown man. Although he was raised Catholic, at Rosa's insistence the entire family attended an evangelical church. Jose especially liked the up-tempo music and the pastor's theatrical sermons, but he wasn't crazy about the restrictions the church placed on his lifestyle all in the name of family values. Like most guys he enjoyed certain pastimes such as having a beer with his friends, going to Dodger games, or watching particular television programs. He especially liked reruns of *Married with Children,* much to Rosa's chagrin: "Joe, why do you want to watch that garbage? You know what Pastor says about shows that promote promiscuity and immoral behavior. We don't want to have a family like that one! You don't want the girls to watch it, do you, Joe?"

Naturally, Jose didn't want his girls, Martha and Maria, now high-school-aged, emulating Kelly Bundy's slutty behavior, or referring to the Martinez family as "losers not quitters." But, he still thought it was a funny show, an escape from the drudgery of his two-plus-hour a day commute to a job that simply involved more driving. Perhaps Rosa was concerned that through osmosis Jose would turn into a beer drinking, potty-mouthed, couch potato like Al Bundy. Jose was too busy for hedonistic pursuits, not to mention needing to meet his dog's fitness requirements.

Prayer was all he could offer this seemingly lifeless man in front of him. Before long, two deputies from the Los Angeles County Sheriff Department's Palmdale station climbed up the trail from the subdivision.

"That's quite a hike up here. You do this every day?" asked Deputy Robert Chin.

"No, just three times a week, before I go to work."

"And, where's that?"

"I drive a Metrolink bus down below. Hey, thanks for reminding me, I've gotta call them right away. Looks like I might be late for work."

"First, we'll need to take your statement, Mr.?"

"Martinez, Jose Martinez."

The second deputy checked the man for a pulse, "Bob, he's DOA."

"He's really dead?"

Deputy Chin and Jose approached the body, but Molly beat them to it and repeated her previous barking antics.

"Sir, could you call off your dog?"

"With pleasure, officer! Molly, get your butt back here right now, you bad dog!" Jose pulled hard on the twenty-foot rope snapping her away from the second deputy, who was conferring with his partner.

"Better call in crime scene and another team to secure

the area. This guy was definitely shot." Then Deputy Chin continued his interrogation of Jose, "When did you find him?"

"I was walking up here with my dog around 6:30. I called you guys right away when I found him. Hey, am I in any kind of trouble, officer?"

"No, but you understand that we have to get all the facts of the case. Have you seen this man before?"

Jose glanced down at the dead man, trying to get a better look. "I'm not sure, it's kind of hard to see his whole face in that position. I don't know. A lot people walk around up here. You can't beat the view."

"I see what you mean. It's very nice. Real shame this guy won't get to see it anymore. Did you happen to notice anyone else walking around this morning?"

"No, not really. Sometimes there are these two forty-something women walking together, a blonde and a brunette, but I didn't see them this morning. I can't imagine them killing this guy. They're always friendly and say, 'Hi.'"

"I'm going to need your address and phone number, Mr. Martinez, for my notes just in case we need to ask you any more questions. Do you live near here?"

"Sure, no problem. I live right down there," pointing toward his house. "It's 38755 Joshua Tree Lane. 661-555-2973. Can I go, now? I'm, like, gonna be really late for my shift."

"Yeah, go ahead. We're pretty much done here," Deputy Chin finished jotting down Jose's contact information, then reached in his pocket for a business card and handed it to him, "If something comes to mind, give us call. I mean anything. We need all the facts."

"You sound like that dude on *Dragnet,* uhh . . . Sergeant Friday!"

"Yeah, we get that a lot."

"Hey, thanks. I hope you guys can figure out what happened," Jose said as he pulled hard on Molly's rope, in an attempt to guide her back down the hill.

"That's a real frisky dog you got there. He's real pretty with all that hair on his legs."

"Feathers. They call them feathers. Yeah, if she wasn't so damn good looking she'd be doin' time in the pound, if you know what I mean."

"Take it easy, Mr. Martinez. We'll be in touch if we have any more questions."

The Tugboat Molly towed Jose toward his home, his anxious wife, sleeping kids, and old green pickup truck.

Chapter 2

The earth trembles. The force of the shock knocks customers and employees to their knees while boxes and cans spill all over the floor of the convenience store. He struggles to pick himself up when another temblor hits, pitching him against the cooler filled with bottled soda. Then the shaking ceases. Mother Nature's reprieve provides everyone barely enough time to hightail it for the safety of the parking lot before a third wave strikes with building collapsing force . . .

ALEX DEMURJIAN'S CELL PHONE went off zapping him out of the subtle lucidity of his personal dream realm back into the heavy materiality of the terrestrial world, its images eerily lingering. Lying on his back, his eyes stuck together with sleep's glue, Alex reached his right hand over to the nightstand and fumbled around for the source of his early morning disruption.

"Hawhhhhhhh, hello."

"Lex, it's David. Have you seen Cal?"

Two nights ago, Alex, David Horita, Cal Stover, John Lopez, and the rest of Alex's Cal Tech comrades had celebrated David's lottery winnings at the Avanti Café.

"No, not since the other night. Why? What's up?"

"Cal was supposed to be here for his shift this morning and hasn't shown. We tried his cell but he's not answering. You know how un-Cal like this is."

"No kidding. He's never late for anything. Didn't he say something about going back up to that mine near Palmdale? He seemed pretty obsessed about it. Did you try Katy? Hell, his own girlfriend ought to know where he is."

"No, I think she's in the Bay Area on business. Hey, but now that you mention it, he just wouldn't shut up about his hypothesis that the mine is putting stress on the San Andreas Rift Zone. I'll tell you, it all seems kind of far-fetched to me, but you know Cal. He can't help himself, always throwing out these wacky New Age ideas about the earth being a living being, and that we humans are like an infestation of termites eating away at the structure, until one day it all collapses. You have to admit, that pretty well pushes the envelope of standard geological knowledge. Even if the mining company is using munitions to extract gold, I can't imagine the explosions being sufficient to trigger a mega-quake like he's always suggesting. When's your first class?"

"Not 'til this afternoon. I was asleep when you called."

"Sorry, dude, I thought you'd already be up. I forget how you professor types are. You just show up for class, pour rocks into the students' empty little heads, and then go home."

"Don't mess with me this early in the morning! I haven't had any coffee yet. If I hear from Cal I'll tell him you've sent the Marines out looking for him."

"Thanks. I'm sure there's a logical explanation for his absence. I just wonder what's going on with him lately. He seemed pretty edgy. Talk to you later. Bye."

Alex clicked off his cell and collapsed back in his bed knowing that the likelihood of getting any more sleep was minimal at best. His thoughts returned to the Avanti Café and Cal's sermon.

"We geologists cannot idly sit by and allow reckless corporate greed to dictate how we treat the planet, especially right here in our own backyard, and given the potential for destruction that this fault possesses. Don't you think it's just insane for a mining company to be exploring for gold in of all places, the San Andreas Fault?"

Of course, Alex had observed that by the time Cal had made his speech he'd already downed his fourth Corona and consumed at least half of a large duck sausage pizza. The toxicity level of this chemical combination would be enough to make anyone say that a mere firecracker could trigger an eight-pointer. Nonetheless, he wondered if Cal's disappearance might be connected with his rallying cry. Maybe he got lost up there walking around the Rift Zone, or worse, fell and had an accident. Alex dismissed these negative thoughts and returned to the day at hand. This morning he would take things in a leisurely manner. His Geology of the Planet Earth class wasn't until twelve-thirty, so he would avoid the early morning rush up into the Valley. After class he had office hours for student appointments, and a departmental staff meeting at four o'clock.

Although many of his geology department colleagues at Cal State Northridge found it beneath themselves to teach elementary geology, Alex actually reveled in it. Sure, Geology 101 was a cakey course, but when you love rocks, mineralogy, and plate tectonics as much as he did, you wanted the first whack at introducing the subject to the blotter-like undergraduate mind. Alex seemed to have a knack for taking the complexity of science and making the subject interesting and immediately usable for a student. "Dr. D," as his students called him, since everybody seemed to mess up the pronunciation of Demurjian, was perhaps the most popular professor on campus. Somehow the word always seemed to get out, even to incoming freshman, that his Geology 101 class was the most enjoyable way to fulfill the basic science requirement. No one fell asleep in his class, plus the field trips he led to Vasquez Rocks and the Devil's Punchbowl helped to underscore that the earth was not just a solid mass of rock, but a living, moving planet. His motto: "You have to leave the classroom and go where the rocks actually lie in order to truly grasp geology."

Alex's passion for geology began when he was just a child. During recess at Los Feliz Elementary School he could be found surveying the rocks on the playground rather than playing dodge ball with the rest of the kids. Later, his high school chemistry teacher, Mr. Stevenson, noticed his interest in earth sciences and encouraged him to pursue a career in geology. His recommendation, plus a 1,490 SAT score landed Alex a substantial scholarship at Cal Tech. Monies from the Glendale Armenian Business Association enabled him to focus on his studies and obtain his doctorate in geology a year ahead of schedule. Having his Uncle George on the scholarship committee certainly hadn't hurt his cause. At age twenty-five he became an associate professor at California State University at Northridge.

Alex's first floor one-bedroom condo was within reasonable driving distance of the campus, and close to all his favorite Hillhurst haunts. After dressing in his signature "Dr. D" uniform consisting of a light-blue dress shirt, gray slacks, and black shoes, he took the stairs down to the parking garage to his car, a silver VW Jetta TDi.

Like most native Californians, Alex was particularly proud of his steed, and had spent hours online searching for a reasonably priced one. Much to his delight the perfect car appeared at a dealership in Ohio for thousands less than he could find locally. A quick phone call sealed the deal and a college student in need of cash flew back East and drove the car out to LA for him.

He slowly turned the ignition key, instinctively paused to allow the glow plugs to engage, and then completed the firing sequence. The mild click-clacking noise of the engine pleasantly reminded him that he could beat just about any car on the road in one department, fuel economy. The commute to Northridge and everywhere else Angelenos drove proved this out. On a bad tank he would get forty-three miles per gallon, and with fuel often pushing five bucks a gallon, only hybrids could come close to these savings. His father, Tevos, would often rib him about his penurious choice of personal transportation, referring to the car as Alex's "Peterbilt" when the only thing it had in common with an eighteen-wheeler was its use of No. 2 diesel fuel. In spite of his father's jest, Alex loved the way the car could patch rubber from a full stop, and the curious glances he received from drive-thru cashiers at fast food restaurants upon hearing its distinctive bus-like sound.

Although the weather was sunny, in true LA fashion, rather than walk, Alex drove the two blocks from his condo on Rodney down Finley to the Bean Head. After hunting for a parking space in the lot the expresso shop shared with the supermarket across from the store, he spotted an empty space someone had recently vacated. In a short time he reached the front of the line.

"Will it be the usual, an extra-large mocha?" asked the cheerful clerk whose nametag read, "Maribel."

"Yeah, you always remember my order don't you. How do you do that?"

"It's my job to know what everyone wants before they ask. Saves time, don't you think? Maybe they should promote me to manager so I can teach all the employees to guess what each customer wants," she said pointing to her head with both index fingers.

"I imagine you would make an excellent manager. I'll be sure to put a word in for you with the company president," Alex joked as he handed her his Bean Head loyalty card for validation.

"Thanks. It'll be ready in a minute. You know where to pick it up," her eyes pointing to the counter on his left.

A minute later Alex retrieved his coffee and headed for an open chair at a table where two men were seated reading newspapers.

"How's it going, Jack? Haven't seen you here in a while," asked Alex.

"Been out on location this past week directing the lighting for that new DiCaprio film. Hey, did you know that his mother lives just around the block from here? He bought her a neat little house. It's nice to see a son take care of his mother like that," Jack stuck his nose back in the paper.

"I'm glad to hear that you're getting some decent work. I was worried we might need to take up a collection just to keep you whole. Got any residuals lately?"

"Residuals!" said the other man, Hans, "Haven't you heard that they're making a DVD out of that mini-series Jack did back in the 70s?"

"Yeah, I might make enough on that deal to keep me stocked up on beer. So, how's our professor doing today? You look dressed for class."

"I'm doing fine, except for this really weird dream I had last night. It's been bothering me since I woke up."

"Lex, we're all ears," said Hans leaning toward him, "Dream interpretation is one of my hobbies."

"Well, I was in this convenience store buying some donuts when an earthquake started shaking the place like crazy, not once, but three times, and each time the quakes were stronger. All I remember before I woke up was being outside the store watching it crash to the ground in shambles. It was a total disaster. Then my cell went off. That was it."

"Hmm, it's quite obvious, Lex, you've got rocks on the brain! Maybe you need a break from all that geology and earthquake stuff you're teaching."

"You should give up eating donuts, even in your dreams. It's bad for the blood sugars," added Jack waving his finger and blinking his eye.

"Maybe so, I've been teaching three classes this semester, plus two field trips. At least I don't have to teach summer school this year."

"You need a vacation. Thinking about going anywhere special?"

"I don't know. I'm sure I'll come up with something worth doing. I kind of liked that trip I took to Missouri a couple of years ago. I walked all around the New Madrid seismic zone."

"Lex, that's not the kind of vacation Jack and I were thinking of. Were we, Jack?"

"Oh, no."

"You need to go somewhere that's fun and frivolous. How about Paris or Berlin? My sister, Frieda, lives in Berlin, and I know she wouldn't mind showing you around, or at least pointing you to Bus 100. You've got to do something totally unrelated to your profession, something that won't give you seismological nightmares. Let me give her a call," Hans pulled out his cell phone and began searching for his sister in his speed dial.

"Hold on, guys! I know you're just trying to be helpful, but is a vacation going to help me? I mean, everywhere you go, there's the earth. And, everywhere I go, there's me."

Chapter 3

DETECTIVE JULIUS JACKSON was only two years away from retirement when a drug bust gone bad marred his distinguished twenty-eight year career with the Los Angeles County Sheriff's Department. As details of the incident trickled out it became apparent that in the resulting firefight with Pablo Rodriguez, kingpin of East LA's notorious Los Tiburones gang, Detective Jackson's gun had caused the death of not only Rodriguez, but also his girlfriend, Melinda Garcia, and an innocent bystander, a nine-year old boy, Hector. Although Jackson was exonerated of all wrongdoing, the outcry from the Latino community was brutal and vociferous. His public and personal apologies to Hector's family were unable to stave off calls for his dismissal from the force as well as demands that criminal charges be filed. The ensuing media frenzy prompted the department to reassign him to the newly opened Palmdale station, seventy miles away from East LA in the hot, dusty, windy Antelope Valley.

Of course, he wasn't thrilled with his reassignment, but took his banishment with the grace of a professional. If only he'd been transferred to the Carson, Compton, or Lennox stations where he could finish his career closer to his South Central home. However, the department brass seized upon his misfortune to beef up the new station with a seasoned veteran like Jackson.

Even though the drive up north each day was reverse commute that was not much solace when driving the 405 any time of the day or night.

"Whaddya got, Bob?" asked the detective as he reached the crest of the hill.

"Crime scene just finished their preliminary investigation and are heading back to the shop. The coroner is due here any moment. Looks like this guy took a slug in the gut possibly from somewhere in that direction," Deputy Chin pointed southeast down the escarpment.

"Any ID?"

"He still had his wallet on him . . . a William Calvin Stover of Punahou Street in Altadena, and get this, he worked for the U.S. Geological Survey at Cal Tech."

"No shit! Cal Tech! What's a genius like him doing up here so far from home? There's nothing up here but rocks. You suppose he was looking at rocks?"

"Could be, but most people don't get shot while looking at rocks. We did find a small pair of binoculars in his sweatshirt pocket, his cell phone, and a pretty fancy digital camera."

"Yeah, and rocks don't shoot people for looking at them, or taking their picture, now do they, Bob?"

"Not in my experience. But, you know how these Cal Tech guys are, always on TV after every earthquake pointing out all the little details and comparing them with the past big quake. As if that's reassuring to the rest of us civilians who are scared shitless. Maybe one of these rocks around here disagreed with one of his seismological reports."

Detective Jackson raised his eyebrow and turned toward Deputy Chin.

"I was just kidding! He was probably up here doing some field work. You do know we're standing right on top of the Bulge."

"Whaddya mean, the Bulge?"

"The San Andreas Fault, man, the friggin' Palmdale Bulge! They say it's going to pop someday, and when it does, you're going to wish you were in Ohio."

"My mother's from Cleveland. You trying to be funny?"

"Nope."

"Didn't think so."

Detective Jackson walked over to the edge of the southerly drop off and pointed down the slope, "Bob, what's that place down there, with all the buildings and the big fence. Looks like some kind of secret government installation."

"That's Stein Mining. It's a gold mine."

"Gold?"

"Yeah, gold, precious metals. The company has been around for years. Bought up all this land back in the 50s when it was dirt-cheap. Now they're digging into the fault. Didn't you see the article in the *Times* about it a couple of months ago? They said that the action of the tectonic plates forces the veins of gold upward. All they have to do is bore down deep enough to extract it."

"I don't read the *Times*. Too depressing. It just doesn't make any sense for this Cal Tech nerd to be lying dead as a doornail all the way up here with his face in the dirt. Rocks don't pull triggers. Make sure crime scene gets the ballistics report to me right away. Find out who he's been calling on his phone, and see if they can get any photos out of that camera."

"Will do, Detective."

"One thing is for certain, this dude didn't get shot by a pile of rocks. Somebody pulled a trigger. I always say, when a lead looks dry, follow the money. You say they mine gold down there. Maybe we should have a look see at what's behind that fence. See you later, Bob."

Detective Jackson carefully made his way back down the hill in his jet black Johnston Murphy dress shoes avoiding the sharp rocks and dust as best he could. The trail led to the top of the Desert Ridge subdivision and his white Cadillac CTS, license plate, "DOC-JAY."

As Detective Jackson opened the door he mumbled to himself, "Looks like this Palmdale assignment ain't gonna be so boring after all."

Chapter 4

ALEX ALWAYS HAD K-EARTH 101 programmed into his car stereo. During commercials he'd punch in Jack-FM to see what they were playing, but K-EARTH played music that he could relate to, even if most of it appealed to a slightly older generation. He sang along with all the classic rockers, like Jimi Hendrix and the Stones, and tapping his fingers on the middle of the steering wheel with the maniacal intensity of Keith Moon. The late morning traffic up the Hollywood, Ventura and San Diego freeways was light as he had anticipated. From the Nordhoff exit it was just three suburban miles to the Northridge campus. CSUN's science buildings were constructed in a row with connecting walkways on the second and third floors. These architecturally uninspiring structures, surrounded by tall, mature trees, were later renamed for trees from the more prosaic Science 1-4. The geology department was located in Live Oak Hall.

"Good afternoon, class! Today we're going to discuss seismology. This shouldn't be something that is new to any of you since we live in this extraordinarily seismologically active part of the earth we call California. Is there anyone here who has not experienced an earthquake?"

Not a hand was raised.

"Didn't think so. Okay, let's get started —"

A hand finally shot up from a girl in the back row catching Professor Demurjian in mid-sentence.

"Yes, uh . . . Miss Daniels, isn't it?"

"Yes, Laura Daniels," came a sheepish voice.

Alex scratched his head in disbelief, "I find it amazing that you have never experienced an earthquake. In all of my years of teaching this class no one has ever raised their hand to that question. Just where are you from, Laura Daniels?"

"Warsaw."

"Warsaw . . . Poland?" cocking his head to the side.

"Indiana."

The entire class burst out laughing.

"All right, I'll grant you that Indiana isn't exactly earthquake country, however, everyone should have already read up on seismology in chapters sixteen through twenty of the textbook."

Moaning echoed across the room.

"Hopefully this little review will help you with the exam next Thursday. First, can someone define the term 'fault' for us? Yes, Roxy," Dr. "D" began his Geology 101 lecture.

Roxanne Romero dropped her hand and responded, "A fault is a fracture in the earth's crust where one side or block moves parallel to the other."

"That works for me, thanks, Roxy. So, let's explore faults further. Who would like to describe for us an event involving a strike-slip fault? Anyone?"

"1906, San Francisco Bay area," Charles Ing beat everyone else to the buzzer.

"Good choice, Charles, now, tell us more about that quake."

"Jee, Dr. D, I think just about everybody knows about that one"

"Hey, man, you picked it, now enlighten us."

"Okay. The quake hit in three phases, the first shaking lasted about forty seconds, followed by a ten-second pause, then a stronger thirty-second temblor. At the epicenter, twenty-five miles northwest of San Francisco, horizontal displacement along the fault exceeded twenty feet. Devastation was widespread, a XII on the Mercalli scale. It's estimated to have been an 8.2 on the Richter scale."

"And why don't we know the precise magnitude of this earthquake?"

"Because the Richter scale hadn't been invented yet?"

"That's correct. Now, can someone tell me the difference between the Mercalli and the Richter scales?"

Richard Ochoa took a stab at the question, "I think the Mercalli scale has to do with how humans experience an earthquake, such as whether you can stay standing up or if a building collapses. The Richter scale is more scientific, and uses seismographs to record and determine the energy released by the quake."

"Thanks, Richard. Okay, let us better understand Dr. Charles Richter's scale, who by the way was a professor where?"

"Cal Tech!" said Roxy.

"Exactly, Cal Tech, my old school, but he was way, way before my time." The class laughed in unison. "Those of you who have rocks on the brain, like me, might consider going to grad school there, even though I'd certainly miss your face around here. Do we still use Dr. Richter's scale when measuring earthquakes? Richard."

"Uh, I'm not sure, Dr. D. I think so."

"Who can help Richard here?"

Utter stillness filled the classroom while the students pondered Dr. D's seemingly simple question. Finally, Charles broke the silence, "The Richter scale was based on using torsion seismometers here in Southern California. It measured ML or local magnitude. With the technological advances in seismometers and their placement into a worldwide network, improved measurements of an earthquake's magnitude have been developed that measure body-wave and surface wave magnitude as well. For larger earthquakes, Mw, or moment magnitude, is the most accurate measurement."

"All right, Charles. Apparently you are the only one who read the chapters in depth," Dr. D. scanned the room looking for a penitent face or two. "Now, for the sake of our discussion, we'll use the Richter scale for the ML, or local magnitude for my next question. If we accept the 8.2

magnitude estimate for the 1906 quake, about how much more energy was released by it than the 7.1 Loma Prieta quake of 1989, which, I might add, was also on what fault system? Charles, you want to help us again?"

"Sorry, Dr. D. I forgot to mention that the 1906 quake was on the San Andreas Fault. To answer your question, with each additional magnitude point there is an exponential increase in the strength of the quake. It's based on a logarithmic scale. The 1906 quake was roughly about thirty-two times stronger."

"Music to my ears! Thanks, again, Charles. Now, let's get closer to home. Who can tell us about a blind-thrust fault? What makes it different than a strike-slip fault? Yes, Brian."

"Wasn't the Northridge quake caused by a blind-thrust fault?"

"Right! I think we can all remember where we were when that one hit, in bed, except for our lone Hoosier comrade. Now, how was this quake different from the 1906 one?"

"A blind-thrust fault is where one side of the fault is moving over another with all the movement taking place below the ground. That's why it's called, 'blind.' There was no surface displacement like in 1906 or 1989."

"Good, Brian. Well said. So, in essence, what's the difference between a strike-slip and a blind-thrust fault? Charles?"

"One fault slips sideways and the other more up and down."

"Well put. In fact, we were the ones who were blind to the fault's existence. Now, can anyone predict an earthquake?" Another moment of silence filled the classroom as no one dared respond.

"If any of you can prove that you have, I'll place your name in nomination for a Nobel Prize and personally pay your way to grad school. You see, no one has ever been able to predict when or where an earthquake will occur, not even your family dog or cat. You may have seen Scruffy or Boots jump around and act crazy before a quake, but no scientific correlation has been made between animal behavior and an impending movement along a fault line. If that were the case every seismologist from California to Japan to Italy would be talking to animals. I think we'll leave that task to Dr. Dolittle."

Everyone laughed.

"Let me throw out another earthquake myth at you. Is there such a thing as earthquake weather?"

"Yeah, I think so. Doesn't it always get kind of hot before a quake? My father always said, 'When the Santa Anas are blowing there'll be an earthquake for sure.'"

Dr. D. turned his head and glanced toward Richard, "My father used to say that to me too. He still does. But, if we look at the evidence earthquakes can happen in all kinds of weather. Let's look at our own Northridge quake in reference to Richard's and my father's weather prediction theory. When did it happen? January 17, 1994, at four thirty in the morning. Not a particularly hot month, even in southern California, and the temperature was a nippy forty-two degrees Fahrenheit when it hit. Ooooh . . . chilly weather!"

Dr. D. rubbed his hands on his biceps and contorted his face as if he were freezing.

"Not earthquake weather. Listen, there is no such thing as earthquake weather! When there's an earthquake in Alaska and it's twenty below zero the local residents don't say to themselves, 'I knew it! Earthquake weather.' We can't use weather to predict earthquakes. I really wish there was a foolproof method of anticipating a quake and warning the public, but weather isn't it," he paused.

"Let's think about it scientifically for a moment. Have you ever been down in a cave, a deep one? On one of my trips back east I went to Mammoth Cave National Park in

Kentucky. And no matter what time of year it is, winter or summer, those caves are a constant fifty-six degrees."

Laura Daniel's spoke up, "We went down there on vacation a few years ago, and, oh, my God, we had to wear sweat tops even though it was the middle of July."

"There's some corroborating evidence for you! Thanks, Laura. My point is that weather only affects the surface of the earth, and not so much the subterranean world miles beneath the surface where earthquakes have their beginnings."

"So, Dr. D., should I tell my father that earthquake weather is a bunch of crap?"

"Richard, don't bother. My father still doesn't believe me when I tell him, and I've got a Ph.D. in this stuff. He learned about earthquake weather from his grandfather who brought the idea over from the old country, so it must be right. Better to let them believe in their Santa Claus and Easter Bunny. Does he also say that California is going to fall into the ocean?"

"God, I hope that doesn't happen," said Roxy, "I don't know how to swim!"

The class burst into laughter, again. "You don't know how to swim? Get out!"

"Shut up, Richard!"

"Don't worry, California isn't going anywhere fast. The San Andreas Fault may be the boundary between the North American and Pacific Plates, and it does cut across much of the state from end to end, but there's no danger of us going under the sea. Since these plates slip past each other at a rate of about fifty millimeters per year if we wait long enough, about ten million years, we should be able to see the Golden Gate Bridge from LA. Just consider the fuel savings alone for anyone having to drive up to San Francisco, and it wouldn't even take an hour!"

The class was in pandemonium.

"Okay, okay. Let me ask you a very serious question. What is the leading cause of death from earthquakes?"

Charles was quick to answer, "UMB's."

There was a moment of silence while the rest of the class pondered the meaning of the acronym.

Finally, Roxy spoke up, "I thought it was UFO's."

"Aliens?" asked Richard.

"No, I read it. Un . . . something, flying, objects."

"Charles?"

"Unreinforced masonry buildings."

"Thank you. Poorly engineered and constructed buildings kill people, especially unreinforced masonry buildings, or UMB's. Sometimes they're called, URM buildings. Roxy was on the right track with her UFO theory, because these buildings break apart into unsecured flying objects during an earthquake. And, what objects are most likely to take flight?"

The class responded randomly, "Bricks, stone, glass, concrete . . ."

"Exactly, just like this brick," Dr. D picked up a red brick from beneath his desk and held it up in the air above his head. "Now, imagine this rapping you across the noggin."

"Ouch!"

"Ouch is right," pointing the brick at the responder slouching in the back row of the classroom. "That's why we don't build brick houses in California anymore like they do elsewhere. Bricks usually become dangerous projectiles in an earthquake. Don't kid yourself, they can kill you. The only fatality during the 1992 magnitude 7.3 Landers quake was a three-year old boy from Massachusetts who was visiting family near the quake. He didn't die because the earth swallowed him up into a deep chasm. He died while he innocently slept in a sleeping bag beneath a fireplace in the living room. Care to guess what the fireplace was made of? Unreinforced masonry, bricks and stone, just like this one."

A hush fell over the class while Dr. D. paced the floor holding the brick in his right hand looking at many of them directly in the eyes.

"The next time you lay down for a nap, or pitch a tent, take a look around you and above you and ask yourself, 'What could possibly hit me or someone else if an earthquake struck?' If you remember anything from this class, let it be this."

He put the brick down on the table.

"Now, let's look at one of the main causes of earthquakes, plate tectonics. Again, what fault lies along which two tectonic plates here in California?"

Brian beat Charles and Richard to the answer, "Like you said, Dr. D., the San Andreas Fault. The Pacific Plate moves northwesterly against the North American Plate."

The lecture continued as Dr. D's subtle interrogative and comedic teaching methods plus a few well-placed PowerPoint slides lifted the class material from his student's minds like the very blind-thrust fault upon which the classroom sat. Once class was done he zipped across the quad to the Sierra Center and wolfed down a turkey panini sandwich. He made it back to his office with time to spare before his first student conference of the day. Just as he was finishing up his last appointment Dr. Eugene Williamson, chair of the Geological Sciences Department, poked his head in the door.

"We need to talk before the meeting."

"Sure," Dr. D. turned to Brian Jones from his afternoon class, "Keep up the good work, Brian. I'm glad you enjoyed the excursion out to Devil's Punchbowl."

"Thanks, Dr. D. See you later."

Dr. Williamson took the now vacant seat, "Lex, I've been looking over everyone's schedules, and, well, you're it."

"What do you mean, I'm it?"

"I want you to host our guest lecturer from Turkey. I was really looking forward to handling her logistics myself, but Jackie didn't tell me about plans she made for us to go to Vegas this weekend. Dr. Karahan's flight arrives at LAX tomorrow at one o'clock. I really need your help, Lex, and everybody else is busy. I'll have a TA cover your classes, and with final exams coming it shouldn't be a big deal. Here's her itinerary."

Dr. Williamson handed him a file folder.

Alex glanced at the folder then shook his head, "Gene, for you, I'll do it, but, you'll owe me big time. It's not that I harbor the old country grudges of my forefathers about the Turks, but I can hear my mother hassling me the minute she finds out I've been playing tour guide for our 'old enemy.' It's hard to keep a secret in an Armenian neighborhood."

"Thanks, Lex, I really appreciate your help. The next time you submit a special departmental request, like a research trip to Hawaii, I'll go to bat for you."

"To study geology, of course."

"Naturally, yes! I mean, where else can you study rock as it's being made in real time?"

"As usual, Gene, your logic is flawless."

"Well, just know that you've got my blessings, provided you bring me back a pound of Kona coffee."

"Deal!"

"Speaking of deal, what's the big deal about the Armenians and the Turks? I know that my grasp of history can be a bit wanting, but I honestly didn't notice any controversy at the conference I attended in Yerevan. You'll recall, that's where I first met Dr. Karahan. Did you fight a war against each other?"

"Much worse, the story goes that the Ottoman Turks exterminated over a million Armenians back in the early 1900s. Before Hitler and the Jews it was the Turks against the

Armenians, at least that's what my grandfather always said. He spent time in an internment camp before coming here."

"Wow, I didn't realize the extent of the bad blood between you."

"But, all that happened practically a hundred years ago. I'm an American, born and bred, just like you, and I certainly don't hold modern-day Turks responsible for what their grandfathers and great-grandfathers did to my ancestors. I'll treat Dr. Karahan as if she were a member of my own family. You can count on it, Gene!"

"I do appreciate your equanimity. I understand that Dr. Karahan is quite the leader in her field at the Istanbul Seismological Institute. Her specialty is earthquake prediction assessment, and she speaks fluent English."

"That's good, because my Turkish is a little rusty. Maybe she can tell us when the Northridge blind thrust fault is going to shake the campus again."

"She just might. I'm sure you'll have a lot to talk about. Thanks again, Lex, you've saved my butt. See you at the meeting," Dr. Williamson glanced at his watch, jumped out of his seat, and sprinted into the hallway, "Shoot, I've only got ten minutes to get ready. Bye."

"Just enough time for me to prep that Hawaii field work presentation."

Chapter 5

IF PAUL BUNYAN sauntered through downtown Los Angeles with a hankering for corn-on-the-cob, no doubt he would set his voracious eyes upon the US Bank Tower. At one thousand eighteen feet, it was the tallest building in California, and the tallest ever built in a major seismic zone. Formerly known as the Library Tower because of its close proximity to the Los Angeles Central Library, it was built to withstand a magnitude 8.3 earthquake. Its immense height dominated the LA skyline making it a prime target for al-Qaeda terrorists seeking to strike the United States as they did on September 11, 2001. Efforts by intelligence agencies foiled these plots making the building reasonably safe for its many tenants, including the occupants of the seventieth floor, Stein Mining, Inc.

Stein Mining was among the oldest mining companies in California, dating back to the Gold Rush, when Walter Stein, an immigrant from the Harz Mountains of Germany, made his fortune in the placer mines of the Sierra foothills. Since 1849, his efforts produced a company that ruthlessly dominated the mining of precious metals throughout the American West. It was as if every ounce of gold or silver was destined for Stein, whether procured through corporate piracy, or by blasting into the bowels of Mother Earth. As old Walter was known to say, "What's yours is going to be mine," meaning, a newly acquired asset of the company. This corporate philosophy extended to the fifth generation of Steins, namely Michael Stein.

"You shot him? Jeezus-Friggin'-H-Christ, Ivan, I don't believe what I'm hearing!"

Michael Stein stood incredulous at the report from his security chief. As President and CEO of Stein Mining, his responsibilities transcended the irritating nuisance of a lone screaming geologist prancing in front of one of his many mines, but the account of the killing zapped him back to the nitty-gritty of the crime's details and its potential impact.

"Look, we tried to reason with him and told him to beat it, but he just wouldn't shut up. That guy was a real *psikh*, you know, *choknútyy*, a goddamn lunatic! He called me and Sergei some pretty bad names, not to mention what he said about you, Mr. Stein. I fired a warning shot, not right at him, just off to his side to scare the shit out of him a little. How was I supposed to know the bullet would ricochet off a rock and whack him?"

"That means he's dead, right?"

"Yeah, he's dead. The bullet hit him in the gut—bled like a stuck pig. We dragged him up on the hill behind the mine after it was dark. Nobody saw us."

"What about all the blood?"

"The guy was standing outside the company fence, so we kicked some sand over it to make everything look normal."

Sergei joined in, "And he was wearing a red sweatshirt that soaked up a lot of the blood."

"So, I wouldn't worry about it. We also had his car towed away, you know, in compliance with the no parking signs. That way the place is clean."

"You're way too confident, Ivan. I'm sure by now the authorities are involved. The last thing we need is to have them snooping around our operation," said Stein staring out the window at the other high rise buildings of downtown. "I went to college with Cal Stover. He was just as big of an environmentalist nutcase back then."

"Mr. Stein. I'm sorry to bother you," popped in his secretary on the intercom.

"Yes, what is it?"

"There's a Detective Jackson here to see you from the Sheriff's Department."

Stein covered the phone receiver and glanced up at Balabanov, "Now, look what you've done, Ivan. The police are already here." He snapped back at her, "Ask him to come back another day, I'm very busy right now!"

Rebecca Gunderson looked up at Detective Jackson, "I'm so sorry, Mr. Stein is in a meeting. May I schedule you for an appointment tomorrow morning? Ten o'clock is open."

"Please inform Mr. Stein that I can have a couple of deputies up here in about ten minutes whose sole purpose will be to escort him down to the sheriff's station. Or, he can answer my questions right now in the comfort of his own office, if you get my meaning?"

"Sorry to bother you again, Mr. Stein, but Detective Jackson insists on talking with you right now, and I don't think he'll take 'no' for an answer."

"I see. Well, then, give me a minute or two, and escort him in, will you?"

"Certainly, Mr. Stein," then she looked back at the Detective, "It just so happens that Mr. Stein's teleconference has finished early."

"That's more like it."

Ivan Balabanov and Sergei Malinovskii quickly escaped the office by slipping into Stein's executive washroom just moments before the detective entered the room.

"Detective Jackson," Stein extended his hand in greeting, "Michael Stein. What can we do for one of LA's finest?"

Jackson firmly shook his hand then backed away.

"We're investigating a crime that was committed near your Palmdale mine. Have you had any problems associated with that facility?"

"Well, no, none that I'm aware of. What seems to be the nature of the crime?"

"Homicide."

"No, I can't believe it!"

"Believe it, Mr. Stein. We found the victim right near your mine. He's laid out down in the county morgue dead as a doornail. You want to go see him?"

"We're ready to cooperate in any way we can, Detective, but why would I need to identify the body? Certainly there's no need for me to see it."

"He's one of yours."

"Oh, no, not someone from our company!"

"Not exactly. He's a colleague of yours, a geologist like you, you know, a Cal-Tech nerd. Are you familiar with a William Stover?"

"William Stover . . . Stover . . . hmm . . . let me think about it a moment."

He strolled back over to his window perch gathering his thoughts, then fired back with his best shot.

"Well, I went to college with a Bill Stover, but we just called him Cal."

"Cal, huh?"

Jackson scribbled down some notes on a notepad.

"Yes, he went by Cal. I heard he was working for the USGS lab over at Cal-Tech. Kind of funny, isn't it, a Cal at Cal-Tech?"

"What?"

"It's a joke, Detective! A play on words."

"A joke?"

Jackson raised his eyebrows.

"Please pardon my feeble attempt at humor in the midst of such an obvious tragedy. You said it was a homicide. How did he die, may I ask?"

"Your buddy 'Cal' was shot. Mr. Stein, we're going to need copies of your employment records for anyone involved in security, including those licensed to carry firearms. It's just routine."

"Please, check the records. Do your investigation. I sincerely hope that none of our staff was involved. I'll have my secretary send them to your office."

"That'll be fine. If we need to talk again, I'll be in touch."

"Please, anytime. I sure hope you catch Cal's killer!"

Detective Jackson barely heard Stein's words as he swiftly left the office, ending the interview as abruptly as it began. On his way to the elevator he swung by Rebecca Gunderson's desk and dropped off his business card.

"Ivan, Sergei, you can come out now. The police are gone." Stein whispered through the door.

They abruptly emerged from the restroom.

"Hey, Mr. Stein, I don't like the sound of that *ment*. You want us to do something about him?"

"Ivan, don't you think you've done enough killing for now? I want the both of you to lay low for a while, and stay away from the Palmdale mine. Just stick around your office here in the tower. No doubt the police will be focusing their investigation up there and I don't want them accidentally running into you. Do I make myself clear?"

"Sure, whatever."

Detective Jackson exited the tower and headed straight for the Starbucks over at the Gas Company Building. After picking up a large cup of strong black coffee, no fancy lattes for him, he gingerly sipped the stimulating elixir, paused, and then glanced up at the towering skyscraper through the bright afternoon sun. Instantly, all of his cop instincts began shouting at him that Stein was sure one lying son of a bitch. Now he just had to prove it.

Chapter 6

KIRAZ KARAHAN STRUGGLED to pull herself out of a fatigue-induced slumber as the Air France Boeing 777 touched down at LAX. The previous evening's flight from Istanbul to Paris had been short and flawless, however, the seemingly endless hours anxiously tossing and turning overnight at a cheap chain hotel near the Charles de Gaulle Aéroport had yielded only a couple of hours of restful sleep. Hence, the eleven-plus hour non-stop flight the next morning had been draining. In a sleepy daze she passed through U.S. passport control and customs and entered busy Terminal Two searching for anyone that resembled her recollection of Dr. Eugene Williamson from a few years earlier. Her tired eyes soon zeroed in on a tall, handsome, dark-haired man in his thirties holding up a homemade sign with the words, "DR KARAHAN."

"You do not look like Dr. Williamson," she said in slightly accented English.

"No, Dr. Williamson had another commitment, so he asked me to be your host. You must be Dr. Karahan. Hi, I'm Alex!"

"Hello, Alex. I am very happy to meet you," extending her hand in greeting.

Alex naturally responded with his own hand, his eyes drawn to her shoulder length auburn-brown hair and penetrating dark-brown eyes.

"Here, let me carry your luggage. My car is just across the way. How was your flight?"

Kiraz Karahan followed Alex Demurjian to his car in the parking garage.

"The flight was good, no problems, but I am feeling quite tired."

"I can imagine. It must be evening in Turkey right now. What's the time difference anyway?"

"I believe it is ten hours."

"Wow, that's more than I thought it was. You must be dog-tired. I'll drive you to your hotel as quickly as I can. The traffic wasn't that bad driving down here so maybe it won't be too heavy going back up to the Valley."

Alex loaded Kiraz's luggage in his car and they soon were on their way out of the airport.

"May I ask, what is that unusual building over there, the one that looks like a spaceship?"

"Oh, that's the Theme Building. It's kind of the symbol for the airport. There's a cool restaurant inside, and they just finished a very pricey earthquake retrofit. Come to think of it, it does have a certain otherworldly look about it. I read somewhere that the buildings in the *Jetsons* cartoon were based on it."

"The Jetsons?"

"Uh, you probably wouldn't know about it. It was a cartoon TV show about a family living in the future. I always thought it was so cool when George Jetson folded up his car into a suitcase. That would sure eliminate always having to find a parking space. Sometimes it's a miracle if you can find one in this town."

"Yes, but then you would still have to carry the suitcase."

"Ha-ha, you've got a point there!"

"Parking in Istanbul can be very difficult too, especially in the old part. The city was designed long before cars. So, Alex, are you from the university?"

"Yeah, I'm one of Gene's geology profs," Alex merged to the right off of Century Boulevard, pulled onto the on-ramp for the 405, and gunned it into the diamond lane. "I understand that you're from the Istanbul Seismological Institute. Where did you go to college?"

"METU."

"M-E-T-U. I don't think I know that one."

"Middle East Technical University, in Ankara. And you?"

"I went to the local school, Cal Tech," pointing to the right in the general direction of Pasadena, "Over that way."

"That is very impressive, Alex. I understand that they only accept the brightest students at Cal Tech, much like they do at METU. May I call you, Alex? Pardon me for being so informal, but I do not think you mentioned your last name."

"Sure, but that's what my parents call me. Most of my friends call me Lex, but my students call me Dr. D because they always butcher my last name. May I call you Kiraz, or would you prefer Dr. Karahan? Am I pronouncing it correctly? It's a pretty name. Does it have a special meaning?"

"Yes, but of course. In Turkish, *Kiraz* means cherry, like the fruit."

"Wow, that's very interesting," Alex nodded, then had an insight, "Kiraz sounds a lot like *Kirsche,* the German word for cherry."

"You are German?"

"No, but I had to take a foreign language in college, so I took German. They say it's the technical language. To be honest, it's been a long time since I've used it. There aren't too many people around here who speak German. In LA it's better to know Spanish, Korean, Chinese, Arabic or Hindi, but not so much German. Funny thing, I remember the word for cherry. Maybe it's because I like them. My cousin, Danny, owns a small cherry orchard up in Leona Valley. Come to think of it, the crop should almost be ready to pick."

The traffic began to slow down as usual when they approached the junction with the Santa Monica Freeway.

"I have learned some German too. My brother, Ahmet, lives in Germany."

"Oh really, where? I actually studied abroad in Germany for a semester at Goethe University in Frankfurt."

"He is not far from Frankfurt, on the Rhine River in the small town of Boppard."

"Boppard. That sounds very nice. What does he do there?"

"He owns a restaurant. Do you like pizza?"

"Doesn't everybody?"

"He makes the best pizza in the world."

"I'll bet he does," smiled Alex glancing at Kiraz, "We've got some pretty good pizza right here in LA, in fact, maybe we could meet up with my Cal Tech friends over at the Avanti Café. It's not far from the USGS lab."

"I would enjoy that very much, Alex . . . I mean Lex."

"You can call me Alex, if you want. Well, we're all looking forward to your lectures. Is there anything in particular you'll be talking about? Gene hasn't told us everything."

Kiraz yawned then she spoke, "Pardon me, my lectures will focus primarily on the similarities between your San Andreas and our North Anatolian fault systems. They have much in common."

"Strike-slip no doubt. We've certainly followed with interest all the quakes you've had there the last several years, especially that big one back in '99."

"Yes, near Izmit. Magnitude 7.6. It was devastating."

"Bad building practices?"

"Yes, we have far too many poorly constructed buildings in Turkey."

A tear began to well up in Kiraz's left eye.

"You know, I really have to say that your English is excellent. Where did you learn it?"

Stealthily wiping the tear away, "Classes at METU are conducted in English, so English fluency was a requirement. But, I've been a student of it since I was very young, and learned a lot watching American and British television shows and movies."

"No kidding! I apologize for not knowing any Turkish words. We all grow up speaking English here in the US, although my grandparents sometimes spoke to each other like they were back in the old country."

"Alex, the whole world is speaking English. You were fortunate enough to have been born into it. And, may I ask, from what old country did your family emigrate?"

Alex took a deep breath and paused before he spoke. He couldn't lie about his ancestry. It wasn't in his nature. However, he knew that an honest response would most likely evoke a reaction from her. The historical animosity between the Armenian and Turkish peoples was undeniable. Between 1915 and 1917, while Europe was in the throes of World War I, the remnants of the Ottoman Empire systematically deported over a million Armenians throughout Anatolia, most of them dying in the process. Over time, the Armenian Genocide was explained away by Turkish historians as an exaggeration of events; the unsubstantiated ravings of an angry and bitter people. That was nearly a hundred years ago. How could he respond truthfully yet conceal his ethnicity? She was bound to find out . . . eventually. Jeezus, Gene hadn't told him what an attractive and interesting woman she was!

"My grandparents came over to the US from Lebanon way back in the 30s."

"You are Lebanese?"

"Nah, just another American, kind of like Keanu Reeves, but he was born in Lebanon, wasn't he?"

"Keanu Reeves?"

"You know, the guy in the *Matrix*."

"Yes, I saw that film. I thought the first one was better than the sequels."

"I couldn't agree more."

Alex had dodged a bullet, but for how long? He had told the truth, but not the whole truth and nothing but the truth so help you, God. Indeed, his grandparents had immigrated to the United States from Lebanon, but Lebanon was not the Demurjian homeland, rather, southern Turkey. His grandparents had somehow endured the pogroms of the Turks only to escape to relative safety in Beirut. Thankfully, Kiraz's jet lag got the better of her and she slipped into a comfortable nap in the cab of Alex's Peterbilt.

The 405 ascended the Sepulveda Pass leading up toward the San Fernando Valley. He hoped that she would sleep all the way to the hotel. Although he had to pay close attention to the stop-and-go traffic around him, he stole glances at her every chance he could. He felt like a regular Peeping Tom, but he just couldn't help himself. The spontaneous affinity he felt for her caught him completely off guard, and transcended their obvious shared profession. Her exotic allure, natural good looks, and pleasant demeanor didn't hurt either. Yet what really struck him was the underlying confidence and strength with which she carried herself, something that most women he had dated never had. Thank God she spoke English! What the hell was he thinking? He wasn't on a date; he was her official university host!

Twenty minutes later, "Professor Karahan."

Alex waited a few seconds before giving her a gentle tap on the shoulder, "Kiraz."

"*Ne?!*"

"We're here."

"What?"

"Your hotel."

"Where?"

"We're in Chatsworth, the Radisson."

"Oh, I must have fallen asleep. My apologies."

"That's okay. You needed to recharge your batteries."

"Recharge my batteries?" looking perplexed, "Oh, I understand!"

"Come on, let's get you checked in right away so you can get a good night's sleep."

Alex came around to the passenger side of the car and let her out. He hadn't done that for a woman in a very long time. Many American women, smitten with years of liberation, were always so eager to handle their own ingress and egress from motor vehicles. After collecting her suitcases from the trunk he escorted her through the hotel entrance to the front desk.

"Yes, may I help you?" said Nikki.

"We have a reservation."

"Your name?"

"It would be under her name, Dr. Karahan."

"Yes, your room is ready. Would you like to leave this on a credit card?"

"The room charge is covered by the university, I hope."

"Here it is. Sorry."

"I've eaten at the hotel restaurant a few times. It's pretty decent. What's it called?" turning to Nikki who was processing the room keycard.

"The Hot Tomato."

"That's it! And, there's room service too?"

"Yes."

"Here's my cell number," handing her his card, "Please, call me if you need anything. I'll be back in the morning to give you the nickel tour of the university, say around ten?"

"Yes, Alex, that would be fine."

Still feeling disoriented from her sudden awakening, a bellboy assisted Kiraz up to her room.

Alex returned to his car for the drive home to his Armenian neighborhood. What would they think about him being attracted to a woman from Turkey?

Chapter 7

Stenger's Towing & RV Storage was a ramshackle business on the light-industrial north end of Palmdale, just east of the Sierra Highway, and a stone's throw from the Palmdale Sheriff's station. After parking his Cadillac just inside the chain link fence Jackson walked across the hot dusty parking lot toward the office. Outside the door stood a tall, husky white man in his early sixties dressed in a red flannel shirt and blue jeans with long graying hair pulled back into a ponytail.

"Holy shit, what the hell youse think this place is, Tobacco Road? Get on back to work!"

The man displayed his annoyance at the lackadaisical attitude of his four undocumented workers sitting on the bench outside the shop's entrance. They quickly tossed their butts on the ground and ambled back to their assigned repair duties in the garage grumbling to one another in Spanish.

Looking at Detective Jackson, "Goddammit, if I wasn't here they'd take an hour for a lousy cigarette break. Aren't youse kinda over dressed to be looking for work here."

"No shit. Detective Jackson, LA County Sheriff's Department."

He showed him his badge.

"No shit. You here about them? Hell, they may look like a bunch of lazy asses, but they actually get work done around here."

"I'm not from INS, and I couldn't give a rat's ass about who you've got working here."

"Good. So, whaddya want? I'm kinda busy."

"Yeah, I can see," rolling his eyes, "You recently towed a car here from Stein Mining. You've got the contract, don't you?"

"Oh yeah, the blue Saab. Brought it in a couple of days ago. It's over there behind that brown piece of shit Southwind. Here to pay for the tow?"

"We might need to impound it for a case we're investigating."

"It's about that guy who was shot up on hill, isn't it?"

"How'd you know about that?"

Detective Jackson walked in the direction of the towed car.

"It's all over the front page of today's AV Press. Got the newspaper right here in the office."

"What do you know about the case?"

"Just that he was one of those Cal Tech smart asses. Seems kind of strange a guy like that getting shot. Youse don't think I did it!"

"You've gotta funny way of talking. Where're you from?"

"Cincinnati, over in Camp Washington. Been there before?"

"Nope, but my mother's from Cleveland."

"Cleveland. People from Cincinnati make jokes about people from Cleveland, but I won't hold it against it youse, since your mother's from there."

"Wise move, Mister? What's your name, for my notes?"

"Johnny Stenger," extending his hand to the detective, "Didn't mean to be so ornery."

After a perfunctory shaking of each other's hands, Detective Jackson jotted his name down in his notepad and began looking through the windows of the car.

"You owned this business long?"

"Fifteen years this June. Bought it after they cut a bunch of us loose from Plant 42. Being an aerospace engineer has its drawbacks. Thought I'd get into a more stable line of work, after all, there are always cars to tow and RV's to be parked. We make some extra money with the repair shop, plus the rack of used tires for sale. Need any?"

"Aerospace engineer, no shit. I had you picked for some low-life lackey. So, you must've gone to college."

The detective put on some latex gloves and checked the driver's door to see if it was unlocked.

"University of Cincinnati, all four years. Started working at the GE jet engine plant in Evendale right after graduation until Lockheed recruited me to come out here. I've never looked back, even after they laid me off."

"How come?"

"What, and give up all of this? Besides, I'm not too fond of snow and cold weather. There's just enough of that here in the high desert for my blood. Being here for thirty years cured me of moving back there."

Just then a cell phone rang. "Jackson here."

The crime lab had downloaded photos from the decedent's camera.

"What do they look like? Uh-huh . . . Uh-huh . . . Uh-huh. So they're all pictures of the mine including some mine employees. Some ugly guys in suits. Uh-huh. E-mail them over. Good, thanks."

Detective Jackson opened the glove box of the Saab and pulled out the vehicle registration that read: William Calvin Stover, 2817 Punahou Street, Altadena, CA 91001. He'd found the car!

"We'll be sending someone from our station house to impound the vehicle."

"So, it's his, isn't it?"

"Could be. Now, I don't want anybody messin' with this car until they get here."

"No problem, Detective. Just wanna make sure I won't get stiffed on the original tow."

"Don't give me that crying shit, you know you'll get paid the standard rate."

They returned to the office. Johnny Stenger resumed his yelling match with his employees and Detective Julius Jackson bid farewell to Stenger's Towing & RV Storage.

Chapter 8

KIRAZ KARAHAN WAS all Alex could think about on his way back home, an infatuation that had caught him completely by surprise. Was it her discerning gaze, or quick wit? Her aura of beauty, or poised presence?

Unable to put her out of his mind, he fantasized that she was still sitting beside him in the car, and that they were driving over to his parent's house for a friendly visit: Hey, here's my new girlfriend, Kiraz. She's a geologist, just like me. Oh, and by the way, she just flew in from Istanbul for a visit. What do you think of her? Plus, he envisioned them welcoming her as if she were an Armenian girl from around the corner, completely forgetting that her forefathers could have been responsible for killing and torturing their relatives back in the old country! The pragmatic side of him seized hold and began to dismiss his hopeful imaginings as completely unrealistic, and yet his heart felt otherwise. Somehow, someway, he felt that he and Kiraz were destined to be more than just fellow geologists.

The red LED light was blinking on Alex's old telephone answering machine when he returned to his condo. A tap on the blue button spit out a message while he changed his clothes.

"Lex, it's David. You must have had your cell turned off. Hey, call me when you get in. It's about Cal."

Alex transferred his cell phone from his gray work slacks to his left hand and punched in David Horita's stored number.

"David, Lex here. Got your message. What's up with Cal? You sounded nervous."

"Man, you're not gonna believe this, but Cal is dead."

There was a lump in Alex's throat while he tried to respond, "Cal's . . . dead?"

"I told you, you wouldn't believe it. Yeah, this detective came by the lab asking about Cal and that's when we found out. And get this, Lex, he was shot."

"Shot? Where?"

"This is even stranger, it happened up in Palmdale, right on top of the Fault!"

"Whoa, I guess if Cal was going to die it would've been there. I can see him lying down in the middle of the Rift Zone and rising up to the Great Seismic Spirit in the Sky, but shot? No, that doesn't make any sense. Everybody liked Cal."

"Everybody, unless you were on Cal's shit list. Isn't the mine right there?"

"Yeah, Stein Mining. Based on our last conversation with Cal, that's where he was headed."

"You don't think that somebody at the mine shot him, do you?"

"Anything's possible. He was pretty rabid about them."

"To put it mildly. He talked like he wanted to take the place apart piece by piece."

"Maybe it was an accidental shooting, a hunter's stray bullet."

"Man, they haven't hunted up there in years. Besides, the detective made it sound pretty ominous, like this was no accident."

"Wow, I still can't believe that Cal's dead. I mean, we just saw him a couple of days ago. Does Katy know yet?"

"Yeah, I called her right away. She was pretty upset, as you can imagine. She's going to call his parents back in Ohio and give them the news."

"So, did the police have anything else to say?"

"No, that's about it. He didn't reveal much, other than he already knew Cal's nickname."

"Well, thanks. I guess I'll see you at the funeral. Let me know when it is, will you?"

"No problem, Lex. Later."

Alex's heart hung heavily in the darkness of his bedroom. On one hand he was thoroughly elated at meeting Kiraz, and on the other he felt the natural shock and grief one feels upon learning of a friend's death. How could it possibly be true? It just doesn't happen. No one shoots geologists. Drug dealers, yes. Gang members, yes. Bank robbers, yes. Police and military get shot. Geologists do not get shot. He shook his head and wondered why someone had shot Cal. His disbelief at the finality of the news dogged him the entire evening. His only relief came at the thought of seeing Kiraz in the morning.

Chapter 9

Kɪʀᴀᴢ ᴡᴀs ᴡɪᴅᴇ-ᴀᴡᴀᴋᴇ at one o'clock in the morning. Upon arriving at the hotel the previous afternoon she barely took the time to put on her pajamas and crashed into bed. Before long she was dead to the world after an exhaustingly long travel day. Now she was conscious enough to survey the sumptuous surroundings of her suite. Not that her apartment in Istanbul was a slum, but every luxury seemed to be available even including a phone in the bathroom. This was a mansion when compared with her previous night's accommodations.

Her thoughts drifted to Alex. Although impressed by his handsome stature, she was most intrigued by his easy going, friendly nature. Were all Americans this nice and well mannered? The more that Kiraz thought about it she determined that it was Alex himself that was responsible for his pleasant demeanor, rather than his American citizenship. The stern looks the US Passport officer gave her when reviewing her travel documents at LAX convinced her of this truth. Perhaps it was a good thing that Dr. Williamson was not available to escort her around. Alex, whatever his last name was, suited her just fine, and she looked forward to seeing him later that morning. She had not spent time in a man's company, other than her colleagues at the Institute, since she was married.

Her two-year marriage to Hamit had been a mistake from the start. After receiving her doctorate in geology from METU, her family simply expected her to settle down and become a homemaker, as had her mother. An educated mother was a better mother, and working at a job outside the home was primarily the domain of the man in Turkey. She worked as a high school science teacher until the Istanbul Seismological Institute lured her away. Finally, after succumbing to family pressure, she agreed to marry Hamit, the son of a long-time family friend from Istanbul. Although Hamit came from an upper-middle class family, he embraced many traditional Turkish expectations of his wife, and never got used to the idea of her having a career. Since Kiraz's work at the Institute demanded much of her energy, there was little time for home and family. A tug-o-war of wills, one demanding the traditional Turkish life, the other a modern, professional one, resulted in divorce just a year ago. Thanks to new marriage and family laws enacted in 2003, granting equality between men and women, unique in the Muslim world, Kiraz was able to come out of the divorce with half of the assets they had accrued during their short marriage. Without this law in force she would have been left penniless and destitute.

Now she was free to pursue her passion, seismology, especially earthquake prediction. The 1999 Izmit quake had been devastating, not only for the tens of thousands of dead Kiraz never knew, but because of the one she did, her younger brother, Mehmet. Her tear, secretly shed in the car the day before, disclosed the extent of her anguish. Days before the tremor she had sensed within her solar plexus an overwhelming queasy feeling coupled with an inner certainty, a deep prompting, that an earthquake would soon occur in the Sea of Marmara. Surprisingly, this sixth sense seemed in complete harmony with her scientific training. She blamed herself for not trusting her intuition enough to warn her family and the media that the quake was coming. Would they have listened to her, even though she was a trained expert? Maybe, and maybe not.

Her father could be headstrong, her mother servile and obedient to him, her younger brother willful and intractable when it came to listening to his older sister. The collapse of a naval barracks in Gölcük took his life. With each passing day her grief for him mounted as she wondered whether his life could have been saved. Now, as both a seismologist and a geo-empath, she was committed to the cause of earthquake prediction. Why should people die so needlessly when forewarning was possible? The mega-quake and subsequent tsunami Indonesia in 2004, and the recent strong temblors in Chile and Haiti haunted her professionally, but Izmit was the one that brought her to tears.

It was years later, at a geological conference on anti-seismic technology in Yerevan, Armenia, that the seed was planted for her trip to America. Scientists and engineers from all over the world attended including Dr. Eugene Williamson from California State University at Northridge. After hearing her lecture on the Broadband Digital Seismic Network that the Istanbul Seismological Institute was installing throughout Turkey, he asked if her schedule could accommodate a trip to the US. She agreed, and now she was finally here. What should she do? It was hours before Alex would arrive. She turned on the TV to the History Channel, lay down on the bed, and drifted back to sleep.

Chapter 10

"HEY LEX, OVER HERE!" waived Hans from an outside table at the Bean Head. Jack was halfway through reading the sports section of the *Times,* but put it down to glance up as Alex walked over to them, with mocha in hand and a bagel in a bag. "You're here early today, and all spiffed up too."

"Lex, you look absolutely gorgeous in that purple shirt. You're not in your usual boring professor attire. What's the occasion, and on a Saturday morning no less?"

Alex sat down at an open chair.

"Hans, I've found her."

"Found whom?"

He looked at both of them almost simultaneously and said, "The woman of my dreams."

"A woman! What's her name? What does she look like? We've just got to know all the details."

"Her name's Kiraz. It means cherry."

"Cherry! Now this is very intriguing. Is she an Armenian, like you? Has she met your folks? Kiraz has that kind of Armenian ring about it."

"You sound like my mother."

"Sorry."

"She's from . . . the same part of the world as my ancestors."

"Tell us, Lex, we want to know what your date was like, don't we, Jack?"

"Well, it wasn't exactly a date, more of a drive up the 405. I picked her up from LAX yesterday afternoon. The department chair asked me to be her host. Next week, she begins a series of lectures on seismology. She's a geologist just like me."

"Jack, will you look at Lex, he's found his soul mate!"

"So, what do you love birds talk about, rocks?"

"Hey, stop kidding me, guys. I only met her yesterday, and I have no idea what she thinks of me. But, we'll see, I'm picking her up from her hotel in an hour, so I can't stay long."

"Hey, you're the one who started all this 'woman of my dreams' stuff," said Jack.

"Just the look on your face when you talk about her tells me all I need to know."

Alex smiled as he raised his eyebrows in agreement and said, "She's like no woman I've ever met. She's smart, pretty, and her eyes. Wow! I just couldn't stop looking at her while she slept in the front seat of my car."

"I guess that doesn't really count as sleeping with her, does it?"

"Hans, don't go there!"

"Not yet."

On that note Alex bid his coffee klatch comrades good-bye.

He had a visiting dignitary patiently waiting for him.

Chapter 11

"*Merhaba!*"

"Mer . . . haba?"

"Good morning, Alex. It is how we say 'hello' in Turkish."

Kiraz greeted her geology department minder in the hotel lobby. Dressed in an open-collared chocolate brown blouse, tan slacks, and a gold necklace, her upbeat tone disclosed her full recovery from yesterday's jetlag.

"Oh, okay, lemme give it a shot. *Merhaba*, Kiraz!"

"Very good. You speak excellent Turkish for a beginner."

"So, how do I say, thank you?"

"*Teşekkür ederim.*"

"Maybe I should stick with English for now. Are you ready to see the campus?"

"Yes, please."

"Follow me."

Alex and Kiraz stepped through the automatic doors of the Radisson and into the mid-morning gloom of a San Fernando Valley spring day, the sun eagerly trying to burn off the marine layer that had crept in overnight. Soon they were southbound on Topanga Canyon Boulevard. By LA standards, traffic was practically nonexistent.

"Did you sleep well?"

"Yes, I'm feeling much better today."

"That's good. How was the breakfast buffet?"

"It was quite good, especially the freshly made omelette."

"I like omelettes too. Was it your first one?"

"Well, no, we eat omelettes in Turkey too, but we call them *menemen*."

"No kidding. Many men?"

Kiraz looked at Alex and enunciated, "Yes, *menemen*. I often make them with green peppers, tomatoes, onions, and spices cooked in olive oil, although my mother likes to use butter instead."

"Wow, I'm already drooling in anticipation of eating one myself. Oh, sorry about the drooling reference. It's just that it sure sounds a whole lot better than that bagel I grabbed and wolfed down in the car driving over here this morning. How was your American-made *menemen?*"

Kiraz pondered the use of "wolfed" to describe the ingesting of a bagel, and then an image came to her, "It was very good, Alex."

"Is this your first trip to the US? I'm sorry, I forgot to ask you yesterday after I picked you up from the airport."

"Yes, my first time."

"Then I can imagine that all of this looks pretty foreign to you," Alex gestured to the modern low-rise apartment and office buildings along their route, "especially all the signs in English. What does Turkish look like?"

"Just like English."

"Nah, really!"

"Yes, really. Turkish has been written using Latin letters for nearly a hundred years."

"I didn't realize that, it's just that my grandparent's language is written so differently . . ."

Alex's fear of revealing his potentially controversial ethnicity, a secret he had concealed thus far from Kiraz's inquiring mind, interrupted the superficial chitchat that had been gushing out of him since they had left the hotel. Written Armenian language looked like Klingon compared with English, or French, or German, and now Turkish, he had learned. Drive down almost any street in Glendale and you would think that you had been magically transported into downtown Yerevan given the many Armenian businesses located there.

". . . From what I remember of the letters they'd saved over the years."

"Since they were from Lebanon the language was most likely Arabic."

"Yeah, Arabic, that's what it probably was," Alex had temporarily dodged the fateful bullet of discovery, for a while anyway. They stopped for a red light at Plummer.

"How far are we from the epicenter?"

"The '94 quake?"

"I have been familiarizing myself with your local earthquake history in preparation for my lectures this coming week."

"As a crow flies, about five miles that a way," Alex gestured to the left. "If you keep going down this street and hang a left at Saticoy then go to Reseda Boulevard, you are pretty much there. Funny thing about it, the epicenter of the Northridge quake was actually in Reseda not Northridge"

"So, why is it not called the Res . . . eeda quake?"

"Probably because the worst destruction was in Northridge, and everybody started calling it the Northridge quake. A few days later the USGS nailed down the epicenter. It's not such a huge error since Reseda is only a mile or two from Northridge."

"I would like to go to Reseda, to the epicenter. Is that possible?"

"Not a problem."

Alex continued down the route that he had just described while Kiraz took in the view. At Roscoe they stopped for the light. To the right was a major chain warehouse store and fast food restaurant, with a gas station and drugstore to the left.

"The buildings here are so much shorter than they are in Turkey, and much further apart."

"Out here in the Valley there aren't that many tall buildings. That's probably what saved our skins."

"You mean lives?"

"Yes, sorry. I'll try to speak better, less idiomatic English."

"Your English is fine."

As the light turned green the traffic suddenly increased as if out of nowhere, with cars shooting their way through the intersection. Alex kept pace all the way until the left turn onto Saticoy. The sun had begun to break through the clouds and was now directly in their faces. Monotonous miles of suburbia whizzed by. Then they passed under high-tension wires after crossing Wilbur.

"We are almost there, aren't we?" Kiraz looked over at Alex.

"Why, yes. But, how did you know that? Did you memorize the directions I just gave?"

"I can sense it."

"Just a few more blocks and we're there. You can sense it?"

"It is difficult to explain scientifically."

"Try me."

"I can feel it in my stomach, a downward pressure that intensifies the closer I come to the epicenter."

"Even years after a quake?"

"That is what is not making sense to me. I usually feel it prior to, not after an event," Kiraz placed her left hand on her belly and took a couple of deep breaths.

"Are you gonna be okay?"

"Yes, I'm feeling better now," Kiraz feigned a smile that hid her inner discomfort.

"You had me scared there for a moment," Alex turned left onto Reseda, "The exact location is just ahead on the left."

Kiraz nodded her head in acknowledgment as they passed by the Southview Apartments.

"It's right behind those apartments. You'd never know by looking at them now, would you? Let's get even closer."

Alex swung his car through three successive left turns at Arminta, Yolanda, and Elkwood and inched down the block. She took another deep breath.

"If we sneak on down this street just a bit more . . . X marks the spot!"

"X marks the spot?"

"What I mean is that this is the exact location where it all happened. The hypocenter was eleven miles below us."

Kiraz looked out her window, "These houses on the right look much newer than the rest. Were they rebuilt after the earthquake?"

"Must've been. They do look a bit out of place architecturally speaking with the rest of the neighborhood," Alex pulled over to the curb at Baird, lowered his window, turned off the engine, and pointed at the ground, "We had no clue there was a fault underneath."

"How could you have known? It was a blind thrust-fault."

"And now we know it's there, the Northridge thrust fault . . .that's in Reseda. Go figure! Well, it's under Northridge too. Am I making any sense here?"

"Yes. It's the faults we can't see that are often the most dangerous."

"Hmm, you've got a point there. Do you think that lightning can strike the same place twice? This extra sense of yours has got me, how should I say it . . . a little spooked!"

"How so? You have electrical storms here in California?

"There I go again, not speaking clear English."

"You are an expert English speaker compared with me, and you are quite funny, Alex."

Alex didn't know what to make of her "expert" and "funny" comments, but he was mesmerized by her smile.

"Thanks."

"I think I understand you now. Will there be another earthquake on this fault?"

"That's what I meant. You kind of brought up the subject a few blocks back."

Kiraz paused, closed her eyes, and spoke, "Yes."

"Yes?"

"Yes."

"When? In the next thousand years, or next week?"

"This coming week."

"Really?"

"Has there been any activity in this area lately. Any swarms of 1 to 3 magnitude quakes?"

"I don't know. We could check with one of my friends over at Cal Tech. Let me see if he's busy."

Alex pulled his cell phone out his shirt pocket and punched in David Horita's number on his speed dial.

"David, it's Lex. Hey, I'm over here in Reseda with Dr. Karahan, a geologist from overseas. She wants to know if you guys have been tracking anything unusual out this way."

Alex turned to Kiraz and relayed his phone conversation, "Uh-huh, six quakes between 1.4 and 2.7 in the last two weeks. The last one was yesterday afternoon, a 2.3. That is a little strange. I've never heard of a pattern like that before, not out here."

Kiraz nodded back.

"How deep? Uh-huh . . . uh-huh, five to twelve kilometers, all over the Valley. What do you make of it? Uh-huh. Wow! Are you going to issue an alert?"

Just then an eight-year old boy emerged from one of the new houses, flopped down his skateboard, and shot right past Kiraz's window.

"Not yet, huh. Thanks. Anything more on Cal's funeral? Uh-huh, Tuesday, three o'clock, church in La Crescenta. Got it. No, I don't think I know that one. Hold on, let me find something to write on."

Alex grabbed a notepad from the center console but unsuccessfully tried to fish a pen from the cup holder.

"Can you just text or e-mail me the info? Yeah, I think I can make it. Dr. Karahan's lecture should be done be noon. I'll catch you later. Bye."

"My apologies for eavesdropping on your conversation, but you mentioned a funeral. Has a friend of yours died?"

"It's the weirdest thing. Cal was on top of his game over at the lab, a real veteran of our craft. I still can't believe that he was murdered."

Alex fired up the car, made a U-turn around the intersection, and commenced retracing their route out of the subdivision and in the direction of the CSUN campus.

Chapter 12

"Rest assured, Emil, the shipments from our Palmdale mine are right on schedule. You heard what . . . about the murder of a geologist near the mine? Not to worry, he wasn't one of our employees."

Ivan Balabanov jumped out of his chair, "Mr. Stein, it wasn't my fault! That guy deserved what he—"

Stein held out his hand silencing Ivan's outburst.

"You saw the story on the Internet. My, my, bad news travels fast, even all the way to Sweden. Like I said, Emil, although the dreadful incident may have happened near the mine, it in no way impairs our operation. You should be receiving your order as scheduled. Give my love to Sonja. *Hej då.*"

After returning the phone to its receptacle, Stein sat down and stared at his chief of security.

"Ivan, do you know why Emil Johansson called me this morning, on a Saturday of all days?"

"No, not really."

"He's worried . . . worried that we won't be able to supply his cell phone company with the gold he needs because of a stupid article he read online about my college chum's sudden departure from the planet."

"Like I said, it wasn't my fault."

"The hell it wasn't! You shot him! When customers get worried they start looking elsewhere for what they need. I don't need Johansson talking to the Chinese, or people in your homeland about a new supplier."

"Sergei said the *ment* who was here the other day had the guy's car impounded."

"You don't take Detective Jackson and his merry men for fools, do you? I'm concerned about this situation not only disrupting business, but stinging me in the ass too. You didn't leave any fingerprints on his car, did you?"

"Didn't even touch it. We left before they took it away. There's no way they're going to find us."

"Let's hope so. No, better yet, let's know so."

"What do you mean?"

"Let's see if we can throw this *ment,* as you say, off our trail. I have an idea that will require some effort from both you and Sergei with perhaps a bit of assistance from your associates in Moscow. But first, let's get this ball rolling."

Stein picked up the phone and dialed a number he had previous scratched down on a yellow notepad.

"May I speak to Mr. Stover?"

"What're you doing?"

For the second time in so many minutes, Stein waved off Ivan's entreaty, "Mr. Stover, my name is Michael Stein. I was a college classmate of your son, Cal. Please accept my condolences on his untimely passing. I can imagine that you must be devastated."

Ivan shrugged his shoulders in disbelief at his boss' acting job.

"I can't tell you how much we miss him out here. He was part of our little fraternity of Cal Tech geologists. I only wish we could've hired him, but those USGS folks snatched him away right after graduation. In fact, what's quite unusual is that Cal was murdered very close to one of our mines. If only he had been able to complete his exploratory work. No doubt his efforts would've helped expand our understanding of the geological structure of the area."

A few moments of silence came over the room as he listened to Cal Stover's father pour forth his grief, "Yes, Mr. Stover, I hear you just fine. If you wouldn't mind I have an idea I would like to suggest for your consideration."

Ivan leaned forward in anticipation of the sales pitch he was about to witness.

"It's my understanding that there's a memorial planned for Tuesday. Naturally, my colleagues and I will be in attendance. What I propose is a tribute . . ."

Chapter 13

THE SATURDAY AFTERNOON lunch crowd was light at Geronimo's dining hall on the north end of the CSUN campus. Alex and Kiraz were seated across from each other at a table devouring the chicken salads they had just picked up.

"How's your lunch?"

Finishing a bite Kiraz responded, "It is very good, Alex. Thank you."

"I hope you didn't mind the walk all the way up here to the dorms, but there's not much open around here on Saturdays."

"I didn't mind at all."

"Good, I was worried you weren't feeling very well when we were back in Reseda."

"Thank you for your concern. The feeling has passed, for now. I appreciate your showing me the campus, and especially the monument commemorating the earthquake. It is amazing that you were able to reopen for classes so quickly, in less than a month."

"It was before my time here, but Gene tells quite a story about all the makeshift classrooms, and meeting the President when he came to visit."

"The President?"

"Clinton."

Alex surveilled the dining room with its movie motif and restaurant like atmosphere.

"They've really done a nice job fixing this place up. I haven't eaten here since the renovation. Students used to avoid this place like the plague because the food was so bad, but it seems they've made some improvements. What I mean is I wish the food had been this good when I was in college!"

"I understand. Last October I visited METU to present lectures, as I am here, and the food tasted much better than I had remembered it."

Alex nodded, "So, this premonition you had earlier. Is this something you're going to discuss this coming week?"

"My lectures will be strictly scientific."

"But you seemed pretty certain that a quake is coming."

"Your friend, David, has already told you about possible foreshocks."

"They could simply be the creeping of the fault without a major event. There hasn't been a warning issued yet."

"The event is coming."

"How can you be so certain?"

"It's difficult to explain logically. I simply feel the earth below me and know what's coming, but not always exactly when." Kiraz gestured to the floor. "After my brother died I promised myself to share what I sense with others in the hope that it prevents harm."

"I'm sorry about your brother. You were close?"

"Yes, he was only four years younger than me. His barracks collapsed."

"He was in the military?"

"Yes, the Navy."

"When did it happen?"

"1999."

"Izmit?"

"Yes, my hometown."

"My apologies for prying into your personal life. I know it's really none of my business, but I was just concerned."

It was difficult for Kiraz to revisit the memory of Mehmet's tragic death, yet again in such a short span of time, but she realized her gracious host's curiosity with her personal story and unique forecasting ability demanded that she explain herself.

"It must sound very strange to the scientific half of you, but have you ever sensed an event before it happened?"

"I keep having these dreams all the time."

Kiraz perked up and looked at Alex directly, "Tell me about them!"

Alex described the collapse of a convenience store in three successive jolts of increasing magnitude as if he were experiencing them in that moment, "My buddies over at the Bean Head think I'm a little touched in the head."

"Touched in the head?" Kiraz cocked her head in puzzlement.

"You know, crazy, a nutcase. They said I need to take a vacation from geology, to get away from California and go somewhere more geologically stable. But, I have this feeling that my nightmares won't stop no matter where I go. I lost count of how many times I've had them."

"You have been given a gift, Alex. It is undeniable."

"You're the only person in the business that I've ever told about these dreams."

"Alex, I don't say too much to my colleagues back at ISI either. They are suspicious of feelings and perceptions that do not fit into their body of knowledge."

"I don't know what to do about them, but I sure wish they would go away."

"Until the events happen I believe the dreams will continue to reoccur."

"Did you have to say that?"

"Would it be possible to visit the San Andreas Fault tomorrow?"

"Sure! Why not?"

Just then the Alex's cell rang, and after noticing whom the caller was, he said, "I've got to take this call."

"Please."

"Hi Dad, how's it going? Uh-huh. Dinner tonight? No, I'm not doing anything, not that I know of. Uh, hold on a sec."

Alex covered the receiver and looked over at Kiraz, "It's my dad. I haven't talked with him or my mother in at least a couple weeks, and now they've invited me over for dinner. I kind of have to go, if you know what I mean, but Gene asked me to chauffeur you around. You're welcome to come if you like, or I can take you back to your hotel. It's your call."

"Alex, go have dinner with your parents. I'll be fine. My Istanbul clock is catching up with me."

She yawned.

Alex returned to his phone conversation with Tevos Demurjian, "What time, Dad?"

Chapter 14

Tevos and Mariam Demurjian were immensely proud of their son. Their dry cleaning business on Glendale Avenue that they had built and toiled in for years helped to provide for a stable home and instill in Alex a strong work ethic and natural friendliness. The day he received the admissions letter from Cal Tech was one of the happiest days of their lives, affirming all their efforts and personal sacrifices. It wasn't just Alex who had succeeded, it was also his hard working father and doting mother. Like most parents, they worried incessantly about his personal life. Most kids in their mid-30s were married, or had already been married and divorced. Alex was still single, and this especially bothered Mariam.

"Alex, have you been out with any girls lately?"

She fired a shot across his bow as he flopped down on the sofa of their Hillhurst home.

"Well, sort of, well, not really."

"What do you mean, not really?"

"I just came from being out with a woman, Mom, but it's not what you'd call a date. I guess you could think of me more as her escort."

"Escort! Tevos, what is the world coming to? Our son has become, what do you call it, a gigolo?"

"No, no, Mom!" Alex was laughing hysterically, "It's work, university work. I'm covering for our departmental chair, Gene Williamson. He had to go out of town, and asked me to escort our visiting lecturer around town. That's all."

"That's my boy!" blurted out Tevos making a fist with his hand.

"So, this is nothing serious then?"

"Mom, Kiraz is a very nice woman, but I only just met her yesterday, and—"

"Kiraz! You're already on a first name basis?"

"Okay, Dr. Karahan, but it's more collegial for us to call each other by our first names."

"Dr. Karahan. Hmm, sounds foreign. Where's she from?"

Alex took in a deep breath and then let out, "The Middle East."

"Where, like Egypt, or Israel?"

"Not exactly."

"Spit it out, Alex, I'm your mother!"

"Leave him alone, for chrissakes!"

"No, it's okay, Dad."

"Hey, just trying to help."

Alex let the cat out of the bag, "Kiraz is from Istanbul."

The living room of the Demurjian home was suddenly enveloped in a silence that even the deepest cave couldn't mimic. Finally, Alex disturbed the stillness of the moment.

"Isn't Cousin Danny's orchard open on Sundays?"

"Yes, your mother and I were up there this morning. The Black Tartarians are coming on pretty soon, ahead of schedule."

"Great! I was thinking of taking her there tomorrow morning as a part of the tour of the Fault she requested. She told me that her name means cherry in Turkish. I wonder if she likes cherr—"

"Oh, she's already ordering you around, is she? And a Turk, no less! History is repeating itself. I don't know what to say."

"Jeezus, Mom, can you lay off even for a minute?"

"I didn't raise you to become a slave of the Turks. Do you have any idea what our people went through, especially your grandparents and great-grandparents?"

"Yeah, Mom, I know the stories like any Armenian, but that was a long time ago. Times have changed. She's really a nice person, and this isn't a date. I'm her host from the university. That's what this is about."

"And you're already taking her around to your relatives. Why didn't you bring her here for dinner?"

"Well, I offered to, but she was still tired from the overseas flight and time zones, so I dropped her off at the hotel after lunch."

"You would have brought her here, into our home?"

"Why not? You act like she's an invader from outer space or something. She didn't have anything to do with what happened back then. She's a geologist, like me!"

"So, this is just a job? It's nothing serious."

"That's right, Mom," Alex lied through his teeth.

"All right, I feel better now."

"Let's eat!" shouted Tevos.

"Mom, try to keep an open mind about her."

"You watch out for her, Alex!"

Chapter 15

EXHAUSTED FROM HER tour of the San Fernando Valley, Kiraz crashed in her room until four o'clock. The disorientation of time and space from her accustomed location on the planet continued to disturb her physical equilibrium. Rejuvenated by her nap, she had freshened up her appearance and gone down to the Hot Tomato for an early dinner consisting of salad, lasagna, and tea. Now, back in her room watching TV she was on her laptop monitoring earthquake activity in Turkey, checking e-mail, and updating her Facebook status when a call unexpectedly came in on Skype.

"Kiraz, *nasilsin?*"

It was Ece Taşkın, her colleague from ISI checking up on her.

"*İyiyim.* You're up early."

"I couldn't sleep, so I thought I might as well start getting ready for work and look to see if you were online. Are you enjoying California?"

"It's been wonderful so far, especially my university host. He showed me around the campus and took me to lunch today."

"That old guy from the conference you went to a few years ago, Doctor . . ."

"Williamson. No, not him, he sent another professor. He's closer to my age, I think."

"Really? What's his name?"

"Alex."

"Alex, what?"

"I honestly don't know his last name. He just goes by Alex, but his friends call him Lex. I heard him talk to one of them on the phone."

"Tell me, what's he like? You look pretty happy about him."

"Alex is a geology professor, and he's . . . very different."

"Different?"

"He's extremely polite, and quite funny."

"Is that all?"

"He's not too bad to look at either. I'm really looking forward to our day tomorrow. We're going to see the San Andreas Fault."

"You're spending a lot of time with this Alex. Why don't you check him out on the Internet? There can't be that many geology professors there named Alex. I'll do it for you, hold on. What's the name of the school?"

"California State University, Northridge, but I can look for myself, Ece, you don't have to . . ."

A few keystrokes later, "Kiraz, his name is Alex Demurjian. He's *Ermeni!*"

"So it seems."

"What do you think about that?"

"If he's really an Armenian, I can't believe he's being so nice to me. They think we're all like Nazis!"

"Kiraz, you're not interested in him, are you?"

She quietly pondered her friend's question before answering. "I feel so at ease around him, so secure. Now that you've pointed out that he's an Armenian, I'm beginning to worry about what he actually thinks about me. I mean, he knows my nationality. Ece, he's even trying to learn how speak a few words of Turkish, no doubt to make me feel at home."

"He must really like you to do that."

"He even tries to open my car door, when I let him."

"Trust me, Kiraz, he likes you. Who knows, you might want to stay California."

"You know that my work at the Institute is the most important thing in my life. I'll be back."

"We'll see. Have a fun day tomorrow with Alex."

"Thanks, Ece, I will. *Hoşça kal.*"

Kiraz sat there in total shock over the revelation of Alex's likely ethnic heritage, and wondered if perhaps his last name wasn't Armenian at all, even if it did end with the telltale "ian." Maybe Demurjian was an Arabic name from Lebanon. She punched it into a search engine and pulled up scores of Demurjians, mostly professionals and their listings on business and social networks. All were Armenians. On page two she spotted a link to Alex's Facebook page and clicked.

Since they weren't Facebook friends, Kiraz couldn't access all of Alex's information, but his dearth of privacy settings allowed her to learn many personal details from her surveillance:

Alex Demurjian

Sex: Male

Current City: Los Angeles

Birthday: June 15, 1973

Hometown: Los Angeles

Relationship Status: Single

Interested In: Women

College: California Institute of Technology, BS, MS, PhD

High School: Marshall High School '91

Employer: California State University, Northridge

Position: Professor of Geology

Time period: June 1998–Present

Looking for: Networking, Friendship, Relationship

Political Views: Moderate

Religious Views: Christian

Friends: David Horita, Cal Stover, Katy Snyder, and 38 others

Pages: Star Trek, Mark Knopfler & Dire Straits, Bill Nye The Science Guy, People for the Advancement of the San Andreas Fault, and 12 others

Chapter 16

"WAS THE *MENEMEN* as good today as it was yesterday?"

"My omelette was about the same. You speak good Turkish."

"I had a whole day to practice. How do you say 'hello' again?"

"Merhaba."

"Merhaba. And how about, good morning?"

"Günaydın."

"I'll catch on someday."

Kiraz continued to be impressed with his attempts at speaking Turkish, especially considering what Ece had discovered last night about his ethnicity.

"If you don't mind my asking, how was dinner with your parents?"

Still reeling from the third degree his mother gave him the previous night, Alex responded, "Oh, pretty good. They live just a few blocks from my condo, so close I could walk there, but I don't. I'm lazy."

"In my short time here I have noticed that people in America drive a lot."

"Do you drive?"

"Of course, I know how to drive, but sometimes I ride the bus, or take the ferry."

Alex and Kiraz had agreed to meet for an early breakfast at the Radisson, which according to the hours of the Hot Tomato meant seven o'clock. The seismology tour that Alex had planned would eat up the entire day, so leaving at the crack of dawn was essential.

After breakfast, they embarked on the expedition up the 405 to the 14 Freeway through the San Fernando Pass toward Canyon Country. Immediately an abundant feast of geological fare began to unveil itself before Kiraz's eyes, both of which were focused on the scenery out the windows of Alex's car.

"The faulting through here looks very complex."

"It is among the most complex anywhere in California, part of the Transverse Range. The rocks around here run from pre-Cambrian to Holocene, something for everybody. We're driving over the San Gabriel Fault right now."

"It is a strike-slip fault."

"Yes, right-lateral. It runs parallel to the San Andreas for about ninety miles."

"I read that this fault was once part of the San Andreas system five to ten million years ago until the rift zone migrated to the north where it is today."

"You've done your homework, haven't you?"

Alex was astonished by her detailed knowledge of the geological history of the area, especially for someone who had literally just gotten off the plane. After crossing the Santa Clara River Basin they began the long ascent toward the Antelope Valley. At Agua Dulce Kiraz spotted something else that aroused her interest.

"For some unknown reason that rock formation looks very familiar to me."

"Oh, that's Vasquez Rocks, one of my favorite places to take new geology students."

"Yes, I thought we passed the sign for it a moment ago."

"You probably recognized it because of Hollywood."

"Hollywood?"

"It's been a popular location for film crews trying to find an otherworldly or Wild West looking set. They filmed lots of *Star Trek* episodes there back in the 60s, plus movies. Did you see *Austin Powers?*"

Kiraz nodded as they began to move out of sight of the rocks.

"Did the *Flintstones* movie ever make it over to Turkey?"

"No."

"They called them the 'modern stone age family.' It was a movie based on a kids cartoon."

"Is everything in California a cartoon about another time period?

"Huh?"

"First the Jetsons, and now the Flintstones."

"You know, maybe you got a point there, or I just have cartoons on the brain!"

They passed the sign for the Escondido Summit, 3,258 feet. Minutes later they rounded the bend entering the Antelope Valley, and stopped at the vista point above Lake Palmdale.

"Check this out, come on."

Alex jumped out of the car and Kiraz followed. From their perch above the valley Professor Demurjian began his San Andreas Fault lecture.

"From here you can see the Fault for miles, starting up at the Mountain High Ski Resort to your right."

Kiraz shaded her eyes as she looked up into the San Gabriel Mountains that towered over the high desert like sentinels standing watch over a vast battlefield.

"How high is it?"

"Let's see, Wrightwood is at six thousand feet, and the ski resort is higher, maybe seven thousand. I'm not sure what that is in meters."

"That would be little more than two thousand one hundred."

"You're pretty quick with that conversion."

"I'm used to it."

"They were supposed to have held the Winter Olympics there back in 1932, but there wasn't enough snow so they moved to Lake Placid. My Cousin Danny loves skiing up there since it's such a short drive."

"This lake in front of us looks like a sag pond."

"You have a good eye. Yes, and they converted it into a small reservoir back in the 1920s. They actually go fishing on it."

"Have you ever fished there?"

"Years ago with Danny, but it's too rich for my blood."

"I don't understand."

"Oh, that wouldn't make sense, would it? It's a private lake. You have to pay a fee."

"You have to pay money to fish?"

"Danny used to belong to the club, and I went with him a few times, but he dropped his membership a few years ago. We caught some nice sized bass and trout from there."

"In Istanbul, there are always men fishing off of the Galata Bridge."

"The Galata Bridge?"

"It crosses the Golden Horn and connects the old part of the city with the new one. It's a great place to buy fish because it's fresh from the sea."

"What do they catch there?"

"*Istavrit*, mostly."

"Istavrit?"

"I think you call it mackerel. Once I saw a seagull steal one that had just been caught. It was very funny. The man was yelling at the bird as it flew away with the fish in its mouth."

"Really! That's hysterical. I'm going to have to add *istavrit* to my Turkish vocabulary," Alex pointed toward the west, "Speaking of seagulls, if you look over this way you can see how the Fault goes right across the freeway and through that landfill. You know how much seagulls love garbage?"

"Even this far inland? I've always lived by the coast, except when I was in college."

"It's hard to believe, but I've seen seagulls as far inland as Missouri, and you can't be further inland in the US than there."

"Missouri . . . the location of the New Madrid seismic zone?"

"Why yes, you do know your stuff!"

"Were you in Missouri to look at the fault zone, or garbage dumps?" asked Kiraz with a smile.

"Very funny. You've got quite a sense of humor, for a geologist."

"So do you, Alex."

"Let's get moving, I've got more faults to show you."

Alex moved from the wooden fence over to the passenger door and let Kiraz into her seat.

"More than one?"

"Maybe a couple, but first you've got to see this!"

They sped out of the vista point and back on the freeway heading north. Moments later Alex slowed down in the right lane as they approached the San Andreas Fault. They soon entered a notch cut through the escarpment that revealed a striking swirl of geological sedimentary stew made up of gypsum, light sandstone, and dark shale.

"What do you think of this one?"

Her eyes were wide open, taking in the contortion of folded rock and a complex array of R shear faults, then she noticed something.

"Can you pull over?"

Traffic was typically light early on Sunday morning. Alex had no problem easing the car onto the shoulder next to a lamppost.

"You see it, don't you?"

She pointed out the window, "The thrust fault in that fold of rock. It's so clear."

"I thought you'd be impressed."

Chapter 17

JULIUS JACKSON SAVORED his days off as did everyone who actually worked for a living, hence the early Sunday morning rousting he received from his supervisor was not what he had anticipated, nor desired. Captain John Fernandez and Detective Jackson went way back, having joined the department the same year. Fernandez had been especially helpful in saving his career following the East LA incident, an act for which he was exceedingly grateful.

"What's up, Captain?"

"J, we got an anonymous tip about the Stover murder."

"Like what?"

"Something about his having worked for a Chinese mining interest. I'd like it you could check it out."

"Can't it wait until tomorrow? I've got plans."

"Change 'em! I've got the Fifth District Supervisor leaning all over my ass wanting some action. You see, the call came into his office not ours. I've arranged a meeting for you with Barbara Rosenfeld, his chief of staff, for eleven o'clock. Can you get downtown by then? She's got this thing about punctuality."

"Shit, John, that's in less than an hour! I'm not Superman when it comes to getting dressed."

"Just throw on anything, after all, it's Sunday."

"Yeah, I noticed. It's the usual day of rest for most folks who've worked all week, unless of course you're a preacher or a hustler, and I'm neither."

"You're the biggest hustler in the department, J! Meet her outside the office on Temple. Remember, don't be late."

Jackson clicked off the phone and in frustration he tossed it clattering across the kitchen table. His brunch date with his daughter and grandkids would have to be delayed. Remembering Fernandez's reminder about timeliness, he snatched back the bruised communication device and called Angela to report the bad news.

"Hi Angie, it's your dad. No, no, we're not canceling, but could we eat at say, twelve instead? Uh-huh. Tell Austin and Mikaylah I'll be there as soon as I can. Okay. See you then."

This time he gently returned the phone to its receptacle and went into his bedroom. The yellow aloha shirt, tan slacks, and brown loafers were the quickest fix to his garment needs. After collecting his wallet, keys, badge, and gun he shot out the front door, locked the deadbolt behind him, and climbed into his car. Within seconds he was hurtling out of his neighborhood heading due east on Manchester. Just as he entered the on-ramp to the Harbor Freeway his cell rang.

"Jackson here."

"Did Captain Fernandez call you about our meeting?"

"Would you actually believe that I'm just now pulling onto the 110 as we speak?"

"Good, how long will it take for you to get here?"

"Is ten minutes soon enough? I don't want the CHP messin' with me on this glorious Sunday morning. That just wouldn't be right, now would it?"

"You can cut the petulance, Detective. I don't like having my day off interfered with either. Pick me up out front. What are you driving?"

"White Caddy."

"See you in ten."

Chapter 18

ALL MORNING ALEX had been completely captivated by Kiraz's company, but since they left the road cut his mother's cautionary words suddenly began to encroach from the back of his mind, like the hanging wall of a reverse thrust fault. He couldn't fathom how it was possible for his mother to prejudge someone that she didn't even know, someone as well mannered, cultured, and intelligent as the seismologist sitting in the seat next to him. At the same time he also wondered if Kiraz had figured out who he really was, and not just "Alex" from the university. These thoughts pestered him as he drove west on Elizabeth Lake Road through the Desert View Highlands neighborhood of Palmdale.

"Alex, what are those buildings over on the left?"

"Oh, that's a mine. Do you remember when I told you about my friend who was murdered?"

"Yes, but I don't remember his name."

"Cal, Cal Stover. He was a charter member of our pizza geologist group until this happened. David said that they found him shot dead right above the mine."

"I'm so sorry about your friend, Cal. They are mining on the San Andreas Fault?"

"Sounds crazy, doesn't it? That's what Cal thought too. Would you believe they use high explosives to extract the ore? I guess the residents have been complaining about the noise for years. The city council finally worked out a deal with the mine to only blast during daylight hours. They didn't want them to leave town and take jobs away from the local economy."

"The economy is depressed here?"

"Isn't it almost everywhere? Jobs up here in the high desert are pretty scarce. Most people commute down to the Valley or LA to work."

"What kind of mine is it?"

"Gold."

Kiraz sighed at the word, "It is sad how our lust for precious metals scars the earth."

"You're beginning to sound like Cal."

"Have the police found his murderer?"

"Not that I know of, but David and I wondered if there might be a connection with the mine. The coincidence between Cal's personal campaign against the mine and his death can't be a fluke."

"Fluke?"

"Fluke, uh, a random event . . . just plain bad luck."

"I understand what you mean now. This valley is quite beautiful, Alex. What is it called?"

"Forgive me for not narrating our tour properly, we have left Palmdale and are now entering the Leona Valley. You can thank the San Andreas Fault for its natural beauty. Notice the escarpment to the right?"

However, Kiraz was fixated on something out of the left window, "Those animals with the long necks. They are like camels. I've seen them at the zoo before."

"You mean those animals standing next to the horses?"

"Yes, what are they called?"

"Those are llamas, from South America. There's a zoo in Istanbul?"

"Of course there is a zoo. It's over in Bayramoglu."

"Where you saw the llamas."

"Yes, where I saw the llamas."

"Just checking. Hey, we're almost there."

Alex slowed down as they neared the center of town turning left down a side street and through the gates of a small farm headed by a sign, "DEMURJIAN ORCHARDS." Kiraz made note of the sign through the moon roof as they passed under it. Alex maneuvered the car in front of a green pole barn on the edge of the orchard and snapped the parking brake into place. A moment later a man fifteen years Alex's senior came out of the side door of the barn to inquire about his unexpected visitors.

"Sorry, picking season doesn't start until next weekend, you'll have to come back . . . wait a minute, is that you Lex? I didn't recognize your car. Must be a new one."

Danny Demurjian expressed his apparent amazement at seeing his cousin show up.

"Hey, sorry I didn't call ahead. My dad said that the Black Tartarians were almost ready and I thought I'd take a chance at pilfering a pound or two."

"Doggone climate change has confused the hell out of these trees. All the growers are bitching about it. We'll be open for u-pick next weekend, but you're welcome to glean the first fruits of the season," Danny suddenly noticed Alex's passenger and said, "Hello. I can't believe you let this clown pick you up."

Alex muttered under his breath, "Not now, Danny," then heightened his tone, "Danny, let me introduce you to Dr. Kiraz Karahan, a visiting lecturer at the university. I've been showing her the unique characteristics of the San Andreas Fault and thought that your orchard would be the perfect place given the character who owns it!"

"Hi again, was it Karass? Did I say that right? Sorry about the clown thing. Alex is like a kid brother to me, and we kinda get our kicks taking jabs at each other."

Kiraz leaned her head forward toward the driver's door and responded to his clumsy introduction, "It is a pleasure to meet you, Danny."

"Alex and Karass. Do you remember Alex Karass? Nah, he's before your time. Played for the Detroit Lions back in the sixties and then became an actor."

"You pronounce her name, Ki-raz, not Karass, Danny."

"Kiraz, welcome to our humble farm!" Danny gracefully gestured with his hand.

Alex turned to Kiraz, "Danny should've become the actor, not this Alex Karass dude."

"Come on, get out of the car and let me give Kiraz the grand tour."

Alex quickly opened his door in an attempt to continue his gentlemanly behavior, but Kiraz managed to get out on her own. They followed Danny into the orchard.

"Here in the Leona Valley we have the only decent spot in all of Southern California that is truly suitable for growing cherries and other stone fruit. The cold winters provide the necessary chilling for the trees, and abundant sunshine every spring brings out the flowers and the bees. The soil is ideal, not to mention all the extra energy the Fault provides," Danny pointed to the ground with both index fingers.

"Danny is convinced that cherry trees in the Leona Valley grow better than anywhere in the world because of the special vibrations emanating from the tectonic plates rubbing together. He's not what you would call your everyday farmer."

"Kiraz, are you fond of cherries?"

"Yes, isn't everyone? My name means 'cherry,' so I'm especially fond of them."

"You know, cherries come from our ancestral home country, especially this variety. I planted out over half the orchard in Black Tartarians, but without a pollinator, they'd be all leaves and no fruit. So, the rest are Bings and Rainiers. You want to try some? They're just starting to turn red this week."

Danny shot up a ladder he had propped up against a tree and selected a handful of the moderately ripened fruit and handed them to Kiraz.

"Here, try some of these."

She popped one in her mouth, "That has a very . . . distinct flavor. Much stronger than I expected. It's very good, Danny."

"They're even better when they turn black. You want some too, Lex? Here's a bucket. You can pick your own!"

"Thanks, Danny. I think I can handle it."

Danny relinquished his position on the ladder and Alex mounted the rungs until he was twelve feet in the air. The morning sun penetrated through openings in the leaves just enough to reveal those cherries worthy of his harvesting efforts. After several minutes of picking his arms tired and he came down with about a pound of the shiny red fruits.

"That'll be five dollars, sir."

Alex turned to Kiraz, "You can see how much Danny likes to joke with me."

Danny jumped in as he poured the cherries into a plastic bag, "Who's joking? Show me the money!"

"Put it on my tab, would you? Professor Karahan and I have more on our agenda today."

"That sounds so official, Lex, as if you were a presidential press secretary or something."

"I'm her official university host, and after lunch there's one more place I want to show her."

"Going up to Lone Pine, aren't you? Where are you taking the doctor for lunch? You're welcome to hang around here a while. I'm having lunch in an hour or so."

"That's okay, Danny. I appreciate the offer. I've already got that figured out."

Danny handed Kiraz the now sealed plastic bag of freshly picked cherries, "Kiraz, these are for you. Know that you're welcome here anytime, and the cherries are always free, even if you come back with this guy."

"Thank you, Danny. I appreciate your hospitality very much. You would be welcome at my home as well."

"Where, may I ask, is that?"

"Istanbul."

Shaking his head in accord, "Ahh, Istanbul. A very historic city. Hmm . . . haven't been there yet. Are sure an old geezer like me would be welcome?"

"You would be welcome, Danny."

Alex let Kiraz into the car and walked over to his cousin shielding his voice from her by turning his back.

"Danny, my mother is having a cow about my escorting her around. You know, the whole Turkish thing."

Danny turned and walked back toward the barn as Alex followed.

"I heard, Lex. My Aunt Mariam called me last night and was spouting off about it. Somehow she knew you'd be showing up here today with her in tow."

"You're kidding. Jeez, I can't believe her!"

"Don't worry about your mother, she can't help herself. You and I, we've moved on from all that ancient history crap. I've gotta tell you, cuz, this Kiraz is a keeper."

"I know, but what do I do?"

"Relax, and let things take their natural course. Just like these trees do."

"Thanks, man."

Chapter 19

As COUNTIES GO, Los Angeles was by far the most populous in the entire United States with over ten million residents, or about the same as the states of Oregon and Washington combined. Economically speaking, if it were a country and not a county, Los Angeles County could be considered for membership in the G-20 club of nations. Governed by five district supervisors, these men and women commanded respect and on occasion, tribute. Detective Jackson wasn't especially good at indulging them, but his boss, John Fernandez, was a master of the art. The familiar silhouette of Los Angeles City Hall loomed in the background as Jackson zipped down Temple Street, but his destination was a less architecturally inspiring government structure, the Los Angeles County Kenneth Hahn Hall of Administration, only a block ahead on the right. After crossing Grand he instantly spotted Barbara Rosenfeld's golden blonde hair. She stood impatiently under a tree yacking away on her cell phone. As he drew closer, in one fluid motion she looked up, walked to the curb, and slipped into the car without missing a beat with her intense conversation with the caller.

"The dedication of the new hospital wing is all set, so let's not go changing it, shall we? Supervisor Shackleford's calendar takes precedence. Are we clear? We'll work out the details this next week."

She turned off her phone.

"No rest for the wicked they say," Jackson said as he pulled back into the traffic lane.

"Ha-ha, you're so funny," Rosenfeld's sarcasm was in high gear.

"My routine at the Improv is world renowned."

"Let's cut right to the matter at hand, shall we?"

"What, you're all business, and here it is the weekend. I thought we'd have a coffee and chat," Jackson turned right on Hill.

"Forget the coffee, Detective."

"You've probably had a bit too much this morning anyway. So, what is it?"

"Last night, our office received a call from a man who claimed that your murder victim was a Chinese agent posing as a geologist. Before we take this information to the FBI, we thought we'd give Captain Fernandez and you an opportunity to affirm or dispel this accusation. You've got seventy-two hours!"

"Hmm, I gotta tell you, that's not what my cop nose tells me about this Chinese nonsense."

"Don't give me that cop instinct bull! Courts of law like evidence. The informant also said that it was the Chinese government who killed Mr. Stover."

"Did he also say why they would take out one of their own?"

"No, but that appears to be your job. Are we clear?"

"What is this, 'are we clear' jive? I'm not your bitch like that person you were just talking to," Jackson pointed at the phone in her hand as he hung a right at First Street.

"Detective Jackson, if it weren't for your friend, John Fernandez, you'd be doing time in Taft for involuntary manslaughter given that business in East LA last year."

"Why'd you have to bring that up? I was cleared."

"You don't have a clue how thin the ice is you're walking on. Don't botch this investigation like you did with the Los Tiburones case."

"The only ice I see is the one surrounding your aura. Ms. Rosenfeld, I'm a pro, not some wet behind the ears rookie with a shiny badge. Tell your boss that Stover's killer will be arrested, Chinese or not. You can take that to the bank!"

"For your sake, let's hope so, or you'll be looking at an early retirement. Let me out here."

"I can take you back."

"Our business is over, for now. Pull up over there and let me out."

He shot a glare of indignation her way, but the salvo missed its mark entirely, "Suit yourself."

When he stopped for a red light at Grand, Barbara Rosenfeld exited the car as swiftly as she had entered it. After slamming the door shut, she whipped out her phone to make another call, and proceeded to march down the sidewalk back toward the county building. Jackson sat there in total astonishment and thought, "Who the hell does she think she is?"

Chapter 20

"SHIT, I HOPED this wouldn't happen!" as Alex pushed down hard on his brake pedal.

Kiraz was startled, "What is it?"

"Sorry about the expletive, but I hate the way these freight trains can shut down the traffic. It's totally ridiculous, and this isn't the first time this has happened to me driving through Mojave."

"Expletive?"

"The bad word I used just a moment ago. It just slipped out of me."

"Oh, that word."

"How do you say that in Turkish?"

"Are you sure you want to learn those kinds of words?"

"It could be handy."

"*Bok.*"

"Okay."

In the hours since breakfast Alex's energy level had diminished to a point where the condition had temporarily dulled his mental alacrity, even in spite of the several cherries Kiraz let him eat from her stash. A few minutes seemed like hours while the Union Pacific switching yard leisurely moved one of its freight trains across the Sierra Highway. Road traffic began to line up behind them compounding everyone's feelings of frustration and impatience. Finally the train passed and they were on their way north for a few blocks until Highway 14 veered off to the right.

"I have this idea for lunch. It's exactly what a geologist would order up."

"Yes, I would be interested in such a lunch."

"How about a picnic? Do you go on picnics in Turkey?"

"Of course we do!"

"You do? Wow, well uh, maybe the place where we'll get our take-out picnic food will be something that you'll find to be uniquely American."

Alex turned into a strip mall on the northern edge of town and parked in front of perhaps the most omnipresent fast food restaurant ever conceived. They got out of the car and entered the establishment marked by a white-yellow-green sign with arrows pointing off the ends.

"They make all kinds of sandwiches here . . . meatball, cold cuts, beef, chicken, turkey, cheese whatever you want, and then you tell them what kind of bread to put it on and what veggies you want. I like the Spicy Italian with all that pepperoni and salami, topped with lots of lettuce and tomato. If you need any help ordering, I'm a veteran customer."

Kiraz studied the menu posted on the illuminated sign above them, and then turned to Joaquin, the counter person, "I would like a fifteen-centimeter, wait . . . a six-inch oven roasted chicken on whole grain bread with lettuce, tomato, and cucumbers."

"*Si señora, quince centímetros.* You are from Mexico?"

"No, I am from Turkey, but we use the metric system, just like almost everyone else, except for the United States."

Joaquin nodded his approval and looked over at Alex, "Señor, your order?"

"How'd you do that? I mean, the menu reads, 'six-inches.' I don't get it."

"You see, in Turkey, Subway restaurants sell their sandwiches in fifteen and thirty centimeter lengths. My mind reverted back there for a moment. I hope I'm not causing a problem, Alex."

Joaquin retrieved a six-inch whole-wheat roll and spread it out on his work surface, "And you, Señor?"

"Yeah, just a second . . . You mean to tell me there are Subways in every town and neighborhood in Turkey, just like here in the US?"

"No, I've only seen a couple of them, but I've been to the one in the Old Town many times since it opened. It's very close to the Grand Bazaar."

"Señor?"

"Yeah, I'll have a foot-long, no, make that a thirty-centimeter Spicy Italian on herbs and cheese bread. These will both be to go."

Joaquin went into action creating their order and within minutes they were out the door and back on the road still heading north.

"Let me crank up the AC on max, it's really hot out here today. Look at the temp on my car's computer, ninety-seven degrees! What's that in Celsius?"

"Thirty-six."

"I sure wish this air was pumping out at thirty-six degrees right now. Fahrenheit, that is."

Sweat began to emanate from Alex's forehead, yet Kiraz seemed unfazed by the heat as the desert landscape flew by. For several minutes they sat in silence while the car's cabin cooled off.

Alex spoke first, "I mentioned that I would be showing you more than one fault, well, we're coming up on fault number two, over on the left. The escarpment pretty clearly defines it."

"That would be the Garlock Fault?"

"Who's giving the tour here? Are you sure this is your first time in California?"

"Your faults are world famous. We studied them in university. I recall that the Garlock Fault is the second longest in California, and differs from all other strike-slip faults because it is a left-lateral not a right-lateral, like all the other major faults. It is also considered to be the northern boundary of the Mojave Desert."

"Then you probably already know where we're having our picnic."

"That is something I actually don't know."

"Good, now I'm feeling useful again."

"I am enjoying the tour, Alex, and appreciate the time you are taking out of your weekend."

"I can't think of anything else I'd rather be doing."

Alex genuinely meant those words, and Kiraz felt his sincerity. Once they crossed the aforementioned Garlock Fault the terrain began to change as the highway rose above the desert basin into a jumble of hills and cliffs, the ubiquitous beige rock now morphed into a palette of reds and oranges, revealing embedded iron oxide deposits. A few miles later a brown and white sign appeared ahead: "Red Rock Canyon, Ricardo Campground, NEXT LEFT." Alex slowed down for the turn.

"Time for our picnic."

"Good, I'm famished."

"Maybe you should've ordered the thirty-centimeter sandwich."

"Very funny. I'll be fine with my six-inch one."

As he turned into the park they crossed a dry riverbed and were greeted with a display of weather carved sandstone that seemed to bubble up out of the base of the flat topped basalt buttes.

"Welcome to the southernmost tip of the Sierra Nevada Mountains, otherwise known as Red Rock Canyon. This is my second favorite place in California. I love bringing my students here to let them walk around, with an assignment, of course."

"Of course! And what is your favorite place?"

"That's coming later this afternoon. Now check this out!" Alex pointed out the window to the left.

Kiraz gazed at the fluted columns of tan rock decorated with multiple ribbony layers of ocher colored strata.

"It's like nothing I've ever seen. What is this called?"

"The Dove Spring Formation."

"How old?"

"Miocene. Paleontologists found the fossils of many extinct animals, and also elephants, camels, and horses. It's hard to imagine them living here today. They filmed a scene from *Jurassic Park* nearby. You know, the one where they're using ultrasonic waves to find buried dinosaurs."

"Can we stop, just for a moment?"

"No problem."

Alex pulled the car to the left side of the shoulder and turned off the motor. Kiraz got out and approached the outcropping, stopping at the edge of the drop-off. While she stood there, shading her eyes from the noonday sun with her left hand, a slight breeze blew her shoulder length hair. For a brief moment, Alex stepped out his professorial persona and observed her simply as a man. He liked what he saw. Drawing in a deep breath of incredulity he paused and wondered, what force of the universe had suddenly dropped her into his life? It had to be benign, creative, beneficent, the same power that had shaped and formed the rock before him into a work of art. The coincidence seemed remarkable. Without warning, his rational mind invaded his momentary reverie, reminding him that he was merely on assignment, like a substitute teacher answering a call at six o'clock in the morning. Once this job was done, he would move on to the next. His schizophrenia was compounded by worries about his mother, her mother, his family, her family, and then her! Maybe his fantasy was just that, a fleeting figment of the mind that passes through and leaves without a trace of substance or reality. Then he remembered his cousin's sage words and relaxed, breathing out a sigh of surrender. He lowered his window and leaned his head out. She noticed.

"A person could spend all day staring at that, couldn't they?"

Kiraz nodded, "I'm sorry for delaying our lunch. I'm coming."

She got back in the car and they took off.

"Just up ahead is our lunch room. It has a decidedly different ambience than the campus cafeteria of yesterday."

The visitor's center wasn't far. Covered picnic tables were available close to the parking lot, although the shade they provided from the sun's intensity was minimal. Alex donned a baseball cap and offered one to Kiraz, which she accepted. After lunch they were back on the road driving north out of the canyon area.

"I've got another place to show you."

"Your favorite place in California?"

"Yeah, that one."

The desert that stretched out before them was pure desolation, mostly devoid of substantial vegetation except for the occasional clump of Joshua trees and the ever-tenacious olive-green creosote bushes. However, with each mile the Sierra Nevada Mountains appeared to grow taller on the left side of the car as if they were there for the sole purpose of keeping them company. But for Alex and Kiraz, the monotony of the scenery didn't really matter. As geologists, they could see the story and magnificence in a single rock; as human beings, they had begun to become aware of those same qualities in one another.

When Highway 14 became US Route 395 Kiraz spoke, "Have you ever been married?"

"Why, no, but it's something that worries my mother to no end. She's always nagging me about it, like I have a disease or something."

"Why haven't you?"

"Well, I've been out on my share of dates, some girlfriends too, but I guess I never found the right person for me. I'm kind of kook, if you haven't noticed."

"A kook?"

"You know, an odd duck." Alex pursed his lips for second, "Um, how can I say it without using a damn idiom?"

"You are unique."

"That's what I meant. Unique."

"I was married once. It didn't last long."

"Really. You're not married now?"

"No. My mother worries about me, just like yours. I'm a thirty-two year old divorced woman, which is not very common in a Muslim country."

"Well, at least you're not a kook like me."

"You mean, unique."

"Right, unique."

"I think I might be unique too."

"A one of a kind."

Kiraz grinned, "We are two one-of-a-kinds!"

"I like that definition. Do you?"

"I do."

They both sat silently for a few moments pondering their foray into personal feelings until Kiraz piped up.

"Tell me, Alex, did you tell your mother about me?"

Alex tensed up, "Yeah, I told her."

"What did you say?"

"Oh, that I was to help take care of your visit, something like that."

"And, what did she say?"

Alex stared out the side window for a moment searching for the best words, but could only muster, "I can't tell you."

"You told her where I was from, didn't you?"

"Yes, I did."

"That I am from Turkey?"

"Uh-huh."

"She didn't approve, did she?"

Exasperated by his own conflicted feelings, and the direct interrogation Kiraz was putting him through, he let loose, "No, she didn't, and I think she's entirely misguided in her judgment of you!"

"Alex . . . Alex Demurjian."

"How'd you find out my last name?"

93

"It is amazing what you can learn from a few minutes on the Internet. I rather enjoyed reading your Facebook profile, not to mention that big sign in front of your cousin's cherry orchard, the one that reads, 'DEMURJIAN FARMS.' You're not Lebanese, are you?"

"Not exactly. My grandparents lived there before they came to America. Does that count?"

"And, before they lived in Lebanon?"

"Same country as you."

"Where?"

"Adana."

"You're Armenian, aren't you?"

"Armenian-American. There's a difference."

"So, do you think that an Armenian-American and a Turk can be friends?"

"I'm an American first, an Armenian second."

"Then, we can be friends?"

"Friends," they both extended their hands and shook them, but neither really wanted to let go of the other's hand.

"How do you say that in Turkish?"

"*Arkadaşlar.*"

"Arka . . . daşlar it is. You know, it's a good thing we're both unique."

"You mean, kooks."

Chapter 21

BEING STUCK IN traffic had become an accepted way of life for most Angelenos, especially during the rush-hour commute, but to be unnecessarily so on a Sunday morning was just plain exasperating. Julius Jackson's mind vacillated between feeling both annoyed at having his Sunday plans altered enough to land him in an ocean of cars on the Pacific Coast Highway, and outraged because of the way Barbara Rosenfeld had tried to verbally smack him around. Eventually he inched his way forward into Pacific Palisades and its landmark Gladstone's Restaurant. He dropped off his car with the valet and dashed into the restaurant. Everyone was waiting for him at an outdoor table.

"Grandpa, where have you been? We've been waiting like forever!"

"Sorry, I didn't mean to be late."

"Mikaylah, I told you that Grandpa would be here soon. You remember, he called just ten minutes ago."

"Well, okay. Don't do it again!" Mikaylah pointed at her grandfather.

"I'll try, I swear."

Jackson leaned down and gave his precocious nine-year old granddaughter a hug and a kiss.

"Yeah, Grandpa, why didn't you put the lights up on your car and make everybody move over for you?" added her older brother, Austin.

"You know I can't do that unless it's official business."

"Aren't we official business?"

"You kids are too much! I would have to take you both in for questioning to make it official business. You wouldn't want me to do that now, would you?"

"Yay, yay!" they both yelled.

"Shhhhush, now, you two! We're dining out not screaming our heads off at a ballgame," said Angie.

Grandpa Julius treasured these moments with Angie and the kids. They were all the family he had left since his wife, Bonnie, had passed away from breast cancer two years ago. Angie's husband, Jamal, a sergeant in the Army, had been killed while serving in Iraq. There wasn't anything he wouldn't do to help them out. The survivor benefits from Jamal's death had run out months ago, and Angie's lone salary working as a secretary in an insurance office barely kept up with their bills. Soon a waitress came for his order. Jackson looked at his watch that now read 11:49.

"Is it too late to order breakfast?"

"Breakfast ends at eleven thirty, sir, but let me check with the manager on duty. You want some coffee while I'm here?" asked Carmen.

"Yeah, please."

"Do you take cream and sugar?"

"No, I like my coffee black, like the president."

"Sure . . . Wasn't his mother white?"

"You got me there."

Carmen finished topping off his cup, and retreated into the main part of the restaurant.

"You look frazzled, Daddy. Rough case?"

"No worse than any other murder."

"Somebody got killed? Who was it?" asked Austin.

"Are you gonna put the killer in jail, Grandpa?" Mikaylah joined in.

"Kids, you know he can't talk about police business."

"It okay, Angie. They're just curious. You read about the geologist that was found dead up in the high desert?"

"Oh yeah, I saw that on the news the other night. That's your new case?"

"And the brass is leaning hard on me for results. That's why I was late."

"They've got some cockamamie idea that he was killed by, shall we say, 'foreign interests.' I think it's total crap, but I still have to check it out."

"Grandpa said a bad word!" shouted Mikaylah just as Carmen returned with a menu.

"Sir, we'll serve you breakfast, but I have to get the order in now."

"I'll have the steak and eggs, medium-well and scrambled."

"Thank you, sir," she plucked the menu from his hands and turned to Angie, "Your food is almost ready."

"Yay!" screamed both kids.

"So, what did you two order?"

"Guess?" asked Austin.

"Pancakes!"

"How'd you guess?"

He pulled his badge from his pocket and waved it in front of them.

"Because your grandpa is a detective!"

Chapter 22

"Tremors."

"Tremors? I don't feel any."

"Every geologist worth their salt has seen *Tremors*. This is where they filmed the movie."

Alex and Kiraz had driven up Whitney Portal Road from the town of Lone Pine into the Alabama Hills and parked on the shoulder just beyond Movie Flat Road. These hills were comprised of heavily weathered granite and metamorphosed volcanic rocks strewn in piles for several miles on the western side of the Owens Valley. As impressive as these hills appeared, looming over a thousand feet above the town, the nearby 14,497-foot Mount Whitney and other high peaks of the Sierra Nevada Range overshadowed them, creating a breathtaking geological panorama.

"Is every place in California a movie set?"

"Just about. They filmed tons of Westerns up here, but my favorite movie is still *Tremors*. I thought Kevin Bacon was awesome. I can't remember the name of the guy who played his sidekick, but he was just as funny. You haven't seen it before, have you?"

"No, I haven't."

"Well, it's set in an old decrepit mining town where a student seismologist is monitoring strange, unexplained earthquakes. Then, people and livestock start showing up dead as the quakes continue to increase. It's a pretty wild movie. You know what's terrorizing the town?"

"Collapsed mines, perhaps?"

"Nothing that logical. Graboids!"

"Graboids?"

"These giant worm-like creatures with huge teeth that tunnel under the earth at high speed."

"Are we in any danger here?"

"Not unless we were in the movie. Do you want to know how the townspeople killed the graboids and saved themselves?"

"Please, Alex, don't spoil the movie for me."

"Okay, I'll behave. I've got it at home on VHS. You want to see it?"

"If I am going to be a true geologist, 'worth my salt,' as you say, I just might."

They got out of the car and walked up on the crest of a rise and took in the view.

"You've got it all here. Mount Whitney up there, the tallest mountain in the contiguous United States, the Alabama Hills around us, the Owens Valley below us, the Inyo Mountains over there, and if you hopscotch over another range you're at the lowest point in the hemisphere, Death Valley."

"This must be your favorite place."

"How'd you guess?"

"You enjoy talking about it."

"Kind of obvious, isn't it?"

"Scientists are trained to be observant."

"So what do you observe, then?"

"There has certainly been a lot of mountain building due to faulting. Where we're standing is fairly new alluvium, Pleistocene, but those granitic rocks which make up the hills appear to be very old, perhaps from the Jurassic Period."

"Late Cretaceous, actually, about ninety-million years old. The rock is similar to that in the Sierras right above us, although there are volcanic rocks to the east that date to the Jurassic."

"Why are they called the Alabama Hills. Isn't Alabama in the Southeastern US?"

"The story goes that local miners sympathetic to the South during the American Civil War named them after the Confederate warship, *Alabama*."

"It seems odd to name a geological formation after a naval ship."

"Wow, I hadn't thought of that before. Well, I think their geologic interests were more focused on extracting gold than finding a relevant name, but the name has stuck. For what it's worth, the Northern ship, *Kearsarge*, sank the *Alabama* during a battle off Cherbourg, France in 1864. They named a town about twenty miles north of here after that ship. I guess you could think of these two places as ships in the desert!"

"How do you know all of these minute details?"

"Do you have any idea how many students I've taken up here on an excursion? I've been asked that question so many times that I had the answer tattooed on the back of my hand."

"Really, you did? Let me see your hand!"

"I was just kidding about the tattoo."

"Oh, okay. The Alabama Hills seem out of place for a rift valley like this."

"They're a bedrock remnant of the Sierra uplift that has been weathered differently. Glaciers shaped the Sierras, whereas the Alabama Hills have been exposed to —"

"Spheroidal weathering."

"Exactly! Come on, I've got a couple more things to show you."

Alex and Kiraz continued up Whitney Portal Road passing the last of the Alabama Hills and stopping occasionally to take in the ever-enlarging view of Mount Whitney. After twenty minutes they reached the top of the Whitney Portal, 7,851 feet above sea level. The coolness of the pine trees and higher elevation was a soothing change for the two geologist's constitutions. After a brief visit to the gift shop and restrooms, they returned to the car for the descent to the valley floor. It was now late afternoon, and Alex had two more items on his agenda before the trek back to LA. Once they were below the Alabama Hills, yet still above the aqueduct, Alex turned left down a winding dirt road into the desert, stopped, and got out of the car. Kiraz followed.

"I've got something interesting to show you."

They walked about a hundred feet until they came to a small but discernible escarpment of loose boulders and dirt nearly twenty feet high.

"We're literally standing on the Lone Pine Fault, the approximate location of the epicenter of what is considered to be the largest earthquake to have hit California in modern history."

"The Owens Valley quake, 1872, with a magnitude of about 8.0."

"Yep. Some people call it the Great Lone Pine quake. It leveled just about every structure within fifty miles. On the Modified Mercalli Scale the shaking here was XI. UMB just blew apart. Unfortunately they didn't know about seismic retrofitting or rebar back then. The quake killed twenty-seven people in Lone Pine alone. They are buried in a mass grave about a mile that way," Alex pointed to the northeast.

"This is a right-lateral fault?"

"Yes, as is its parent, the Owens Valley Fault, just a few hundred yards over there. There's scientific dispute about the amount of displacement. Early geologists said that the vertical movement was over twenty feet, and the horizontal nearly forty, but modern investigation downgraded those numbers significantly suggesting that the total displacement occurred in successive events over tens of thousands of years. Regardless of the numerical speculation, this quake was a big one. Everybody living in California that day felt it to one degree or another."

Once back in the car they returned the way they had come from Whitney Portal Road, and turned left across the aqueduct into town. At US 395, they went north a couple of miles passing the gravesite of the 1872 earthquake victims.

"My friend, David, told me about this place only a few more miles up the road that I've really wanted to check out. Would you mind if we took just a few more minutes? How are you holding up? I've really put you through the paces today."

Kiraz tried to force back a yawn but it broke through nonetheless, "I'm doing fine, Alex, let's go see it."

Then, she suddenly felt a twinge in her stomach.

Chapter 23

JOSE MARTINEZ WAS SNORING away in his recliner as the Dodgers came to bat in the bottom of the eighth inning. With his hand still firmly grasped around the television remote control, he enjoyed a sacred sliver of peace in his otherwise busy life. Rosa was down in the Valley visiting her parents for the afternoon, while Martha and Maria were with friends at the movies. Although he loved them all dearly, he needed his down time too. If only his dog were more cooperative. Without warning, Molly began barking and running around the room trying to get his attention. Startled by her noisy behavior, Jose dropped the remote and jolted out of his chair.

"What the hell are you doing? Let me guess, you want some of these, don't you?"

He held up a large bag of barbecue flavored potato chips that had been resting on the small table next to his recliner. Molly persisted in barking and then started doing something he'd never seen before. She itched her head on the carpet as if a spider had crawled inside one of her ears.

"I don't know if you deserve any, you're such a naughty dog waking me up like that."

Then, the house shook. Not too hard, but enough that you knew a seismic event of respectable magnitude had occurred. For twelve long seconds Jose watched his new flat-screen television dance around on its stand. Instinctively, he ran toward it with arms outstretched like a mother rescuing a falling baby. The game was now interrupted with comments from the veteran sportscaster, "That was quite a jolt! I'm sure everyone here today at Chavez Ravine felt it. Shades of the World Series nearly twenty years ago. Now I'm being told that programming is shifting back to the news studio."

A women reporter spoke, "A powerful earthquake has just rocked the Greater Los Angeles Area. It's too soon to tell where the epicenter is located, but the shaking was very strong at our newsroom here in Studio City . . ."

He looked at Molly, "Dang, maybe you're not as dumb a mutt as I thought. Jee, I wonder how Rosa is."

Jose ran back to their bedroom and fished his cell phone out of the mound of things piled on his dresser. After several failed attempts to get through there was finally an answer.

"Hi, Joe."

"Are you all right?"

"We're fine. We all ran outside when it hit. I guess we shouldn't have done that. You know what they say, get under a doorframe or table. Are the girls home yet?"

"No, they're still at the mall, but they're probably okay. It wasn't too bad up here."

"It was here. Mom's favorite lamp fell down and broke . . ." Rosa paused from her report when the earth under her feet began to rumble then stop as quickly as it began.

"Rosa, what's happening?"

"Didn't you feel that, Joe?"

"Not really. Hold on, let me go see what they're saying on the news."

Jose hustled back into the living room and plopped down on the recliner, his eyes and ears fixated on the screen.

"Reports are now coming into the newsroom from all over the Southland. It appears that everyone felt it, including that strong aftershock, the first of many for sure," the female reporter nervously spoke.

"You must be closer to the earthquake. Maybe you better come home now."

I want to make sure mom and dad are going be fine. I'm calling Cousin Mario."

"Hold on a sec. They're saying something more about the earthquake."

"And this just into the newsroom, the U.S. Geological Survey in Pasadena has issued the following statement: 'At 4:52 p.m., Pacific Daylight Time, an earthquake with a preliminary magnitude of 5.7 occurred in the northeastern San Fernando Valley near Panorama City. Aftershocks are likely. Residents are urged to take caution. This almost looks like a repeat of the Northridge quake, but thankfully on a smaller scale," said the female reporter turning to her male counterpart.

"Yes, Panorama City is right next door to Northridge. I'm not a seismologist, but my bet is that this quake was caused by the same fault, one that the experts didn't even know existed until 1994 . . ."

"Honey, you're right on top the quake. Forget Mario, can you bring your folks back up here with you?"

"I'll try talking to them, but you know how attached they are to the house."

"Do your best. I'll go check on the girls."

Chapter 24

FOR UNTOLD CENTURIES the land that comprised the Manzanar National Historic Site had been the home of the Owens Valley Paiute Indians. The encroachment of white settlers interested in farming, mining, and ranching precipitated a two-year long war with the Paiute, one that led to their involuntarily removal by the Union Army to Fort Tejon on July 22, 1863. Around the turn of the next century, the area was developed into a large fruit growing enterprise and the town of Manzanar, meaning "apple orchard" in Spanish, was born. But by 1930, the City of Los Angeles' thirst for Eastern Sierra water had brought most of Manzanar's land under its domain, and the town disappeared into the history books until the outbreak of World War II.

Alex turned left off of US 395 and through the front gate of the park.

"What is this place?"

"David told me his parents lived here when they were kids."

"There's nothing here except desert."

They passed a wooden sign suspended by cables between two posts that read, "MANZANAR WAR RELOCATION CENTER." A little further along they came to a small rock hut with a sign, "INTERNAL POLICE SENTRY POST." A gust of wind blew dust across the road.

"This place gives me the creeps."

"The creeps?"

"It's kind of spooky . . . uh, scary."

They continued to roam about the complex passing signs for various municipal buildings of the former relocation camp.

When they came to the sign marked, "HIGH SCHOOL," Kiraz said, "This is like a small village, but there are no buildings or people, only signs. How could anyone have lived here?"

"I think it was all torn down later. Let's check out that building up ahead."

They parked at the interpretive center. A woman park ranger greeted them at the door, "You still have time to catch our last showing of the film."

"How long is it?" asked Alex.

"Only about twenty minutes."

"Sure," Alex answered for both of them looking at Kiraz for agreement.

They hurried into the small auditorium just as the film began. For twenty-two minutes images of the deportation and internment of Japanese-American citizens during the years 1942–45 flashed before their eyes while the narrator told the story.

"You know, I'd heard about this stuff back in high school history class, but it's quite another thing to actually see it in-person. It's terrible what we Americans did to our own people."

Kiraz remained silent as they walked out of the interpretive center toward the car.

"And I didn't realize that the guy who played Sulu on the first *Star Trek* was a little kid here. That just weirds me out. You know, my grandparents—"

"Alex, what is it?"

"Oh, nothing, nothing."

"Your grandparents were in a camp like this one, weren't they?"

"Are you psychic or something? Actually, I don't think it was this nice."

Kiraz looked into Alex's eyes, "Your grandparents?"

"One time, when I was about fifteen, my grandfather told me about his 'time in the desert,' as he called it. He said he imagined that he was kind of like Jesus, who spent forty days and nights in the wilderness being tempted by the devil, or Moses, living in the desert for forty years with his fellow Israelites. Maybe that association with biblical figures helped him cope with how bad it was for him and his mother. But anyway, he told me about the horrific heat of the Syrian Desert, and lice covering their heads."

"What happened to his father?"

"He was killed a few years before during the Adana riots. So, it was just the two of them, Gramps and his mother. She carried him on her back when he got tired. What a tough lady she was, and he was lucky to have her. There were so many other kids who were orphans. He said they lived in these makeshift tents with almost nothing to eat or drink. They were starving to death, but so was everyone else."

"What happened to them?"

"Somehow they made it to Beirut to a shanty town called Bourj Hammoud. I guess it was pretty bad there too, but better than baking out in the desert. That's where he met my grandmother. She was a survivor too. They got married, then moved to LA back in the 30s."

"They would be your mother's parents?"

"Yeah. My dad's family has been in California since the 1880's, and lived up in Fresno until the Depression hit. Then, they moved to LA. He's as American as apple pie."

"You like your father."

"He can be a real comedian, always joking, which balances out my mother's insane lack of flexibility and sense of humor."

"And you are lot like him, I think."

"A chip off the old block? Maybe."

"What happened to your family was detestable. No one ever deserves to be forced from their home and taken somewhere to die. The Armenian people suffered greatly during those years."

"How do you know so much about what happened to Armenians? I thought that Turks—"

"Alex, I've been to Armenia. It was several years ago for the geological conference in Yerevan, where I first met Dr. Williamson. The local host organization held special excursions, one to Spitak where the big 1988 quake happened, but there were also others offered around the city including one to the Armenian Genocide Museum. I went on that tour with another woman at the conference, Anna, from Ukraine. We're still good friends."

Alex shook his head in disbelief.

"Alex, Turkish people don't like to talk about what happened, or what might have happened, but after seeing the displays in that museum my eyes were opened and I know that something terrible did happen. The Assyrians, Greeks, and later the Kurds suffered as well, but what was done to your ancestors was the worst of it. I never felt ashamed of being Turkish until that day."

"You didn't cause the genocide!"

"I know that logically, as a scientific thinker, but like you said, there's nothing quite like seeing something in person to impact you on a deeper level, to put you in the event as if it were happening now. For a few hours I became an Ottoman soldier driving your family into the desert. Later, when I was back in my hotel room that night, I couldn't sleep. The horrifying images of dead people swirled around in my mind. Then it occurred to me that the Ottoman Empire was crumbling, and that kind of disintegration almost always seems to make people do bizarre and often unconscionable things."

"How so?"

"This film we just saw about your government's response toward its ethnic Japanese citizens after the Pearl Harbor attack is the same kind of thing, although less violent. Your country, for all its faults, has a warm heart, but people gave into their fears and no one questioned the decision. When will we humans grow up and learn from our atrocities? We have enough suffering to go around when a natural disaster happens, so why do we make life worse? We are many peoples, but one human race. It's no one person's fault that these things happen, but it's everyone's responsibility to see that they're not repeated. I can understand why the Jews say, 'never forget' given their barbaric treatment by the Nazis during World War II, but why must Palestinians now endure hardships and deprivation because of Israeli policies and practices? It is a terrible cycle of evil begetting evil. Bosnia, Rwanda, and Darfur. The list seems unending."

Blown away by her spontaneous lecture on the evils of genocide Alex offered a response, "I couldn't have said it better myself. It's amazing to me that we seem to hurt our own people the most."

"Anna said exactly the same thing when we were at the museum. She told me about the famine in her country during the 1930s that killed all of her family, except for her grandmother."

"How can a famine be considered killing?"

"Stalin used hunger as a weapon. The peasants' harvest was taken from them and they starved to death."

"I see what you mean. Hey, that reminds me of when I was in Missouri a couple of years ago. I found this state park by the Mississippi River kind of by accident. It was a memorial to the Trail of Tears."

"Trail of Tears?"

"I didn't know what it was either, but I learned that my own country's cruel behavior didn't begin with this place," pointing at the ground. "It was called the Indian Removal Act, and during the 1830s the US government forced Native American tribes to move from their homes back East to reservations hundreds of miles away in what is now Oklahoma. It was nothing but a simple land grab, and thousands of people died because of it. It made me think of my grandfather back in the old country and what he and his mother went through. Even though my country came to the rescue of the Jews in Nazi concentration camps, we're not so squeaky clean when it comes to human rights. I guess every country has its darker moments."

What had begun as a field trip to study geological faults had turned into a deep discussion of human ones. Just then a fresh gust of wind blew some dust around the parking lot, their cue to get back in the car for the long drive back to LA. Immediately, Alex's cell went off. It was a familiar name on the ID.

"Hey David, would you believe I finally made it Manzanar. I can't believe what your parents —"

"Lex, that's cool, I'm glad you saw it, but here's what you're not going to believe, we just had a 5.7 magnitude quake in the San Fernando Valley."

"No shit! Oh, sorry," glancing at Kiraz, "What was the Turkish word again?"

"Bok."

"Got it. Bok."

"Those little quakes we've monitoring will probably be classified as foreshocks, and we've already had one strong aftershock, a 4.9."

"Hold on a sec," Alex looked at Kiraz, "You know your premonition about a quake coming? Well, you should hire out. There's just been a 5.7 right where you said it would happen."

Kiraz searched her thoughts, then spoke, "Ask him when it happened?"

"When did it hit?"

"About an hour ago. Why?"

"Nothing. We didn't feel it up here, not that we noticed. We were on the road, and you know how hard it is to feel a moderate quake while driving. I didn't even know the Whittier Narrows quake had happened until I got to the campus that morning and saw everybody freaking out in the parking lot. Besides, we're almost two hundred miles away."

"Dude, you've got a long drive ahead of you."

"Yeah, I know, we're about to head back right now. Thanks for the head's up. I'll catch you later."

Alex clicked off his phone and asked her, "Why did you want to know when the quake hit?"

"I felt it happen then."

Chapter 25

MICHAEL STEIN HAD experienced his share of earthquakes in his forty-seven years as a Los Angeles native. This latest one he classified in the routine category. It was nothing to be alarmed about, yet strong enough to remind one that they lived in earthquake country. Its movement had done no more than merely intrude upon a vigorous tennis match with a newer Brentwood Country Club member, Herschel Brockman, tossing both of them to the court surface with rackets and free hands outstretched. Once the tremor ceased, Stein stood up, pulled a fresh ball from his pocket, and served match point without missing a beat, much to the surprise of his opponent.

"This isn't the French Open, you know! You can pause more than twenty seconds between earthquakes, after all, we're only playing for the right to buy the first beer."

Still kneeling on the ground, he watched the ball assertively bounce through the service box and sail over the baseline.

"Hersch, you better stay focused to claim that prize," Stein pulled another ball from his pocket and served, "but I'll give you another shot at it if you insist."

His tennis partner returned serve and a fierce rally ensued until Stein's backhand volley whizzed by Brockman's ear bringing the match to a satisfying end.

"Okay, you win. Make mine a tall, ice-cold Stella. Can you afford such high-end brew?"

"What's the price of gold?"

"I haven't a clue."

"I can afford an entire brewery."

Stein further annoyed Brockman by bouncing an extra ball on his racket striding toward the bench.

"You're a terrible show off, you know."

"You mean about the brewery, or this?"

With the next bounce he popped the ball up into a perfect parabolic trajectory and it dropped into his open tennis bag. He snatched a fresh towel to wipe the perspiration from his face.

"Now you've outdone even yourself."

The two men headed through the pool area and into the clubhouse for their showers. Freshly rinsed and clothed in clean shorts and shirts they sat in the bar each partaking of the grand prize.

"I'll beat you next time, and I won't rely on an earthquake to do it."

Brockman had already downed most of his first beer and was motioning for a second.

"You might get lucky, or catch me on an off day."

Michael Stein had more on his mind than basking in the glory of winning a simple game of tennis. His plan to divert the police away from himself now nagged at him with even greater force than any concerns about the quake's possible damage to his gold mine.

"Your confidence is unfounded."

"Hersch, how about next Sunday, same time? I've gotta run and ensure that the little geological miracle I just performed during our game didn't disrupt any of my enterprises."

"You're on!"

Stein put down his half-full glass of beer and was out the door and into the driver's seat of his Nordic Gold Metallic Porsche 911 Turbo Cabriolet, the fastest convertible sports car in the world. With a 0–60 time of only three seconds and top speed of nearly two hundred miles per hour, there wasn't a car in Brentwood, Bel-Air, or Beverly Hills that could keep pace with it, driving or parked as it was now. He retrieved his cell phone and scrolled to a number he'd called the day before.

"Vladimir, sorry to wake you up so early. What time is it in Moscow?"

"Not a problem, Mr. Stein, please call us at any time. We are a 24/7 agency."

"Have you had any success with my idea?"

"Yes, one of our associates witnessed a brief meeting between the parties just this morning. Hold on . . . here it is. 'At precisely eleven o'clock Jackson was seen picking up Rosenfeld in his car in front of 500 West Temple Street. He then turned right on Hill Street and disappeared from view. Three minutes later Rosenfeld was seen on foot walking up Grand Avenue and returned to the Temple Street location.' We have great confidence that the plan has been successfully set in motion."

"Good."

"Mr. Stein, we have had a discussion with our colleague, Mr. Balabanov, regarding the situation last week at your mine. He is to refrain from future frivolous use of firearms."

"I appreciate the help, Vladimir. Although Detective Jackson has proven to be a shrewd policeman, perhaps we can prevent Ivan's transgression from becoming a legal matter."

"*Da*, we understand your special need to be shielded from the problem. We will contact you if something new develops with the Jackson-Rosenfeld surveillance. Is there anything else we can help you with today?"

"None that I can think of. You know, your customer service skills are incredible. How do you do it?"

"Thank you, Mr. Stein. You have a good evening."

"I will now," Stein clicked off his phone.

Feeling buoyed by his tennis game win, and his chat with Vladimir, Stein fired up the Porsche and gracefully exited the country club parking lot through the security post, the turbocharger kicking in briefly as he gunned it up Burlingame toward his Mandeville Canyon estate.

Chapter 26

"YOU MUST BE STARVING BY NOW."

The drive back toward LA went by in a flash. Alex was all over his car's radio searching for updates on the quake. As late afternoon grew into evening KFI and KNX's fifty thousand-watt clear channel signals summoned them home. Alex turned down the sound.

"Yes, I'm very hungry."

"Good, I've got just the place in mind, and I absolutely guarantee that you've never eaten at one of these before."

"How can you be so certain? We have all the famous American restaurants in Turkey—McDonalds, Burger King, Pizza Hut, KFC, and you know we have Subway."

"I seriously doubt that you have one of these in Istanbul." Alex aimed the car down the off-ramp.

"Right now, I could, how do you say it, 'eat a horse?'" Kiraz tried her hand at speaking American.

"Sorry, I don't think horse is on the menu. You eat horse?"

Kiraz teasingly backhanded him on his right arm as he shifted the car through the left-turn onto Palmdale's main drag, "You know what I mean!"

"I guess I do, but I don't know about this horse eating thing of yours."

"I don't eat horse meat!"

"You can't always be sure when someone says, 'I could eat a horse!' Do they eat horses in Turkey? Just curious."

"No, horse is not a food in Turkey," Kiraz was becoming quite exasperated with Alex's humor, "but I believe it is in Kazakhstan."

"Kazakhstan, huh," Alex turned right into a small lane between two fast food establishments, *"Voilà, madame, we have arrived at our culinary destination."*

"I said that we have Pizza Hut in Turkey."

"Wrong direction."

Alex glanced to the right and pulled into the parking lot of the other eatery, In-N-Out Burger.

"You're right, we do not have one of these."

"Didn't think so."

Alex bolted out of the car and let Kiraz out of her door before she could open it. He felt like a sixteen-year old out on a first date with a girl from his high school. Soon they were through the doors of the restaurant and up to the counter.

"Welcome to In-N-Out Burger! May I help you?" asked Martha.

"You can't come to LA and not have a Double-Double. That just wouldn't be right."

"What is a Double-Double?"

"Just the best hamburger in the entire world, that's all!"

Kiraz raised her eyebrows and looked at Martha.

"They're like really good, I promise."

"And, we have to eat it here. There's no way you can eat one driving. It'll just all run down your arm. I've tried before."

"It is not made with horsemeat? You know how much I could eat a horse."

Martha shot Kiraz a perplexed look.

Alex butted in, "Private joke. Did you feel the quake?"

"Yeah, me and my sister were at the movies, but it didn't last long. My dad was like freaking out about it though, calling us on my cell like a whole bunch. Oh, my God, he almost didn't let me work my shift tonight."

"Really? We were up north when one of my friends from the earthquake lab called me about it. I was wondering how strongly it was felt up here in the high desert."

"Are you like a, what do you call it, a geologist?"

"Yes, we both are."

"That's cool. Um, do you want to order now?"

"Yeah, two Double-Doubles, two fries, a chocolate shake, and a . . . ?"

"An ice tea, please," Kiraz completed Alex's sentence for him.

"Two number-one meals, chocolate shake and ice tea."

"Right."

"It'll be just a couple of minutes."

Alex turned to Kiraz, "They make every burger as they are ordered."

Kiraz looked up at the yellow neon sign above the counter that read, "Quality You Can Taste." A few minutes later a red tray appeared on the counter with their freshly prepared order. Alex picked it up and brought it over to their table.

"Now, tell me this isn't the best hamburger you've ever eaten."

Kiraz opened the wrapper and took a bite, chewed, swallowed, nodded, and said, "It's very good, Alex, the best I've ever eaten!"

"I told you so."

"And, you are correct. We don't have any In-N-Out Burger restaurants in Turkey . . . not yet anyway. They haven't found enough horsemeat available."

Chapter 27

"THE U.S. GEOLOGICAL SURVEY in Pasadena has upgraded yesterday afternoon's earthquake in the San Fernando Valley to a magnitude 5.9, and pinpointed the epicenter at the intersection of Arleta Avenue and Osborne Street in Panorama City, only two blocks from the Golden State Freeway. Caltrans officials are inspecting the roadway for damage. So far, none has been discovered. Now we switch you to an exclusive report from our own Paul Abernathy who's coming to us live from the epicenter. Paul, can you tell us what's happening?" the female news anchor reported.

"I'm here with Mr. Juan Garcia, who manages this convenience store, and was inside when the tremor hit. I can imagine that sitting directly on top of the quake shook things quite a bit," he held up the microphone.

"Yes, it happened real fast. Almost everything on the shelves began falling all over the floor. The doors to the coolers were banging back and forth like this," Mr. Garcia demonstrated for the viewers. "The place was a mess, but fortunately we didn't lose too much merchandise."

Click.

Alex was in a hurry after the previous day's motoring blitz of his favorite California geological sites. Unfortunately, the Double-Double hangover from their visit to the *Mecca* of hamburger restaurants lingered, bogging down his efforts to finish his accustomed morning routine. It was already 7:45, and there was simply no time for a stop at the Bean Head. Instead, he grabbed an apple from the fridge and soon was sailing down Hollywood Boulevard toward the freeway along with hundreds of his fellow Angelenos in their Monday morning commute.

Simultaneously, miles away, Kiraz had turned off the same television report and refocused her attention to her laptop's screen and the slides that she would soon be presenting at the morning lecture. Images of her day with Alex paraded through her mind, not only the geological sites, but, more importantly, the close personal moments. The prediction of the earthquake reaffirmed her empathic gift. What overshadowed even this experience was how unlikely it was that an Armenian and a Turk could get along so well, enjoy each other's company, and even share the same interests. Okay, he was an Armenian-American, but still, the whole concept of their interaction seemed unimaginable. She sighed and wondered where their relationship could be heading. One thing of which she was certain—she didn't want it to end. When she returned to Istanbul, Kiraz Karahan wanted Alex Demurjian in her life.

She logged off her laptop, slid it in the carrying case, and went down to the Hot Tomato for a quick breakfast of oatmeal and hot tea. Thirty minutes later Alex's taxi service pulled up to the front of the hotel and she got in the car.

"How are you doing this morning?"

"I'm fine, Alex," looking down at the half-eaten apple resting on the center console, "Your breakfast?"

"Yeah, I was in sort of a hurry this morning, something about my having to escort a famous seismologist from out of town to a lecture hall."

"Didn't your mother teach you to always eat a good, substantial breakfast?"

"Are you sure you want to discuss my mother on this sunshiny morning? The fog might roll back in if we did."

"Yesterday, you said that your mother is an unhappy person."

"That's putting it mildly, although I wish it were otherwise," Alex turned left onto Nordhoff.

"We can't make our parents happy. They must find it for themselves."

"Sometimes I think my mother expects her happiness to come from what I do. What about your mother and father?"

"They have their lives, and are content, but I understand what you mean. They probably wish I was married and had children instead of working for the Institute."

"It sounds like our mothers would be the best of friends, except for —"

"The fact that my mother is Turkish?"

"How'd you guess?"

"My mother would probably have some difficulty as well. She wouldn't understand your mother's perspective."

"It makes you wonder what would happen if they were both locked in a room for an hour. Now, that would be interesting!"

"Perhaps they would become best friends, just as you said."

"You really think so?"

"Look at us!"

Alex nodded at Kiraz encouragingly, "What's that old saying, 'hope springs eternal?'"

He parked the car in the faculty parking lot on the south end of the campus, and they walked across the quad.

"Gene has reserved a lecture hall in the library for your presentation. It's not huge, but big enough for all the geology students to attend plus a few more. There should be a decent sized crowd. I know most of my students will be there . . . what the hell is . . . ?"

As they approached the front of the library they were greeted by an unexpected display of protestors walking up and down the steps carrying placards that read:

STOP DENIAL OF ARMENIAN HOLOCAUST! WHY IS KARAHAN HERE? GO BACK TO ISTANBUL!

Assembling on the lawn in front of the protestors were those television news crews not covering the earthquake.

"Quick, follow me, I know a back way in!"

They hurried to the left toward Bayramian Hall and then around the west end of the library to a side entrance. Once inside he pulled her aside.

"This is not what we had planned, trust me!"

"I trust you, Alex."

The Presentation Room wasn't far and soon they were welcomed by Dr. Gene Williamson's friendly face.

"Dr. Karahan, it's so good to see you!"

"Dr. Williamson, the pleasure is mine as well."

"Has Alex been taking good care of you?"

"Quite well indeed."

"Good. He is our most popular professor. We all wish we had his magic."

"Gene, what's up with the business outside?"

"What are you talking about? We've been in here all morning setting up."

"It just so happens that half the population of Glendale is out there on the library steps rolling out the 'red carpet' for our guest, if you get my meaning!"

Alex pulled out his phone and tuned into a live webcast from one of the local television stations.

"We are live on the steps of the Delmar T. Oviatt Library on the campus of Cal State Northridge where protestors apparently of Armenian heritage are upset about the arrival of a Turkish geologist by the name of Dr. Kiraz Karahan. Here's a flyer we found outlining the lecture series that begins this morning. In an ironic twist, Dr. Karahan is here in Los Angeles to discuss, of all things, earthquakes . . ."

"I helped design that flyer!" Gene pointed at Alex's phone.

" . . . A spokesperson for the group is unhappy with the Turkish government's unwillingness to call the persecution of Armenians during the First World War, genocide. Given the large number of students of Armenian descent who attend the university, and last month's commemoration of the holocaust, the arrival of Dr. Karahan has provided an opportunity to bring this issue to light . . ."

"I've heard enough, I'm calling in the campus cops. We'll get this cleared up."

"Gene, I swear I had nothing to do with this!"

"I know you didn't."

"I just can't figure out how this came about so suddenly. I mean, I can't imagine that the university's Armenian Student Association would be so crass as to take advantage of her lectures just to prove a point. They must be acting independently. How are you feeling?"

Kiraz looked him directly in the eyes, "Alex, just like we talked about yesterday, what happened in my country almost a hundred years ago was terrible. They are understandably upset, but I don't view their protest as a personal attack on me."

Gene broke in, "Dr. Karahan, are you up to presenting the lectures given this unwanted publicity? If you want to call off this morning until we get this under control I'll completely understand."

"We are professionals, and I am ready to talk about the seismology that links our two countries."

He nodded, "Impressive."

Just then two police officers arrived, "Dr. Williamson, I presume?"

"You presume correctly."

"Frank Donavan, Campus Police Chief," offering his hand in greeting.

Shaking his hand, "I was just about to call you. What are your options about the protest? Can they take it somewhere else on campus, like the soccer field?"

"We're trying to avoid an incident if possible. You know, handle this with kid gloves."

"Oh, by the way, this is our distinguished guest whose arrival has caused such a stir, Dr. Karahan."

"Pleased to meet you, ma'am."

"Yes, thank you."

"Safety is our first concern, public relations second. Since you're securely in the building, Doctor, we've already jumped over one hurdle. These people out there don't look violent, but we must take all precautions. We'll position officers at this room, the library entrance, and outside. When is your lecture over?"

"Twelve o'clock," said Gene.

"Okay, we'll escort the Doctor out of the library to wherever she wants to go on campus. How many days will she be here?"

"Through tomorrow."

"We'll find out more about the demonstrators' plans, but in the meantime it would be wise for us to handle security before and after each lecture. Before we're done today, let's establish a game plan for tomorrow."

"Agreed."

"Good. I'm going to leave Officer Mendoza here at the room, and head outside to check on my other troops. Felipe, you're in charge."

As Chief Donovan left the room Gene commented, "Well, that was timely, wasn't it? Officer Mendoza, how can we cooperate?"

"I'll be here at the entrance to the hall observing the crowd and establishing a presence. If there are any hecklers we'll hustle them out."

"Thank you for your help."

"Just doing my job, Professor."

The three geologists moved toward the front of the room where an IT tech met with Kiraz about her slide presentation, saved on a flash drive from her early morning rehearsal. While she discussed logistics, Alex and Gene continued to check-in.

"You two look pretty cozy, calling each other by first names. Are you becoming an item?"

"Gene, not so loud. We're becoming good friends, although I wouldn't be opposed to our becoming even better ones. Do you have any idea how bright she is?"

"Of course I do! Why do you think I scraped together the departmental funds to bring her all the way over here? That wasn't easy to do in these times of budget cuts, but there's nobody on earth more knowledgeable about quake prediction than her."

"You got that right, in fact, she predicted yesterday's little wakeup call the day before it happened."

"She found out about the swarms, didn't she? Wow, she really is on top of things. USGS could really use someone like her, although she's immensely useful to her own outfit."

"That's not exactly what I meant. You're going to have to think outside the scientific box for a moment. She sensed the swarms before we even knew about them."

"What do you mean, sensed?"

"She can feel quakes before they happen, including their magnitude."

Students began filing into the Presentation Room raising the noise level. Alex spotted some of his own, and left his boss hanging on those cryptic words to greet them. Soon the time came for the start of the lecture.

"Greetings everyone, and welcome to our special end of the semester series, *The Tale of Two Faults: The San Andreas Meets the North Anatolian*. I am Dr. Eugene Williamson, chair of the Geological Sciences Department here at Cal State Northridge. We are in for a treat these next two days. Our guest, although youthful in age and appearance, is wise beyond her chronological years. I first met her many years ago during a professional conference and came away thoroughly impressed by her knowledge and dedication to our craft. She holds a Ph.D. in geology from Middle Eastern Technical University in Ankara, Turkey. As the assistant director of the Istanbul Seismological Institute, she pioneered the broadband quake detection system throughout her country. We are honored and privileged to have with us Dr. Kiraz Karahan."

Dr. Williamson paused, then continued, "But, before she begins, it is unfortunately incumbent on me to mention something else, and I don't mean yesterday's quake. Upon entering the library this morning you probably couldn't help but notice the protestors. Let me be clear at the outset that we are not here today to comment about the merit of this activity, nor the pros or cons of their position, but are here for the sole purpose of science and the mutual cooperation between the peoples of our different lands. With that said, I now turn the podium over to Dr. Karahan." The Presentation Room, filled to its 150-seat capacity, burst into applause.

"Thank you, Dr. Williamson, and thank you everyone for bringing me to your distinguished university to talk about a subject that links our two countries. When your invitation arrived suggesting this series of lectures I was naturally overjoyed at the prospect of visiting the United States for the first time, but especially to come to your university given all the rebuilding you've accomplished since 1994. You have a very beautiful campus, and thanks to my gracious host, Dr. Alex Demurjian, I've been able to visit its many sights. I even sampled the food in one of your cafeterias."

Laughter ensued from the audience punctuated by a yell, "And you survived?!"

"Yes, actually, it was a very good chicken salad, but you didn't come here this morning to hear me critique your school's cuisine."

Instantly, on cue, a slide flashed on the screen showing images of two rift valleys.

"Fellow geologists, do you recognize these faults? Can anyone identify them? Yes."

Roxy, from Alex's Geology 101 class, raised her hand, "The one of the left is the San Andreas Fault, and the one on the right, well . . . looks a lot like it too."

"You have made a good observation and assessment, except for one small fact. The fault on the left is my North Anatolian, and the one on the right, your San Andreas."

Voices responded in unison, "Huh?"

"It's easy to mistake one fault for the other, for they behave like twin sisters, traveling above ground for hundreds of miles before diving into the sea, and on occasion wreaking havoc on the lives of nearby residents usually without warning."

Kiraz advanced to the next slide entitled, "Comparison of the North Anatolian and San Andreas Faults."

"I borrowed this slide from the U.S. Geological Survey website, but I didn't think they would mind."

Laughter circled the room.

"For millions of years, these two right strike-slip faults have been fracturing their respective lands at a rate of twenty to forty millimeters per year, completely unbeknownst to each other. Of course, I speak as if they were sentient beings with the potential for meaningful communication, but scientifically we know they are simply a dynamic part of the earth's crust. Notice how California and Turkey when laid against each other appear to mirror one another. Today and tomorrow we will examine the destructive impact of these faults and the potential for early detection of large seismic events . . ."

Kiraz launched into her lecture with the entire audience's attention riveted on her every word.

Chapter 28

AFTER LUNCH WITH Angie and the kids, Detective Jackson drove back to his South Central home with one thing on his mind—putting Michael Stein in shackles. The preposterousness of a Chinese connection in the Stover murder case was making about as much sense to him as if Mao Tse-tung had risen from the grave and shot him himself. Stein continued to display as the largest blip on his radar screen, and in the fresh light of Monday morning, it had grown considerably during the overnight hours. He decided to report in to his boss.

"John, it's J. I met with Madame Dragon Lady yesterday, and I gotta tell you, this business about the Chinese is total bullshit."

"Really? She said her source was rock solid. So, what's your strategy?"

"I've got a suspect, but he's sly, rich, and very capable of throwing us a red herring with Cantonese sauce on it. It's gonna take some time, more than the tight leash she tried to put on me."

"J, you do what you think is right, and I'll run interference with Supervisor Shackleford's office. I dance that dance all the time."

"You're such a politician, John, but are you sure you can dance with her? Hell, that bitch wears steel-toed stilettos! She might stomp on your tender little feet."

"Don't you worry, J. I'll put on a pair myself. Who's your prime suspect?"

"Michael Stein, head of Stein mining. Got a fancy office downtown up in the Library Tower."

"Why him?"

"Stover's body was found very close to Stein's Palmdale mine, and when I interviewed him he fessed up to knowing him. They even went to college together. It's kind of weird, but thinking back on it, I swear he already knew Stover was dead."

"Anything else?

"Personnel records don't show any of his employees owning guns, except for his tin cops, and they checked out. He doesn't even appear to have a security department. What's a gold-mining company doing without security?"

"Maybe they contract with somebody."

"I'm already on that."

"Ditch the Chinese thing, J. Put the heat on Stein!"

"That's my plan, John. Have fun at the dance, and don't forget to wear your special shoes!"

"You're bad, J. Really bad!"

Chapter 29

EVEN THOUGH ONLY the first day of lectures was behind her, Kiraz was already feeling emotionally exhausted. Scenes of the demonstration had stunned her. She knew she shouldn't buy into the messages she had seen and heard, but her empathic nature zeroed in on the crowd's animosity. If only she could shield herself better. Somehow she managed to conceal her distress from her colleagues.

"That was outstanding, Dr. Karahan. I don't know when I've enjoyed a lecture as much as this one. Lex, wouldn't you agree?" Gene Williamson broke into her inner world.

"You were 'amazing,' to quote one of my geology students."

"Thank you. It was my pleasure."

"We better get you back to your hotel. Lex, can you continue to be her host for the duration of her stay, especially after she gave you such a public endorsement?"

Gene looked at Alex with a slight wink in his eye.

"Absolutely!"

"Good. Make sure he doesn't take you back to that cafeteria for lunch! See you both in the morning."

Chief Donavan arrived at the door of the Presentation Room with three additional officers just as Dr. Williamson was making his exit.

"Chief, we need to talk about tomorrow."

"Here's my card, call me this afternoon. Dr. Karahan, are you ready?"

"Yes."

"Where are we headed to?"

Alex took command, "How about back to my car? I'm in the south lot off Darby."

Kiraz looked up to him and nodded affirmatively.

"Okay, let's take you out the back away from the demonstration. I need to warn you that the crowd has grown a little since earlier this morning, but perhaps we can avert a confrontation."

Kiraz's stomach tightened upon hearing the chief's update.

"Felipe and Mark in front, the rest of us will trail behind."

The entourage of police officers and geologists efficiently made their way through the halls and out the side entrance of the library. Kiraz stuck to Alex like glue. Once outside they hustled down the sidewalk around the back of Bayramian Hall eluding the demonstrators in front of the library. Soon they were marching down Etiwanda making a beeline for the parking lot, drawing curious looks from students passing by.

"How are you doing? Here, let me carry your laptop."

Kiraz willingly handed it to Alex and he flung the strap over his shoulder. The procession continued unabatedly without incident until Officer Mendoza spotted something that caught his attention.

"Chief!"

"I see them."

As they approached the front of the Sierra Center a half-dozen placard carrying protestors, having arrived late for the festivities, had just walked across the street from the parking garage and were now on a collision course with them.

"What do we do now?" the officer asked his boss.

"Just keep walking, nice and steady. Look straight ahead." Stares and glances shot from the eyes of the oncoming group as they began to awkwardly wiggle past each other until one of the protestors shouted out, "Hey, Dr. D!"

Alex immediately recognized the young man, a former student of his from the fall semester.

"Hi Sam," Alex replied as he tried to keep step with the lead flank.

"Wow, you look like you've got an army around you. What's up?"

They slowed momentarily as Chief Donovan assertively placed himself between them.

"We don't want any problems here. Just move along."

"Hey, wait a minute, that's her isn't it?" He pointed at Kiraz.

All at once they slowed to a crawl. Two more police officers came forward, creating a human shield around the two geologists.

"Like I said, keep it moving, son!"

"No way!" He turned to a fellow protestor, "Arakel, text Maral at the library and tell her to bring everyone over here fast!"

If the protestor's signs had read "FREE BEER" the crowd couldn't have assembled more quickly. The electronic message had done its trick. Waves of protestors soon flooded through the Sierra Center complex towing in their wake students eating lunch at the nearby tables as well as the television news crews.

Chief Donovan pulled out his phone and called the dispatch center, "We have a situation over here at the Sierra Center and I need every available officer here, and I mean everyone, including parking enforcement! Alert LAPD up at Devonshire in case we need more help."

Alex and Kiraz were at the mercy of the moment. Certainly the police had done all they could in preventing the showdown that was unfolding before them. How could they have predicted encountering a group of stragglers? Fortunately, the CSUN Department of Police Services was only a block away, and within a matter of minutes twenty-five uniformed officers, including several police vehicles joined the ranks of their comrades drawing an impressive line in the sand along Etiwanda Avenue.

"The cavalry has arrived."

"Cavalry?"

"Reinforcements."

"I understand."

Kiraz moved closer to Alex's side.

Alex bent over and whispered in her ear, "I was thinking that maybe we could just slip away from this throng of 'well-wishers' and find us a nice outdoor table at an In-N-Out. I know where there's one just a few blocks from here."

A small smile emerged on Kiraz's face filtered through the anxiety coursing through her body, "Two Double-Doubles?"

"Yeah, and do you think one order of fries will do?"

The police chief's voice blasting through a megaphone thwarted her reply, "This is Chief Donovan of the campus police. We know your constitutionally granted rights under the First Amendment to freedom of speech and assembly, and we're here to uphold that right as long as laws are respected. But, we all need to consider the rights of Dr. Karahan, who is our guest here at the university."

A yell shot from the crowd, "Who was the asshole that invited her here in the first place?"

Another shouted, "Yeah, and what rights does she have anyway? She's a damn foreigner!"

Suddenly, the mob ignited into a robust burst of chanting, "GO BACK TO ISTANBUL! GO BACK TO ISTANBUL! GO BACK TO ISTANBUL!"

Chief Donovan turned to Alex, "This is getting ugly. Got any ideas?"

"Yeah, in fact, I do. Give me the bullhorn!"

The chief handed him megaphone, "Good luck."

"Hey, everybody! Hey! Can we all just chill here for a moment?"

The last utterance of "GO BACK TO ISTANBUL!" trailed off the lips of the crowd.

"Guys, this isn't going to solve anything, or bring back our ancestors. I mean, really, it isn't. When I say our ancestors, I mean mine too. Some of you know me, and I recognize many of you from my classes. For those who may be wondering who I am, I'm Dr. Alex Demurjian, a professor of geology."

At a dry cleaning business in Glendale an anxious mother watched her son speak on live television for the first time.

"Tevos, come here!"

"That's right, Demurjian. I'm an Armenian-American like many of you. And, like with many of you, members of my family were killed or abused back during the genocide. When I was a kid my parents would take me every April 24th to the memorial in Montebello. So, I get what bothers all of you, but to rail against someone who had absolutely nothing to do with what happened is totally ridiculous and unfair. These past few days I've gotten to know Dr. Karahan, and let me tell you, she's what you call, good people."

"Tevos, get in here!"

"She came here to the university at our invitation, not to cause anyone injury, or to rub our collective Armenian noses in the muck and mire of history, but to freely share new and helpful ideas on the subject of seismology. Given that little shaker we had yesterday, maybe, just maybe, we could benefit from what she knows."

"Wow, would you look at that!" said Tevos.

"Ahh . . . you're thinking, yeah man, but she's a Turk. Some of us grew up hearing that word spoken derisively. I know I did. Yes, she's Turkish, but more importantly, and get this, she's also a human being, just like you and me. Like someone you'd catch a movie with, or drink coffee with, or just hang out with. Yesterday, we were talking about the genocide, and she told me that what happened to our people was totally wrong. So, let me ask you, why are you picking on her? She didn't do anything to our ancestors. She's not the enemy!"

Alex looked at Kiraz, then at his watch and said, "Protest if you want, but it's getting pretty close to one o'clock, and I don't know about all of you, but we were kind of looking forward to grabbing some lunch. Not sure where we're going yet, but we were just discussing that when you guys showed up."

Alex handed the megaphone back to Chief Donovan, took Kiraz by the arm and said, "Let's go!"

He boldly led her down the sidewalk in the direction of the faculty parking lot. The chief motioned to his officers to follow while the gathering of protestors, onlookers, and news crews stood motionless with their collective breaths inhaled. Upon exhaling they gradually began to disperse leaving behind little trace of the encounter.

Back at the dry cleaning shop Tevos was beside himself, "That guy should run for office, and what a handsome devil too. And she's quite the looker, don't you think, Mariam?"

"Tevos, be quiet! I'm trying to listen."

Chapter 30

"WHEW! LET'S GET OUT OF HERE!"

Alex nervously inserted and twisted the key in the ignition, and then jammed his fingers on the power window buttons. In seconds they zipped out of the parking lot onto Darby Avenue.

"I know we talked about lunch, but if you want me to just drop you off at the hotel, I can understand. After what you've been through this morning you might want your own space."

"Alex, I need some air."

"Hold on a sec, let me turn up the AC. I just thought that rolling down the windows would help cool off the car. It's been sitting out in the sun all morning and—"

"No, I don't mean air conditioning! Can we drive somewhere, away from this place?"

"Sure, let me see . . . uh . . . hey, I've got an idea!"

Kiraz held her hand to her head and gently closed her eyes while Alex drove away from campus. Miles of San Fernando Valley suburban sprawl silently passed by until she came out of her trance.

"Where are we going?"

Alex had just turned left off of Tampa and onto the onramp for the westbound 118 Freeway.

"Someplace where we can get some air. You know, you're starting to master English idioms just like a native. How do you that?"

"Television."

"You said that the other day."

"Where are we going for lunch?"

"Oh, that's kind of up in the air."

"Ha-ha! You are trying to cheer me up."

"Maybe just a little."

"You don't know where we're going? That is, it is up in the air. Right?" she held her hands up.

"Not so fast. Why don't we go to—"

Alex's cell phone rang. He instantly recognized the phone number.

"Mom?"

"It's your father."

"Hi, Dad. What's up? Are you okay?"

"Your mother and I saw you on TV. You know, that little one here at the shop she watches the afternoon soaps on. They interrupted her show for you."

"Oh, my God, you're kidding!"

"Nice job, son. You said what needed to be said—things that many people in our community ought to hear. Even your mother was impressed."

"Mom actually liked what I said?"

"I don't know if she loved it, but she was pretty excited to see you on TV, even if it did mess up her soap. She's busy with a customer right now, but she can tell you herself if you and the Doctor have time for dinner tonight. Seven o'clock at Louise's, our treat?"

Alex looked at Kiraz, "Lunch might be up in the air, but I think we've got dinner figured out."

"Yes?"

"My parents have invited us out to dinner tonight. Are you game?"

"What?"

"Sorry, uh, would like to have dinner with—"

"Yes, Alex, I would."

"We'll be there at seven, Dad. See you then. Bye."

Alex turned off his phone and stared out the window at the rocky scenery as they topped the crest of the Santa Susanna Pass and began their descent into Simi Valley.

"They call this the Ronald Reagan Freeway."

"Why is that?"

"Perhaps because it leads to the Ronald Reagan Library. All the ex-presidents have libraries that store archives from their presidencies. I've been to Clinton's back in Arkansas, and Reagan's just up the road. The Nixon one is down in Orange County."

"Is that where we're having lunch?"

"No, I wasn't thinking about eating there. I don't know what I was thinking. Pretty cool rocks out here don't you think?"

Alex motioned with his head out the window where reddish slabs of rock adorned the slope at a gentle angle. Kiraz examined the scenery as they passed a sign that read, "118 West, Ronald Reagan Freeway."

"Sandstone?"

"Sandstone."

"How old?"

"Cretaceous, part of the Chatsworth Formation. I sometimes take new geology students on hikes along the trails around here. It's just a hop, skip, and a jump from campus. Real easy to get to."

"It is one of your favorite places in California?"

"I'd rank it around fifth or sixth, just ahead of Vasquez Rocks and Devil's Punchbowl. The road cut here exposes the original grayness of the stone, but when it's weathered it turns reddish-tan, sort of like the rock we saw yesterday at the—"

"Alabama Hills."

"Yes, but the change in appearance is from the oxidation of iron minerals present in the rock and not—"

"Spheroidal weathering."

"Right."

Their geological repartee helped draw his attention away from selecting a suitable lunch site as well as the shock of his father's phone call. Suddenly, his impromptu, televised speech to his clan had begun to open doors that previously appeared to be shut tight. For his parents to have invited Kiraz, a Turk, to dinner at Louise's was a shift in reality akin to the San Andreas, Garlock, and Sierra Nevada faults all slipping a hundred meters simultaneously. He felt both dread and delight in anticipation of the forthcoming gathering.

"This city that we are driving through now, Simi Valley. It feels very calm here."

"It is a nice place, very . . . Midwestern."

"Midwestern, I don't understand."

"Look around you. It's pretty flat like most of the Midwest, except for the surrounding mountains. In my travels I've driven through many small Midwestern cities and they all remind me of Simi Valley. Mostly white, family-oriented, conservative, harmonious, peaceful, and safe. Maybe that's one of the reasons the Reagan Library is here. Most people think he was from California, but he was actually from a small town in Illinois. They call it the safest city in America. Nothing really bad ever happens here."

"Nothing? That is difficult to believe."

Kiraz continued to look out the window at the passing noise walls that provided a sound barrier between the freeway and city.

"One big thing did happen here several years ago."

"The Northridge Earthquake?"

"I wasn't thinking of that, but you're right, it did shake Simi pretty hard, a solid VII to VIII on the Mercalli scale. No, it was a couple of years before that when I was still a student over at Cal Tech. They held the Rodney King Trial at the courthouse here in Simi rather than in LA."

"What was this Rodney King accused of that they came here for his trial?"

"No, hold on, let me explain it better. The trial wasn't for Rodney King but for the police officers who beat him up. Didn't you see the video?"

Kiraz searched her memory sorting through images of the mob scene on campus, her time with Alex, back to

Turkey, watching television, "Yes, I saw it, we all did. We couldn't believe how brutal the American police could be toward one of its citizens. Your country is known everywhere for protecting its citizen's rights."

"It was pretty bad what happened, and when the not guilty verdicts came all hell broke loose."

Kiraz looked confused, "I don't understand."

"The riots that came afterward. Dusk to dawn curfews. It was the first time I ever heard one of those emergency broadcast system alerts on the radio that wasn't a test. It all started right here in pleasant, peaceful Simi Valley."

Alex turned off the freeway as State Route 118 continued its path westward into Moorpark. A familiar fast-food restaurant marquee with a yellow arrow pointing down toward itself came into view on the left side of the car.

"Lunch is no longer up in the air. Check it out, over there!"

Given the lateness of the lunch hour a repeat of the previous day's dinner was quickly ordered and rapaciously consumed. Following lunch, their journey continued for yet another half-hour until they could drive no further. Alex welcomed Kiraz to their intended destination.

"You wanted some air. This is the best air in Southern California."

She stood up from the car and drew in two lungs full of a pollutant-free mixture of nitrogen and oxygen.

"Come on, the air is even better over there."

Alex led the way as they walked the short distance from the parking lot along a narrow path cut through the diminutive dunes. The squishiness of the sand caused their footing to become unstable. Kiraz stopped, reached out her hand to his, alternating between them as she took off her shoes.

"What am I thinking? It's pretty stupid walking on the beach in shoes, isn't it?"

Kiraz nodded in agreement, and motioned with her head toward his feet.

Alex propped himself up against the dune. He slipped off his loafers, stuffed his socks inside them, rolled up his shirtsleeves, and then picked up his shoes with the fingertips of his left hand.

"You want me to carry yours?"

"No, I can carry them."

She returned her hand back to his and nudged him in the direction of the strand.

They stood for a few minutes hand in hand admiring the view of the ocean and the wide expanse of San Buenaventura Beach. The waves were lightly breaking creating the familiar seashore percussion. Kiraz pulled her sunglasses over her hair and shielded her eyes to look up toward the mid-afternoon sun, now shining brightly after having done its job of pushing the morning's marine layer out of sight.

"Alex?"

"Yeah."

"Do you like me?"

"What do you mean, like you? Of course I do!"

"What I mean is, do you like me, and are being nice to me because it is your job, your assignment?"

"I stopped thinking about you as an assignment from the very moment I saw you at the airport."

"You did?!"

Alex closed his eyes, shielding him momentarily from the penetrating intensity of hers, then he opened them, "Yeah, I did. Really, I'm not making this up. You're not what I expected. While you were sleeping in the car on the way to your hotel I couldn't take my eyes off of you. It was hard to pay attention to the traffic."

"Alex, I like you very, very much too. I don't know when I've felt so secure. I felt protected when you stood up to that crowd and told them to leave me alone."

"I spoke from the heart, and I'd say it again."

"I know you would."

They began to stroll along the edge of the beach toward the pier, the afternoon breeze encouraging them with its freshness and vitality. Two seagulls that had been circling around in the air just ahead of them unexpectedly landed next to each other and strutted along the shore.

"Look at them!" Alex pointed with his shoe-laden hand, the other gently holding hers.

"They look very happy."

"Just like some people I know."

"I think I know them."

Chapter 31

UNLIKE HIS GRANDKIDS, staring at a computer screen all day was not something Detective Jackson especially enjoyed. Even though he was wearing reading glasses his eyes had begun to blur from the hours of sifting through a seemingly unending pile of Internet generated reports of private security companies. As a reward for his effort he decided to knock off for a coffee break when something captured his attention. Interpol reported monitoring the activities of two Russians now working for the fledgling Moscow-based agency, Fortress Solutions. Questioned in the investigation of a steel executive's murder in Luxembourg City, Interpol continued to show interest in these former FSB Academy rejects. Jackson gleefully noted that their current whereabouts had been traced to none other than his own turf, Los Angeles. He printed off their photos and dossiers, alleviating his computer screen fatigue, and began comparing them with the photos from the victim's camera.

"China my ass, look at these bozos!" he smacked the papers with tips of his fingers.

"What'd you say?" Deputy Chin was working on a report at the adjacent desk.

"Check it out, Bob. Give me you unbiased opinion." Jackson held up the photos.

"For a moment I thought you were defaming my ancestral homeland."

Deputy Chin studied the Interpol photos and those from Cal Stover's camera and nodded in agreement.

"They're the same, but I'm not a photo expert."

"You're a cop, and that's what matters."

"This cop says the men in these photos are a dead-on match. This is from the Stover murder, isn't it?"

"What else?"

"So, who are these guys?"

Jackson read the report, "We have here Misters Ivan Balabanov and Sergei Malinovskii. I think I said that right."

"Russians?"

"Yeah, Russians."

He googled Fortress Solutions and up popped a very professionally executed website, both in English and Russian.

"Here's the outfit they work for. Pretty slick. They do it all—bodyguards, corporate security, monitoring, the whole nine yards."

Deputy Chin got up and moved behind Detective Jackson to get a better view.

"Check out their list of clients. Click there. Scroll down. Oh, my God, would you look at that!"

"Stein Mining!"

"This case is practically solving itself, Mister Holmes."

"And let me guess, you're . . . what was his name?"

"Doctor Watson. Hey, I've heard those Russians can be some pretty badass characters."

"Not as badass as this one!"

Deputy Chin stood up and pointed his thumbs toward himself, "Well, if you need some backup don't forget to call."

"Don't worry, I've got your number."

Chapter 32

THE BULDING AT 4500 Los Feliz Boulevard had long been a popular dining establishment before it began serving Italian cuisine. Originally a chicken restaurant, the property had been developed into one of the famous Brown Derby restaurants owned by Hollywood legend, Cecil B. DeMille. As the last remaining Brown Derby still functioning as a restaurant, with its distinctive silver domed top remaining where the hat was once perched, it had survived the wrecking ball thanks to the efforts of local Hillhurst angels who came to its defense a few years before. It was now an official Historic Cultural Monument of the City of Los Angeles.

Whether the restaurant donned the signature Brown Derby hat, or a Michael's or Louise's sign, it had become a life-long Demurjian family favorite, particularly for noteworthy celebrations. This salient fact had secretly gnawed away at Alex since his father suggested they meet there for dinner. Was this a unilateral invitation of a curious parent enticed by what he saw on television, or had his mother been consulted as well? Given her parting words to him the other night, he has his doubts. Could it be that his parents somehow magically tuned into the relationship that was emerging between them?

"Sorry we're late. You know how the 5 Freeway can be this time of night."

"No problem. Your mother and I were just studying the menu."

Tevos rose from the table and offered them the open seats in front of him.

"Mom, Dad, this is my friend and colleague, Dr. Kiraz Karahan."

"Please, call me Kiraz. There is no need for formality," she greeted the elder Demurjians with a kindly smile.

Tevos took her extended hand, "I'm Tevos. Alex has told us so much about you. I must say that you look as lovely in person as you do on television."

"Thank you."

Mariam lagged behind her husband in the greeting process, but hoisted herself into a partial standing position before breathing out a, "Nice to meet you," as she sat back down.

"I hope you don't mind eating inside by the window. I'd rather sit outside on the patio, but you know how your mother is about those space heaters, so we compromised."

"You don't have to tell all the family secrets in the first five minutes!" Mariam rapped him on the arm.

"This is fine, Dad," turning to Kiraz, now seated next to him, "When this restaurant was called the Brown Derby people used to drive up and were served in their cars, right there, didn't you say, Dad?" pointing out the window.

"That's right. Back in the late 50s my father would bring the whole family here in his Studebaker. He'd park the old heap right where those people are eating."

"But not anymore? Why is that, Mr. Demurjian?"

"Please, call me Tevos! You didn't want me to call you Dr. Karahan?"

Alex answered for his dad, "You don't see drive-in restaurants much anymore, at least not in LA, but I ate at one when I was back in Missouri a few years ago. What was it called, uh . . . Sonic! That was it!"

"When you were at the Trail of Tears?"

"Yeah!"

"Trail of Tears?" asked Tevos.

"It was a state park."

"I don't remember your mentioning it before. What kind of park is called that?"

"Like I told Kiraz the other day, it commemorates the forced march of Native Americans from their homes in the East to the Indian Territories out West. That's why they call it the Trail of Tears."

Mariam cross examined her son, "So, what did you eat at this restaurant?"

"The usual, burgers and stuff. It was pretty decent as I recall."

She shook her head, "Not good food, Alex."

"You're right, Mom, it wasn't nearly as good as In-N-Out. I just thought it'd be kind of cool to eat at a drive-in, just like you and Dad did back in the old days. Then I came back home and discovered there were actually a few of them here in LA!"

"That was your father's side of the family. We couldn't afford such luxuries."

Just then a female server came to the table for their drink order.

Tevos led off, "How about a nice bottle of red wine?"

"May I suggest the Chianti Classico?"

"That'll work."

"Hey, you look familiar," said Alex.

"Hello, extra-large mocha!"

"Wait, you're Maribel! You work here too?"

Mariam asked, "You know our waitress?"

"She's from the Bean Head."

"We haven't seen you around for a while. Your two friends look for you every morning."

"Tell them I'll be there real soon, maybe Thursday. I've been kind of busy these past few mornings," subtly glancing Kiraz's way.

"I see. I'll report that you haven't totally disappeared from the planet."

"Uh, I'd appreciate that."

Once Maribel left, Mariam began the inquisition, "Do you come from a large family?"

"There are four of us, my parents in Izmit, and my brother, Ahmet, who lives in Germany. Let me show you their photos."

Kiraz reached into her purse and retrieved a bright red wallet with an extensive photo section. Mariam leaned forward keenly and watched her describe each image in detail.

"This is Ahmet in front of his restaurant with his wife and children. It's only a few blocks from the Rhine River."

"I didn't see your husband's picture."

"I am divorced and no longer carry a photo of him."

"I see."

Tevos looked encouragingly toward his son while the two women continued to discuss their respective families.

"My parents came from Turkey you know."

"Yes, Alex told me about your father's exile to the desert with his mother. That must have been awful for them."

"Thank you for showing me your family. They look like nice people."

"You're welcome, Mrs. Demurjian."

"You may call me, Mariam."

"Mariam."

Kiraz allowed a smile to arise through her anxiety.

"You and Alex have much in common."

"Yes, we both have, as he likes to say, 'rocks on the brain!'"

"Sometimes I think he has rocks for brains, right son?"

"Mom!"

"Oh, I get it!" Kiraz began giggling out loud, sparking everyone's laughter.

Maribel arrived with the wine and four glasses, "It appears that you won't be needing any of this, will you?"

Tevos stopped her from walking away, "Go ahead, pour the glasses. We have much to celebrate."

Those cryptic words shot through the table like a P-wave on its way through bedrock.

"To warm friendships, happy families, healthy lives, and abundant prosperity. *Genatset!*"

"Genatset!"

"So, how do you make a toast in Turkey?"

"We would say, *sagliginiza!*"

"Sagliginiza!"

Two hours sailed by as the senior Demurjians drank in not only the wine that had been poured, but also this darling, young, bright woman their son had brought to dinner. Before dessert was served the two women excused themselves for a trip to the restroom.

"Alex, my nephew called me."

"Danny?"

"He warned me about her."

"Warned you?"

"He said that in all the years you've brought girls up to the farm this was the only one he's ever been impressed with. I thought he was just pulling my leg, like he always does, until I saw you two on TV today."

"I know, I know, but what about Mom, and the rest of the family?"

"If you believed half of what you preached to that mob today, you wouldn't give a crap about what anyone thinks, even your mother. Besides, don't you wonder what they're talking about right now?"

"They do seem to be getting along pretty well."

"When she laughed at your mother's joke about your rock-brain that was the clincher."

"You think so?"

"Make your move, boy. Hell, you're almost thirty-seven for chrissakes!"

"Well, for what it's worth, we're already becoming a bit more than colleagues, if you know what I mean."

"Son, don't let this one get away like all the others."

"She goes home on Wednesday. What do I do?"

"What? You don't have the same access to air travel? Aren't you done teaching for the summer?"

"Yeah, and I think my passport is still good."

Just then Mariam and Kiraz returned to the table.

"Kiraz was telling me about your trip up to the desert yesterday. That's an awful place to take a girl on a date."

"It wasn't a date, Mom, it was a geological expedition!

"Right."

Kiraz fought back a grin.

Chapter 33

"WE'RE HERE ON the quad in front of the Delmar T. Oviatt Library, the site of yesterday's protest against university sponsored lectures presented by Turkish geologist, Dr. Kiraz Karahan. With me this morning is one of the organizers of the protest, Maral Asadurian, a student here at the university. We understand that the demonstration has been called off for today. Why the change?" the female reporter asked.

"After what happened with Dr. D and the police we realized that our issues aren't with Dr. Karahan, but with the Turkish government and their obstinate refusal to acknowledge the historical fact of the Armenian Genocide. For him, an Armenian, to stand up and scold us with this truth was sobering."

"That would be Professor Alex Demurjian?"

"Yes. Everybody here on campus calls him Dr. D. We have a lot of respect for him and hope that Dr. Karahan will accept our apologies. We wish her no harm."

"There you have it in a complete turn of events. Reporting live from Cal State Northridge, Amy Chang with 'NEWS-ON-THE-GO,' Now, back to the studio."

Alex, Kiraz, Gene, and Chief Donovan had huddled around Alex's cell phone watching the webcast from the Presentation Room.

"Like I was telling you, she and some others came to us yesterday after things cooled off and said they were sorry. In all my years on the force I've never seen this happen before. We don't anticipate any more problems with the Doctor's visit."

"Lex, you saved the day! You're not going to start bucking me for a pay raise, are you?"

"Not today, but that field trip to Hawaii suddenly came to mind."

"Later."

"Nonetheless, I'm going to station Officer Mendoza here again as a precaution. Use the radio if you need backup," the chief glanced toward his subordinate who nodded his acknowledgment of the orders.

"Dr. Karahan, you've been such a good sport about all the fuss we've put you through. Thank you for enduring our rather unpredictable and sometimes messy democratic process."

Kiraz glanced at Alex and then spoke to Gene, "Dr. Williamson, I have felt well supported the entire time I've been here, and will take home only good memories of my visit."

Noticing that the clock on the wall read almost nine o'clock he said, "The room is nearly full. Are you ready to start the lecture?"

"Yes."

"Then let's get this ball rolling."

After her reintroduction, Dr. Kiraz Karahan launched into her second lecture with a slide of a collapsed apartment building.

"In just thirty-seven seconds nearly twenty-thousand people died, twice that many were injured, and hundreds of thousands left homeless. The August 17, 1999 Izmit quake was an enormous wake up call for my country, and for those of us who work at the Istanbul Seismological Institute. We should have known a quake of this significance was not only possible, but also an absolute certainty. Could we have predicted its arrival? There have been so many earthquakes recorded in the history of my hometown that its residents should each be given a 'Frequent Shaker Card' at birth."

A moment of laughter was hushed as more images of demolished buildings paraded themselves on the screen.

"The historical account is telling. Since the beginning of the Common Era there have been twenty damaging seismic events in this section of the North Anatolian Fault, and yet we have completely failed to learn our lessons about how earthquakes kill."

She paused the flow of images then advanced to a slide of a fully intact mosque surrounded by the debris of collapsed apartment buildings. A gasp came over the audience.

"If these modern apartment buildings in the town of Gölcük, places where people lived their lives, had been built as well as this fourteenth-century mosque, the death toll would have been significantly lower. Notice the fifty-meter tall minaret, still standing. Many consider it a divine miracle, and it was when you take into account the destruction around it. You must admit that the Ottoman architects and builders knew how to construct structures that would endure."

"We all know that earthquakes alone don't kill, but poorly engineered and badly built buildings do. Sadly, the newest buildings suffered the greatest damage in this quake, a fact that seems totally illogical. As scientists, we can share our knowledge with policy makers and businesses, but they must heed our recommendations. The decisions that were made to build these shoddy buildings are what doomed their inhabitants. Those were criminal acts."

For a brief moment, Kiraz fought back the tears as she thought of her brother, Mehmet, who had been buried under the rubble of a naval barracks only a short distance from the mosque.

"Geology is more than just rocks, sediment, and fault lines; it is about helping our fellow human beings live their lives well and safely."

"Yes," came from the audience.

"I'm so glad you agree with me! California and Turkey are earthquake countries, and we must learn to cope with that reality. My office made the decision to expand the use of broadband technology to more accurately monitor earthquakes in real time using software created by . . ."

Kiraz's second lecture whizzed by as a receptive audience soaked up her expertise in seismology and its impact on human life. By eleven-thirty she was shaking hands at the door.

"Another brilliant presentation, Dr. Karahan! We're so glad you came all this way to assist us helpless Californians cope with our beloved San Andreas Fault. Don't you agree, Lex?"

"She can come here anytime . . . to assist us , that is."

"Thank you for the compliment, Dr. Williamson, but you appear to have things well under control. After all, we obtained the software to run our monitoring computers from your USGS."

"Speaking of which, are you up for attending the funeral for my USGS colleague, Cal? We could grab a bite and head on over to the church afterward," asked Alex.

"Yes, give me a moment to retrieve my laptop and make a trip to the restroom."

"I'll get it."

"Thanks."

Kiraz headed to the restroom while Gene followed Alex back to the front of the Presentation Room.

"You two have become quite a team, or dare I say, you even look like a couple."

"Gene, what are you driving at?"

"Got any plans to visit Istanbul anytime soon, perhaps starting tomorrow?"

"The thought had crossed my mind a few times. Okay, maybe a hundred times since my father suggested it last night at dinner."

"You took her to meet your folks. Very old fashioned."

"The dinner was my father's idea. He kept pestering me to go after her."

"In front of her?"

"No, while she and my mother were in the restroom, kind of like you're doing now!"

"I'm with him. You've got the whole summer off starting right now! No summer school to teach, no exams to score."

"I still have a few of those to look over and grades to post."

"And, what are department chairs for, to just sit around and drink coffee and complain about university administration politics? I think I can manage to get your end of semester loose ends tidied up."

"Thanks, Gene. Now I owe you one."

Kiraz returned from the restroom and left with Alex carrying her laptop bag.

Gene thought to himself, "They really do make a nice couple."

Chapter 34

SANDWICHED BETWEEN THE San Gabriel and San Fernando Valleys, and perched upon the shelf between the Verdugo and San Gabriel Mountains, the Crescenta Valley was comprised of the suburban communities of La Cañada Flintridge, Montrose, Verdugo City, La Crescenta, Tujunga, and Sunland. With an average elevation of 1,600 feet, the valley provided a small-town respite above the urban congestion and sprawl of Greater LA. Perhaps that is why the Medina, Ohio native, Cal Stover, found his weekly refuge at the Crescenta Valley Creative Living Center, a church located midway up the slope of the valley along Montrose Avenue.

Before coming out to Cal Tech for his freshman year, his minister back home had encouraged him to attend their services. The church's upbeat message and the earth friendly meme of many of its members naturally resonated with Cal's psyche. Following graduation and landing the USGS job, he stuck around as the church's sound tech. No doubt his weekly visits to the area had inspired him to write his doctoral thesis about the geological impact of the highly destructive 1934 New Year's Day Crescenta Valley Flood. Understandably, everyone at the church had been in mourning since learning the news of his untimely death.

"Friends and family, we are gathered here to reaffirm our faith in life eternal, as we bless this loved one, William Calvin Stover, on his way into his next experience in divine unfoldment. It is our prayer that from this time forward that we may never think of him as limited by time or form, but always as a living soul, continuing on the pathway of life, ever in our heavenly Father's wise and loving care," Reverend Alan Tucker began the memorial service.

Well over two-thirds of the church's one hundred-seat sanctuary was full. His parents, Ed and Joanne, and his girlfriend, Katy, were seated up front on the left next to the piano. Cal's USGS colleagues were to the right near the stained-glass windows, now illumined with early afternoon sun. Two elderly men were stationed at the entrance to the foyer handing out programs as latecomers arrived.

"Sorry we're late," Alex said to the usher wearing a nametag marked, "Jim."

He handed Alex and Kiraz programs, held his hand up to his mouth, and softly said, "It's okay. Come on in. The service just started. There's plenty of room over on the right."

"Thanks."

They quietly entered the sanctuary and slipped around to the right aisle finding seats just behind the USGS crowd.

David spotted them, turned around, and whispered, "Lex, I was hoping you guys could make it."

Alex nodded.

"One of the greatest challenges that all of us meet is the challenge of change, and indeed the most mysterious of all changes, is the one that we call death. Let us approach this time of challenge, of change, of readjustment by turning to God's Presence within ourselves. Let us give Cal the strength of our own spiritual understanding as we bless him on his way. As we do, listen now to these comforting and reassuring words of the Master Teacher, Jesus Christ, from the Gospel of John: 'Do not let your hearts be troubled. Believe in God, believe also in me. In my Father's house there are many dwelling places. If it were not so, would I have told you that I go to prepare a place for you? And if I go and prepare a place for you, I will come again and will take you to myself, so that where I am, there you may be also.'"

He paused for a moment, allowing the audience to prayerfully ponder his last words, then continued.

"I think everyone would agree with me that Cal was more than a member of this congregation, he was family. I remember when my colleague and friend back in Ohio, Reverend Anderson, told me about Cal. Apparently Case-Western made a big pitch for him to attend their school, but Cal Tech made an even bigger one. I guess that's what happens when you're a certifiable genius—you've got people fighting over your brains!"

The audience chuckled.

"We all know how smart Cal was, and how he helped drag our church kicking and screaming into the modern age. You'll remember how he single handedly transformed our old vacuum tube sound system into the one we're blessed with today. Perhaps you can still see him in the back there behind the sound board. I know I can, and it's going to take a while for us to get used to his not being there. By the way, we're looking for volunteers. Is anyone interested in the job?"

More laughter came from the audience.

"But, there was another side of Cal that transcended his mental aptitude, and that was his passionate quest for environmental justice, something that inspired us all. I'm sure you'll join with me in praying with the police for divine order in finding those responsible for his tragic death."

Just at that moment a well-dressed man in his forties twitched, while the two men seated next to him adjusted their posture. Another man seated in the back row carefully observed these non-verbal clues.

"Ed and Joanne, all of us here at the church can't imagine the grief you must be feeling right now, but please know that you're among family. We're so glad that you shared Cal with us these past twenty years, and if there's anything we can do to support you please don't hesitate to ask."

The Stovers politely smiled and nodded.

"And now, I'd like to open up the floor to anyone who has something they'd like to share about Cal. Is there anyone?"

The man in the fancy suit assertively walked up to the lectern and began to speak.

"I first met Cal when we were students at Cal Tech. If memory serves me right, it was Igneous Petrology class."

David leaned back to Alex, "Who is this guy?"

Alex shrugged his shoulders.

"No one loved geology as much as Cal, and over the years he served our profession with authenticity and distinction. I know that we all wish we could bring him back to life, but that is not possible in a corporeal sense. As a tribute to him, and to the work of geology, the Stover family has agreed to allow us to consecrate a place where Cal spent much of his time, his beloved San Andreas Fault. I have directed my company to erect a plaque in his honor at our mine in Palmdale where his ashes will be scattered. In this way, Cal and his spirit will live on forever in each one of us. Thank you."

The man returned to his seat.

"Thank you, Mr. Stein, for generously arranging this special blessing for Cal. We hope that many of you can attend the committal ceremony following this service. Is there anyone else who'd like to share?"

David raised his hand and began to approach the platform. "Yes, please come on up," motioning his hand toward the lectern.

"Hi, I'm David Horita, one of Cal's friends and co-workers. He worked with a bunch of us over at the lab. I must admit that he didn't talk a lot about your church, but now we know where he spent all of those Sunday mornings. For the life of me I don't know how he got here in time for services given some of our late Saturday night parties."

Laughter filled the sanctuary.

"He may not have spoken much about his religious beliefs, but he was rather vociferous about his political and economic views. Although he worked for big government, he wasn't a big fan of it, nor of big business."

David loathingly glared at Stein, then looked down toward the front row.

"Katy, Mr. and Mrs. Stover, I think I speak for all of Cal's friends when I say that we miss Cal almost as much as you do, and we're here for you. That's all I have to say."

Teary-eyed, David took his seat.

Reverend Tucker reclaimed the pulpit, "Is there anyone else who'd like to share something about Cal? Anyone?"

For nearly half a minute silence encompassed the audience as no one offered another word.

"Okay. I invite you to join me in affirming this prayer. As I say each line of it, repeat it after me, and as you do, think of Cal wherever he may be in God's great universe. Let us begin: The light of God surrounds you . . . the love of God enfolds you . . . the power of God protects you . . . the presence of God watches over you . . . wherever you are, God is, and all is well . . . Amen."

Reverend Tucker came down from the platform to the front row to console Cal's family, and everyone else began to file out of the sanctuary into the outdoor patio area where tables had been set up with light refreshments. The usher, Jim, went to the soundboard, punched a button, and Norman Greenbaum's, "Spirit in the Sky," began to play over the PA.

Michael Stein spoke to the other usher, who was handing out maps, "I appreciate your help."

"Hey, it's no problem. I think we printed enough for everyone," said Bob.

Just then the man from the back row came into Stein's view.

"Detective Jackson, I didn't see you come in."

"It's so easy to get lost in such a large building as this one," he said with a hint of sarcasm.

"Come to pay your respects to the dead?"

"Well, you know how we cops like to attend the funerals of murder victims. It's amazing how many suspects we find."

"And has your visit been a success?"

"Extremely!"

"Really? Anyone I know?"

"Quite possibly."

The two men who had been sitting next to Stein approached them.

"Ivan and Sergei, allow me to introduce Detective Jackson of the Sheriff's Department. You're LA County not LAPD?"

"Yeah."

The Russians muttered meager greetings to the *ment* who gave them a slight nod.

"Ivan and Sergei are associates of mine, and help me solve various security problems."

"Oh, I doubt they do much of that."

"You jest, Detective!"

"Not really. I've become well acquainted with your associate's CV's. It's fascinating reading, but I doubt you've bothered. Fortress Solutions has really taken you for a ride, Stein. I hope for your sake they gave you a discount."

Jackson began slowly walking out of the patio area toward the parking lot. Stein, Balabanov, and Malinovskii followed behind him.

"How so?"

"They really scraped the bottom of the barrel when they rustled them up for your detail. They're nothing but a couple of FSB's waste products. I'm surprised an astute CEO, such as yourself, hasn't noticed their complete lack of professionalism."

"What the . . . ?"

"Hold on there a minute, Ivan, we'll have plenty of time to talk down at the station house. Of course, you've seen the inside of one those back in Luxembourg."

"*Chush' sobách'ya!*"

"Watch your tongue, Ivan, you're on hallowed ground here at church."

"Detective Jackson, what is the point of your disturbing this peaceful assembly of mourners with your taunts and impoliteness."

"That's why we're taking this out here, right next to your shiny new Porsche."

Jackson pulled out his radio and spoke, "Now!"

Almost out of nowhere a swarm of LA County sheriff's deputies and Glendale PD officers descended on the group with guns pointed.

Deputy Robert Chin reported in to Detective Jackson, "I was wondering when you'd call."

"I told you I had your number. Search these two boys for weapons."

"You got it. Okay you two, spread 'em!"

Deputy Chin and his fellow officers recovered a handgun from each of them.

"A couple of Makarovs. You guys are so Russian."

Ivan formed a fist and tried to punch Deputy Chin, but was immediately wrestled to the ground by the other officers who quickly handcuffed him.

"Naughty, naughty, Ivan," Jackson waved his finger back and forth, "Have those pieces sent to ballistics, will you, Bob? My bet is that one of them is our murder weapon."

"My pleasure."

Then Detective Jackson looked the Russians in the eye, "Ivan Balabanov and Sergei Malinovskii, you're under arrest for suspicion of murder. Ivan, you also get assaulting a police officer and resisting arrest. Bob, mirandize them!"

"*Tvoyú mat'!*"

"Oh, are you talking about my mama? Sorry, you're my bitch now!"

After Deputy Chin read them their rights, Ivan and Sergei were stuffed into a Sheriff's Department SUV for transport to the station.

By now the crowd began to notice the arrest. Detective Jackson flashed his badge and made an announcement.

"Folks, sorry to trouble you, but we ask you to remain in the patio area for the next few minutes. No need to worry, we have everything under control. Unfortunately, it became necessary for our investigation of Mr. Stover's murder that we apprehend these suspects on the spot since they pose a credible flight risk. We'll be out of here shortly, and thank you for your cooperation."

Reverend Tucker asked, "Does this mean the committal service is off?"

"That's up to you, Reverend, but keep this in mind, Mr. Stein employed our prime suspects."

"Reverend, my offer still stands."

"I think not," shaking his head.

He left them and returned to the patio to share the abrupt change of plans with the gathering of well-wishers.

"Stein, no doubt we'll have more questions for you as the investigation proceeds, so don't get too comfy."

"I am free to go?"

"What do I have to do, walk you to your car and open the door?"

"No need to mock me, Detective. You'll be hearing from our legal team."

"I'm counting on it."

"Why is that?"

"Cuz you're gonna need 'em!

At that moment one of the mourners felt a sharp spasm in her solar plexus.

Chapter 35

THE AVANTI CAFE on North Lake Street in Pasadena had been voted year after year as LA's "Best Gourmet Pizza." Its wood-fired ovens and fresh ingredients brought in the customers, even in the middle of a Tuesday afternoon. Cal's USGS comrades David and John, Katy, plus Alex and Kiraz had gathered there for a geologist wake. In honor of Cal, a round of Coronas and two large duck sausage pizzas with black olives were ordered. Once the beers arrived the conversation erupted.

"Here's to Cal!"

"To Cal!"

Bottles clanked at John Lopez's call.

"Can you believe the gall of that guy sticking his nose into Cal's service? What an asshole!"

David articulated what nearly everyone around the table was thinking.

"At least they didn't go through with it," said Katy.

"Go through with what?"

"The ash scattering up at that mine."

"It's a good thing Cal was already ashes. If he had been in a casket I think he would've busted open the top and snatched the mike away from him," added John.

"Or walked back to the sound board and turned off his mic!"

"You've gotta admit that having the cops show up right then and bust those hoodlums was poetic justice," said Alex.

"Cal would've liked that," David nodded.

"I got a weird vibe off those two," said Katy.

"Hoodlums?" Kiraz looked at Alex.

"Criminals."

Kiraz did her best to follow along with the table conversation. Discussing the funeral service and the unforeseen police action required a completely different mind-set than her morning geology lecture. Continuing to gnaw away deep in her body and mind was the queasy pulsation that had begun back at the church. Images of fissures opening up in the ground and powerful earth movements flashed across her inner screen, images of Southern California shaken to its foundations with the San Andreas Fault looming large as the primary culprit.

"How did you like the service? It was quite different than the usual kind, very upbeat. I know Cal would've liked it," Katy attempted to change the tone of the conversation.

"Yeah, the Reverend was not what I expected either. Most of funerals that I've been to are pretty grim," said David.

"I really liked that prayer at the end. How did it go? Something about the light of God surrounding you," Katy remembered what she could.

David looked at Kiraz, "What are funerals like in Turkey?"

Kiraz was instantly propelled to Mehmet and the anguish and helplessness she felt sitting back in her apartment in Ankara hundreds of miles away hearing the news of his death over the phone from her wailing mother. The subsequent mass funeral, as was the case for the thousands killed on that hot August day in Kocaeli, only added to her sense of vacant disconnection. If she had stayed in Izmit where her premonition had occurred only days before, she herself might have perished.

She refocused and answered, "In Turkey they seem to happen much more quickly than here in the US. There is no cremation or service many days later. The body is ritually washed, wrapped in linen, placed in a coffin, and taken to a mosque for prayers, then the burial follows at the cemetery."

"What, no rock music?"

"No music at all, but lots of tears," she fought them back again.

"Oh."

"Kiraz's brother was killed in the '99 Izmit quake," Alex tried to rescue her.

"I'm so sorry. I didn't mean to open any wounds."

"It's quite all right. Perhaps I'm holding on to the past more than I should. It has been a long time now."

The pizzas arrived saving Kiraz from further explanation of Mehmet's death. Still the connection between her premonition eleven years ago and today's eerily stalked her. Should she say something to her colleagues about her ever-unfolding intuitive episode? Would they understand, or ridicule her? What would Alex say if she broached the subject? Although conflicted, as she often was when her geo-empathic nature was active, she mustered a simple question.

"Have there been any micro-quakes on the San Andreas Fault lately?"

"Funny you should ask. We're still monitoring aftershocks from Easter Sunday's 7.2 down in the Imperial Valley. They're following a predictable modified Omori's law decay rate, but lately we've been noticing a new swarm stretching from Wrightwood to Fort Tejon," David reported.

Alex perked up, "Really? What magnitude?"

"Mostly in the 2.0-3.5 range. There was a 2.7 in Lake Hughes this morning, and 3.2 in Valyermo the day before."

"Fort Tejon. That is the location of the 1857 mega-quake?"

"You know our history."

"What is between Wrightwood and Fort Tejon?"

David paused before answering, creating a mental map of the Rift Zone and then shook his head in amazement.

"I don't believe it! Why didn't we ask that question back at the office?"

John answered, "Sometimes it takes someone on the periphery to see what is so obvious."

Katy jumped in, "What the hell are you rock heads talking about?"

Kiraz looked at Alex for a less cryptic response.

"Do you remember when we drove up to Danny's orchard and we pulled off at the scenic lookout along the side of the highway?"

"Yes, by the sag pond."

"Remember that ski resort I pointed to up in the mountains? That's Wrightwood."

"And Fort Tejon?"

"About fifty miles the other way."

"The middle is Palmdale?"

"Exactly!" said David pointing his index finger at her.

John followed up, "Makes you wonder if Cal was on to something wandering around up there next to that mine."

"The mine, it is directly on the San Andreas Fault, isn't it?"

"From stem to stern," said David.

"I don't understand."

"From one end to the other," Alex translated.

"Perhaps we should shoot an e-mail to the gang up in Menlo and get their read of it." John suggested.

"Menlo?"

"Menlo Park, our regional headquarters in the Bay Area. We're more of a local branch office down here," David explained, then looked at John, "I'm sure they're monitoring them as well, but it wouldn't hurt to touch bases."

Kiraz felt somewhat satisfied with the subtle prompting of her colleagues, but wondered if stopping short of revealing the entire picture was the right thing to do. The timing of earthquake prediction wasn't a perfect process, but her hunch said this event was perhaps a week away, two at most. Here she was boarding a plane the next day and flying away leaving everyone to their peril, including her adorable, handsome, charming host seated by her side! Her heart prayerfully searched for an inspiration.

"David, do these micro-quakes follow any pattern?"

"Starting about a month ago we've noticed one about every twelve to fifteen hours, but lately their frequency has increased. Why are you so interested?"

"Kiraz specializes in earthquake prediction, and she's pretty good at it too, Alex looked at her, "Do you want me to mention the other day? It's up to you."

"Go ahead, perhaps you would be more convincing than I."

"She can feel significant quakes before they happen, perhaps tuning into small foreshocks, but it's probably more complex than that. You know that 5.9 we had on Sunday afternoon?"

"Duh."

"She told me it would happen on Saturday morning. Remember when I called you and asked about swarms?"

"Well, yeah, so?"

"We were sitting in my car in Reseda not more than a couple of miles from the epicenter."

"No shit!"

John entered the fray, "You mean that you can feel an earthquake coming?"

"I can understand how incongruent this is with modern science and sound geology. I am a scientist too, but it has also been my experience that if I'm near where an earthquake is imminent, I feel nauseous and then information about its strength, duration, and location begin to come into my mind. These are the facts."

"With accuracy?" asked David.

"Yes. I am not always certain of the timing, but they always happen within a month of my sensing it."

"Remarkable!" said John.

"So, why all the questions about the San Andreas Fault? I mean, we just had a pretty significant event that you apparently predicted. Is something else coming?"

"Yes, David."

Alex turned to Kiraz, "Really, another one?"

"Yes. Back at the church, after the service —"

"Come to think of, you did look a bit peaked on the drive over here. Why didn't you say anything before now?"

Kiraz could feel everyone's eyes upon her, "I wasn't clear about what I was seeing yet."

"What do you see now?"

"The San Andreas Fault will move five meters, followed by a pause of a week or two. Then another shift of thirty meters displacement will occur with the Garlock Fault responding with a movement of fifteen meters."

"Oh, my God, that's unbelievable!" said David.

"I wish it were not true, but the message has been clarifying itself to me since it began."

"There hasn't been a significant quake on the Garlock Fault in over five-hundred years, maybe a thousand."

"Does the Panorama City quake play into this?" asked John.

"Like your Landers quake of 1992, there was another three hours later at Big Bear Lake, then one in Mojave two weeks later. As you know, earthquakes can trigger others. We've seen this kind of seismic symbiosis in Turkey as well."

David countered yet again, "But that scenario would be reversed, with a smaller quake triggering larger ones. Not just larger ones, but cataclysmic ones! Jeezus Christ, thirty meters of movement on the San Andreas Fault all at once! I have no idea what the moment magnitude would be for a whopper like that. The estimated movement for the '04 Indian Ocean quake was twenty meters, and that was a 9.3. You're talking about a quake measuring up to ten."

"9.5."

"You're shittin' me! Oh, sorry."

"It's quite all right."

"How do you live with yourself? I mean, you must be constantly bombarded with doom, especially living in earthquake ridden Turkey."

"I have always had this gift, and it is why I became a geologist, to understand what I was feeling, and perhaps help others."

John noted, "You're like the Mother Teresa of geology. We're all just in it because of our obsession with granite and the security of a government paycheck."

Laughter burst from their table for the first time since they sat down, relieving the pressure of the moment.

Katy leaned across the table to Kiraz, "You really believe we're gonna have the Big One?"

Kiraz nodded sympathetically.

David asked, "When do you fly home?"

"Tomorrow."

He looked to Alex and John, "Given the enormity of this information, and Kiraz's impending departure, there's only one thing we can do, and you know Cal would agree, right?"

"Right. *Tremors!*"

"Where?"

"My place."

"Right."

Each patron threw money at the restaurant bill, except for Kiraz, and departed for their respective vehicles arriving twenty minutes later at Alex's condo for the big show.

Chapter 36

"WELL, I'M GLAD that you didn't forget about us here!" Maribel sassed Alex for his Bean Head delinquency.

"I missed your fabulous mochas, what can I say? By the way, how do you say, 'fabulous' in Spanish?"

"Fabuloso. Muy grande?"

"Why not, I'm feeling pretty good! Can you add a blueberry bagel?"

"Sure. You are looking good. Might it have anything to do with that pretty young lady I saw you with the other night?"

"Jealous, are we?"

"Maybe."

"Maybe?"

"Here's your bagel. They're both waiting for you at the usual table. Mocha'll be up in a couple of minutes," she pointed to her right.

"Thanks."

Alex joined his coffee comrades, deeply buried in various sections of the *Times.*

"Well, if it isn't our long lost prodigal come home to roost," said Jack from the top of his paper.

"Where have you been, Lex? It seems like weeks since you've graced us with your presence."

"I've been occupied with various university duties."

"The girl from Turkey? How's the romance going?" asked Hans.

"You can't bullshit us, son. We have our spies," Jack shot a glance toward the front counter.

"What are you people, the local Hillhurst FBI?"

"Just keeping tabs on our community project."

"That would be me?"

"Who else? In these matters you need a wee bit of encouragement."

Hans added, "More like a swift kick in the ass!"

"Speaking of that, guess where I'm going today?"

"The airport. It's her last day in LA, isn't it?"

"True, but that's not my final destination."

"What do mean, Lex?"

"You guys have been beating on me about taking a vacation."

"You didn't!"

"The results of your project are encouraging, shall we say. See you later, but not sure when though."

Alex got up, snatched his freshly prepared beverage, and headed for the exit.

"Be sure to write," said Jack.

"I will, if I have the time."

"A postcard a day, no less," Hans pointed at him.

"Where should I send them?"

"Right here. The address is on your loyalty card."

Alex grinned as he rushed to his car for the drive up to the Valley to retrieve his precious cargo. Last night he had arranged to pick up Kiraz the next morning at ten o'clock. She was waiting for him in the lobby.

"Günaydın!"

"Good morning!"

"Let me make sure everything is good with the hotel bill." Kiraz patiently stood by her luggage while Alex talked with the front desk staff. Satisfied with the billing, he was back to her in a jiffy.

"Ready?"

"Yes."

Like the perfect gentleman that he had proven himself to be, he picked up her suitcase and laptop and walked her out to the car, momentarily putting the bags on the pavement while he ushered her into the front seat. Once she was inside, he opened the rear passenger door and laid them on the back seat. Within moments they were southbound on Topanga Canyon Boulevard.

"There's an accident on the 405 at Van Nuys, so we're going down to the 101 instead. There's no sense sitting in traffic unnecessarily. How are you doing?"

"I'm fine."

"You look very nice today."

Alex admired her black business suit, the same one she had worn the day of her arrival, but with a fresh blue blouse.

"Thank you," her smile instantly took his breath away.

"You were pretty wiped out last night when I drove you back. Is LA time still bothering you?"

"It's been easier each day. This morning I woke up at four instead of three o'clock."

"Of course, and now you're going back, or is it forward, ten hours."

"Yes, I'm going back home, but ahead in time."

"It's strange how precise we can be about time, yet it seems so intangible and unreal when we travel from one place to another, especially by plane. It's almost as if time didn't really exist at all. What did you think of the movie?"

"It was very, very . . . crazy!"

"Crazy in a bad way?"

"In a good way. I can see why you wanted me to watch it."

"Required viewing for all seismologists."

"And for those who love the Alabama Hills."

"Yeah, I think almost the entire movie was filmed up there."

"How would you classify the movie?"

"I don't know, it's kind of a comedy and a horror film. Maybe crazy is a better term. Did you like it?"

"I liked it, although some of the American humor did not make sense to me. For instance, every time the character, Earl, used a swear word he would say, 'Pardon my French.' but he was not speaking French, not that I noticed."

"Ah, that's just another idiom that is said to excuse using rough language."

Kiraz paused before responding, "If you said it before the profanity, then it would be a warning and an apology, but afterward it's just an excuse."

"I like the way your mind works."

She grinned, "Thank you for noticing. What was your favorite scene?"

Alex pondered his response for a moment, "There are so many, but I think the one where the graboid throws the bomb back at them was pretty hysterical."

Miles of San Fernando Valley real estate blew by as they crossed Roscoe, Saticoy, Sherman Way, Vanowen, Victory, and finally Burbank.

"Here we are, the famous Ventura Highway, or Freeway."

"It is famous?"

"Like the song, 'Ventura Highway.' Have you heard it?"

"I don't think so."

"Hold on."

Alex fished through his CD collection, found the right one, popped it in the player, and advanced it to the fourth track.

"Now you can experience this road properly."

America's Greatest Hits album played in the background for the rest of the drive. "Lonely People" was playing by the time they exited at the Century Boulevard.

"Did you have breakfast?"

"A light one. Some yogurt, toast, and coffee."

Kiraz picked up the crumpled paper bag from beside her seat and discovered Alex's half-eaten blueberry bagel inside.

"You didn't finish yours."

"I guess I forgot. Are you hungry?"

"Actually, yes, a little"

"Maybe we better do something about that. I didn't eat all of my breakfast, and you didn't have much either."

Alex drove toward LAX's lower level arrivals and past several traffic signals until the Theme Building came clearly into view. He pulled into the valet parking for Encounter Restaurant.

"We're eating lunch with the Jetsons?"

Alex nodded, "They just happen to be close and personal friends of mine and have opened the kitchen early just for us."

The valet attendants beat Alex to Kiraz's door, and soon they were transported upward to a window table in the space décor restaurant above the hustle of the busy airport.

"This restaurant used to rotate, but now it's stationary. They just finished a huge seismic retrofit of the whole building."

"How did they strengthen it?"

"Tuned mass damper."

"Alex."

"Yes?"

Kiraz eyes welled up with tears. Alex quite naturally held her hand in response.

I don't know what to do. We are friends?"

"The best."

"Do you want me to leave and go back to Turkey?"

Alex shook his head, "No, I really wish you could stay, but I know you can't. I've never met anyone like you. You drive me crazy."

"In a bad way?"

"Only in a good way."

"Are you sure, even with my horrible predictions of doom and destruction?"

"The whole enchilada!"

"Huh?"

"All of you, devastating predictions, everything! But, I've got a confession to make. I lied to you a while ago."

"About what?"

"About my favorite scene in *Tremors*."

"Oh, which one is your favorite?"

"The end scene."

With that remark their lips met just as a jumbo jet lifted off the runway. When they finished kissing Alex was nearly in tears himself.

"You have no idea how long I've wanted to do that."

"How long?"

"Too long. Since I met you right down there," pointing toward the terminal, "By the way, while I was up last night on the Internet I happened to snag one of these."

Alex reached into his pants pocket and out came his passport and several pieces of paper stapled together.

"Here."

Kiraz's amazement at Alex's surprises increased upon reading the paper:

Passenger: Alexander Tevos Demurjian

Air France Flight 65 Departs 3:30 p.m. Los Angeles (LAX) Arrives 11:00 a.m. Ch. De Gaulle (CDG) Seat 27D

Air France Flight 1890 Departs 12:35 p.m. Ch. DeGaulle (CDG) Arrives 4:55 p.m. Ataturk (IST) Seat 34B

"Alex, those are my flights! Those seats are next to mine! You're coming with me?!"

"You didn't think my job as university host would end by my merely dropping you off at the airport and waving good-bye? We offer complete door-to-door going home service. Gene would be seriously disappointed if I did any less."

"You are kidding me!"

"Maybe a teensy bit," holding his thumb and index finger closely together.

"Alex?"

"What?"

She hugged him so hard he could barely breathe.

"I take it your approve of my travel plans."

She nodded enthusiastically. He took her hands in his.

"Do you think I'm crazy, Kiraz?"

"Yes, you're crazy."
"Crazy in a bad way?"
"Only in a good way."

Chapter 37

"IVAN, YOU'RE GONNA be doin' some serious hard time if you don't fess up!"

"Kiss my ass, cop! Our lawyers will have us out of this *mentóvka* before your first donut break."

"Apparently you haven't heard the latest."

"I got nothing to say to you."

"First, about your gun, that Makarov. It's the murder weapon all right. Ballistics confirmed it. Unless, of course, you just handed it off to your buddy, Sergei, and had him shoot Stover, but my money is on you. Why wouldn't he just use his own gun?"

"*Valí otsjúda, ment!*"

"Uh-uh-uh! You're not being very cooperative for someone who's being sent up the river."

"What are you talking about?"

"Your friends back in Moscow barely even acknowledge your existence."

"You lie."

"Let me see here," Detective Jackson flipped through a file folder, "Ah, Fortress Solutions, says that yours and Sergei's employment was terminated on the sixteenth of this month. That was . . . yesterday! My, my, they are efficient. Here's a copy of their e-mail if you don't believe me."

Ivan grabbed the paper out of Jackson's hand and read it. "This is more of your cop bullshit. You probably typed it yourself."

"Think so? You're quite right about my typing ability. I've been writing police reports since before you were born."

Jackson snatched back the e-mail and shook his head back and forth, "No, didn't do this one. We have been following your former assignment since we picked you boys up at the church, and already your replacements have shown up fresh off the plane from Mother Russia. You must be feeling quite deserted."

"Suck me!"

"Such language, Ivan, and I haven't used one bad word during this entire interview. Why do you persist in using them yourself? That's no way to talk with a friend. Although I wouldn't mind an English translation from Russian every now and then, just as a courtesy. On second thought, forget it, I pretty much know what you've been saying. So, how about you tell me what really happened up there at the mine. I mean, wouldn't you like to stick it to ole Stein after he abandoned you for new heat? He hasn't exactly sent his best legal team down here to spring you out of lockup."

"He'll come through for us. Stein is a first-class bitch."

"I wouldn't be so sure of yourself. Unless you've got wheelbarrows of money stuffed somewhere other than in your mattress, your next attorney will most likely be a public defender."

"You don't know where I live!"

"We had a blast going through your apartment, legally, of course, with a proper search warrant. Sadly, we found no money in your mattress, and we were so looking forward to your making a generous contribution to our local Palmdale FOP lodge."

"*Ischézni!*"

"You're not the law and order type, are you, Ivan? Ah, but Sergei, there's a sensible person."

"What about him?"

"I gotta admit, he's not the mental titan that you are, but he does appreciate the logic of his situation."

"He didn't tell you shit, you're just on a fishing trip."

Jackson referred to his file folder, "'Ivan didn't mean to kill him, it's just that the guy was being such a dick. So, he shot at the ground near him, just like in the cowboy movies.' Got anything else to add?'"

"That *suka!*"

"I take it that means, my best friend? Right now, buster, you're looking at assault with a deadly weapon and manslaughter for starters. At least in this country you won't have to sit in a cage in the courtroom like a wild animal while they try your case. Oh, and did I mention the marvelous gourmet food they serve up at San Quentin?"

Ivan stared off into space, the vacancy of his deep blue eyes concealed his brain's machinations, and then he spoke,

"Stein's covering this up. He called Moscow for help after I wasted the guy."

"*Spasibo*, comrade."

Jackson left the interrogation room and called Deputy Chin on his cell, "Bob, you up for another collar?"

"Where?"

"Library Tower."

"You're on."

Chapter 38

THE AROMA OF BREAKFAST cooking wafted down the hallway awakening Alex to his first morning on the continent of Asia. Kiraz's fourth floor apartment in the Çengelköy section of Istanbul had been her abode since the divorce from Hamit, and for the first time ever she had an overnight male guest. It was this guest who now suffered from a severe case of jetlag and time displacement, whereas Kiraz seemed to have easily slipped right back into her Istanbul rhythm. Still in his pajamas, Alex trudged down the hall and dropped into a chair at the small table in the kitchen.

Kiraz served him his first course—yogurt with honey, "This is good for you."

"Good morning, my dear."

"I don't have any blueberry bagels as you are accustomed to eating for breakfast, but I do have some fresh *simit, tereyağı and reçel.*"

Alex lurched to get up.

"I left my dictionary back in the bedroom. Let me go fetch—"

"Turkish bagel, butter, and jam. Oh, and I hope you like your omelette made with tomatoes and peppers."

Slumping back in his seat he yawned as he spoke, "Don't you mean, *menemen?*"

"You're learning Turkish very well even without your dictionary. Coffee or tea?"

"How about some tea for a change of pace."

"Now, you are going to eat your first good breakfast in years, or at least since you left your mother's home!"

"Yes, ma'am," Alex saluted.

Kiraz had taken complete control of Alex's morning nutritional regimen. He willingly succumbed as he dove into his first taste of her cooking. To his delight he discovered that her skills closely rivaled even his own mother's.

"How do you like it?"

Chewing away, "This is fantastic! Where did you learn to cook like this? Certainly not at the university."

"I learned a few things from my mother. Wait until you taste her cooking firsthand. My parents are really looking forward to our visit."

"I am too, but I wonder what they'll really think of me. I mean, if you had promised to bring them a souvenir from the US, I doubt it was another geologist."

"Very funny. Like I told you once, they leave me to live my life as I wish."

"And, are you?"

"Most definitely."

"It was sure nice of Ece to pick us up from the airport last night. Now I understand how you felt when you came to LA. Those flights were brutal."

"She is a dear friend. We try to help each other out, like sisters would. She even bought some of the food we're eating now."

"Where do you go shopping for groceries around here," shoveling in another bite full, "at a farmer's market or corner grocery store?"

"Just like you do, at a supermarket. There's one about five minutes from here in a big shopping mall."

"Shopping mall?"

"Maxi City, and the entire bottom floor has a Tansaş supermarket. You can get anything there. Even American food."

"Really, like what?"

"Let me see, there's a Burger King in the food court."

"That's pretty American," he nodded.

"We could go there for lunch if you wish."

"What, no In-N-Out Burger?"

"You really would like a Double-Double?"

"Get out, you have an In-N-Out here?"

"I was just kidding you."

"That's okay, I'd rather try something new, something Turkish!"

"Good. I was thinking, we could stop by the Institute this morning, and then I can show you around town."

"As my tour guide?"

"Yes, you have to follow me now."

Alex let out another long yawn, "I'll do my best to keep up with you."

"This will keep you awake."

She poured him another glass of tea and joined him at the table. Alex took a sip.

"Ah, you're so good to me."

"I'm only getting started."

After their hearty breakfast and quick showers, they went outside to the apartment complex parking lot where Kiraz's car was parked. Alex was in shock at the sight of it.

"You never told me you drove a VW!"

"You never asked."

"I guess I didn't, did I?"

Alex walked around the little red car, "A Polo," scratching his chin, "Don't think we have these in the US."

Kiraz opened the driver's door, got in, and motioned at Alex to join her.

"I'm coming, hold on!"

Alex jumped in the passenger's seat and put on his seat belt.

"I didn't see even one Polo during my entire visit to California."

"Too bad. They'd sell like hotcakes in LA. What year is this one?"

"It's a '96, which is much older than your car. I bought it second hand just this past year. It's my first car."

She started the engine and put it in reverse.

"Really. It's very, very nice. I would even say, cute."

"Cute?"

Kiraz shifted into first gear and drove out of the parking lot and turned left onto Kaldirim Caddesi.

"It suits you well."

Kiraz upshifted through second and third gears as they sped down the street.

"Just curious, what does a car like this go for?"

"I paid seven thousand five hundred lire."

"What's that in dollars?"

Kiraz did the mental math in a flash, "Five thousand, more or less."

"Ouch, that is a lot of money."

"Hey, it was a good deal! Cars are expensive in Turkey, but Ece has a friend who owns an open car market. This was the cheapest Polo they had."

Alex faithfully agreed with her, although the sticker shock of the Turkish used car prices lingered in the back of his mind. Kiraz entered a traffic circle and took the first right onto Selvi Yolu Caddesi. He looked out the window as they passed by blocks of four to five-story cookie cutter apartment buildings. Shortly thereafter they turned left through a gate entering the palatial wooded grounds of the Istanbul Science & Engineering Institute.

"What a beautiful campus this is, and such a short commute.

What is it, maybe five minutes?" looking at his watch.

"When the weather is nice like it is today, I sometimes walk, or ride the bus."

"We could've done that."

"Then I couldn't have shown off my cute car!"

Kiraz drove deeper into the woods and parked along the street in front of ISI's main building, a long newer two-story tan structure with a red tile roof.

"Come on, I want to introduce you to everybody."

Kiraz and Alex entered a room abuzz with several working seismographs and people sitting at computer stations.

"This is where we monitor the broadband network — "

"Kiraz!"

"Hi Ece!"

Ece got up from her chair and approached them, "I didn't think you two would be here today."

"Well, I thought Alex would like to see where I work. Is the Director in?"

"He's here."

Just then, the other workers left their workstations and joined the party in the middle of the room.

Kiraz handled the introductions in English, "This is my friend, Dr. Alex Demurjian, from California. He is a professor of geology at the university where I gave my lectures. Alex, this is Dr. Akdoğan, Dr. Yazıcıoğlu, and Dr. Berberyan."

Alex greeted each person one by one, limping his way through their Turkish surnames, while Kiraz disappeared down the hall into one of the many private offices.

Drs. Akdoğan and Yazıcıoğlu returned to their workstations, but Dr. Berberyan, the youngest of the three, dressed in jeans and casual shirt, protracted the conversation.

"Just call me, Vasil. You're from Northridge, aren't you?"

"Yeah, I've been teaching there for quite a while."

"Cool. What was the quake like?"

"Which one? You mean the '94 quake?"

"No, the one on Sunday."

"Oh, I missed it. We were too far away to have felt it."

"My sister, Tamy, lives in Burbank. She called me up in the middle of the night and was like totally freaking out about it."

"Wow, small world."

"I went to see her last year. LA is such an awesome city. I mean, you've got it all—the beach, the mountains, the desert, and the clubs. What brings you here?"

"I was invited, well, sort of. I heard you have some rather impressive sights."

"Istanbul is okay. I mean, it's big, like LA, but very old too. My family has lived here since the Ottoman days. Your first time?"

"Yeah, we flew in last night."

"Cool. So, you and Kiraz are good friends?"

"I was her tour guide when she was in California, and now she's reciprocating."

"Oh, very nice."

Alex tilted his head in response, "I think she is."

Vasil smiled and winked, "Way to go, man! Hey, I gotta get back to work."

"Good talking with you."

Kiraz returned to the room with a short man in his sixties dressed in a dark suit.

"Alex, may I introduce our director, Dr. Mustafa Sargut."

"Pleased to meet you, Doctor. I'm Alex Demurjian."

"Yes, Kiraz has told me much about you. Allow me to thank you for taking such good care of her during her visit to your country."

"You're welcome. It was my pleasure."

"Alex, Dr. Sargut has permitted me to take the next month off from my work here at the Institute. I told him about us."

"Really?"

"Dr. Demurjian, I couldn't refuse her. Besides, she deserves the time off. All of these people you see working here are quite capable, mainly because of the excellent training she has given them."

"I have trouble saying 'no' to her myself."

"She can be quite convincing. Watch out for her!"

Kiraz rolled her eyes, "Let me show you my office. Come on!"

Alex threw up his hands, *"Evet."*

Down the hall they went and into a small office. Attached to the walls were maps of the World, Europe, Turkey, and California. Kiraz sat behind her desk and turned on the computer. Alex slid into the chair in front of her desk.

"I never did get around to showing you my office, did I?" Kiraz looked up and off to the left, "No, I don't think you did."

"It really is not all that impressive. Your office is much nicer, and you have a fantastic view of that large evergreen tree," Alex pointed out the window.

Kiraz glanced over her shoulder toward the tree, "It's a cedar of Lebanon." then returned to typing on the keyboard.

"I think I've seen a few of those back in LA. What'cha doing?"

"I'm resetting my automatic e-mail response message."

Alex surveyed the maps hanging on the wall, "I really enjoyed talking with Vasil. Did you know he has a sister living in LA?"

Kiraz continued to type on her keyboard, "I thought you two would discover one another. Did you notice anything special about him?"

"He's quite a bit younger than the others, and very friendly."

"He's Armenian."

"Armenian? You mean, like me?"

"His last name is Berberyan. That's Armenian, isn't it?"

"I guess I missed that detail when you introduced us. I probably need more tea."

"We'll take care of that soon."

"He said he was an Istanbul native. Where did he go to college?"

"Istanbul University. He's our newest hire, and quite adept at computers."

"I assumed there weren't any more Armenians living in Turkey, at least that's the impression I got as a kid growing up."

"There are at least two, as you can see."

"Two?"

"Vasil, and you, my dear."

She finished typing and logged off her computer, then reached her hands toward him.

"Alex."

He took them in his, "Is it okay to hold hands at work? I mean, I don't want to get you into trouble with Dr. — "

Kiraz held his hands even more tightly, "I wish I could stay in the moment forever."

"Me too!"

He looked back into her dark, penetrating eyes. They sat for a while undisturbed by the busyness outside the office door.

Kiraz spoke, "Are you ready for another ride in my cute car?"

Alex started to smirk, "I would love it."

Kiraz and Alex said their good-byes to her ISI colleagues and drove down the hill to the Bosporus shoreline. Their route took them past the Beylerbeyi Palace, then along Paşa Limanı Caddesi to the ferry docks in Üsküdar where they parked in a nearby garage. Once onboard they found a spot along the railing on the port side of the ferry.

"You have to see Istanbul from the Bosporus."

"I see what you mean, what a view!"

"That's the Topkapı Palace on the left, where the sultans lived."

"Wow! What are those two huge mosques?"

"That the Blue Mosque to the right, and in the middle is Aya Sofya."

"I think I've heard of Hagia Sophia before, from a college art history course I took back at Cal Tech."

"It was first a Christian church, then a mosque, and now it's a museum."

"Can we go there? I don't know, but it's kind of calling me."

"Let's go there first."

Minutes later Kiraz and Alex stepped off the ferry at Eminönü at the entrance to the Golden Horn. They were back in Europe.

Chapter 39

"WE NEED SOME STRAIGHT answers right now, Mrs. Gunderson!"

Unnerved by the looming presence of Detective Jackson and Deputy Chin's official police uniform, Rebecca Gunderson repeated herself, "Like I told you, Mr. Stein isn't here, but—"

"But what?"

Looking at her watch, "I shouldn't say this, you know, because I could be fired, but he left the office about ten minutes ago for the airport."

"LAX?"

"No, Mr. Stein has a private jet at Van Nuys Airport."

He whipped out his cell phone and hit the speed dial, "This is Detective Jackson, put out an APB for Michael Stein. He is considered a flight risk. Notify Van Nuys to ground his aircraft."

"What was he driving today?"

"I don't know for certain, but probably his Porsche. He's in love with that car."

"Alert CHP for a late model gold Porsche. Check with DMV for license plates. Vehicle is probably northbound on the Hollywood Freeway by now and may be accompanied by private security," glancing back at her, "What do the Russians drive?"

"Mercedes."

"What color?"

"Black."

"Security team likely driving a black Mercedes sedan. Consider them armed and dangerous," he clicked off his cell phone, "Bob, let's go!"

They dashed out of the office toward the elevator for the seventy-floor ride down. Once inside Jackson muttered, "I wonder how he knew we were coming."

"Balabanov, who else?"

"You're probably right."

"Loyal to the end."

"Did you ever think about becoming a detective. You're pretty sharp for a young guy."

"Need a partner?"

"You're on."

This time there wasn't a moment to waste. In spite of the police officers' need for additional caffeine they bypassed the nearby Starbucks—adrenaline would have to suffice. They mounted Jackson's Cadillac CTS and bolted out of the Library Tower's parking garage onto Fifth Street, immediately taking the right hand fork of the northbound Harbor Freeway onramp. Traffic was beginning to back up for the morning rush as they crossed under the Third Street overpass. Jackson flipped on his lights and siren and aimed his car toward the exit for US 101 North. Vehicles scattered out of his way. He got on the radio.

"This is Detective Jackson in pursuit of Michael Stein. We are now entering the Hollywood Freeway. Any news of his whereabouts?"

Five seconds later a female voice with a slight Hispanic accent came over the radio, "Chopper Six is airborne and tracking the suspect's car now entering the Ventura Freeway westbound. Black Mercedes sedan following behind. CHP is shadowing in a black and white unit."

"We're gonna get that son of a bitch, Bob!"

"He's going for the plane."

Back to his radio, "Tell CHP to keep their distance. We don't wanna spook him."

Just then Michael Stein's cell rang, "Yes, Dmitri."

"Mr. Stein, I think we've got a problem."

"What is it?"

"There's a *ment* vehicle to the rear of us, about three car lengths back."

Stein looked in his rearview mirror and noticed the CHP cruiser lurking behind a red minivan and a silver sedan.

"He could be on a routine patrol. It's probably nothing to worry about."

"If you say so, Mr. Stein," Dmitri Somov looked back behind him once more while his partner, Andrei Ulianov, continued to drive, "but now there's a second car next to the first one."

An LA County Sheriff's cruiser had joined the parade. Stein glanced in his rearview mirror for a look.

"That's probably not a coincidence, is it?"

"In Russia, we would be worried at such a coincidence. They are monitoring us."

Stein thought for a moment about his personal secretary and her compulsively honest nature, "Dmitri, I think the plane is out."

"What do you suggest we do, Mr. Stein?"

"I've got an idea. Let's take them where they think we're going."

"You mean, take them on a, how do you Americans say it, a goose chase?"

"Precisely. Here's the plan . . ."

A slow speed chase, reminiscent of the 1995 OJ Simpson case, continued down the Ventura and then onto the San Diego Freeway, while Jackson and Chin pulled within two miles of the group.

"Calling Detective Jackson," the radio squawked.

"Yeah, Jackson here."

"Chopper Six reports suspects have exited the 405 and are now westbound on Sherman Way."

Deputy Chin remarked, "They haven't spotted the black and whites. Awesome!"

"Don't start counting your chickens yet, Bob. This Stein is a crafty mutha," back to the radio, "Copy that. Are the units still in pursuit?"

"10-4."

"Good, we're about five minutes behind them. Suspects are definitely heading toward Van Nuys Airport. Repeat, the Van Nuys Airport. They are to apprehend them immediately!"

Jackson approached the impending bust by his fellow California peace officers with a sense of glee. In fulfillment of their marching orders, they immediately switched from silent approach to Code 3. Stein's cell went off.

"I see them, Dmitri. Remember, right when we enter the tunnel you go into action."

"Yes, Mr. Stein."

The speed of the four vehicles suddenly increased as they shot into the tunnel beneath the airport. Fifty yards in, Andrei put the Mercedes into a left-hand slide causing the two police cars to slam on their brakes stopping within inches of impact. They quickly got out of the car and nonchalantly raised their hands in surrender. Officers leapt from their vehicles and pulled out their weapons.

"My apologies, but I believe the anti-lock brakes on my car are defective," Dmitri offered an explanation for their unorthodox driving maneuver.

When Stein emerged from the tunnel he pulled the Porsche into a hard U-turn at Hayvenhurst. Now heading eastbound, he drove through the other side of the tunnel obscured from the police officer's view by a concrete wall.

Stein silently remarked to himself, "Dmitri and Andrei are definitely an upgrade from that bumbling Ivan and Sergei, in spite of their ridiculous devotion to me."

"Detective Jackson, this is Chopper Six."

"Go ahead, Chopper Six."

"We're not sure what happened, but we're now following the lead vehicle back onto the San Diego Freeway northbound."

"What, say that again?"

"The pursuit went under the airport. Only the Porsche came out of the tunnel and then it went in the opposite direction, eastbound. He's now northbound on the 405."

Jackson turned to Chin, "I told you Stein was a clever SOB."

"I stand corrected."

"Chopper Six, we copy that last report. Keep the Porsche under surveillance. We're going after him!"

Jackson clicked off the radio.

"Let's see what this Caddy can do, shall we?"

Lights and sirens blaring, the duo of Jackson and Chin closed to a half-mile behind Stein, who was now weaving in and out of the HOV lane and adjacent traffic lanes to maximize forward movement.

"There he is! Doesn't he know he could be arrested for driving there all by himself? That ain't no hybrid," joked Chin.

"I see him. I wonder what he's up to."

For years, Michael Stein had maintained a secret getaway, a luxury chalet tucked along a back road in the community of Pine Mountain Club up in the Los Padres National Forest. Having eluded the initial police pursuit, he felt confident that his high performance sports car could outdistance the authorities. Unbeknownst to him, thousands of feet above, LA County Sheriff's Chopper Six kept a watchful eye on the speeding Porsche. Traffic began to loosen up north of the 118 Freeway.

"Suspect is now northbound on I-5 heading out of the Valley," reported Chopper Six.

"We're losing him," said Chin.

At that moment Jackson's cell went off, "Yeah!"

"J, it's John."

"Well, Captain Fernandez, it's so nice to hear from you." Jackson whipped the Cadillac into the HOV lane and floored it, "Checking up on me, are you?"

"I heard that you've been having a little bit trouble with a routine arrest."

"Maybe, just a little. You can tell Madame Dragon Lady that we've nearly wrapped up the Stover case, except for this minor detail."

"Need some help?"

"I would be much obliged, John. This Stein has got himself quite a rod, and it appears he's taking the Commander Cody Tour."

"He isn't driving a Lincoln, is he?"

"What the hell are you guys talking about?"

Jackson looked at his sidekick, "It's just some old fart LA cop talk. You're too young to understand, Bob," then back to his cell, "If only he was, I'd have passed him by now, if you believe the song. He's driving some pretty serious Kraut iron, and he's gonna lose us pretty soon."

"Affirmative, J. Chopper Six tells me you're coming up on the split with the 14."

"Where do you think we can corral this sucker?"

"Santa Clarita would be the first opportunity, but I don't think we can put that together in time."

"Shit, I always wanted to bust somebody at Magic Mountain."

"Save that trip for your grandkids, J. You got any idea where he's going in such a rush?"

"Beats the hell out of me, John."

"Well, once he passes the 126 exit he's pretty much home free up the Grapevine. Hold on a sec . . . Lieutenant Alvarez from Santa Clarita tells me he's got a free black and white leaving a call in Stevenson Ranch and is now getting on at McBean."

Chin jumped in, "Ask him about setting up a roadblock, the Frazier Park exit would be best. We could get units from CHP, Antelope Valley, and maybe some other county mounties from Kern or Ventura."

"Did you hear that, John?"

"Yes, J. Who is that with you?"

"Some guy bucking for a promotion."

"Tell him he's got it. That's a good idea, Deputy . . . ?"

"Chin, Robert A."

"We'll get busy on our end."

"Let's hope he doesn't deviate from his present course," Jackson returned to the discussion.

"Yeah, we'll pray for that. Talk to you later, J."

Jackson hung up his cell and jumped back on the radio, "Chopper Six, do you read?"

"Chopper Six here."

"Where is suspect now? We've lost visual contact."

"He's just passing Valencia Boulevard."

"Man, Stein's really hauling ass!"

"Give us an estimate of his speed, if you could?"

"He's got to be doing at least a hundred."

"Thanks. Keep us posted of any changes."

Jackson clicked off the radio, "Stein's not going to give us much time to prepare a proper welcoming committee."

Chin shook his head, "Doesn't look like it."

Meanwhile, Michael Stein was finding out just what his car really could do for the very first time, and the exhilaration was narcotic. He'd had it out once on I-10 for a run to Palm Springs, giving it a burst up over a hundred on occasion, but he was always mindful of the CHP lurking about. Not today. He didn't care. The pre-rush hour traffic was fairly light, allowing him to push past the exits for Santa Clarita and Castaic at a speed double the average car, with more pedal available. For the next twenty-five miles nothing could touch him as he wound up the twin turbos to their factory limits. Although each vehicle was equipped with a 3.6-liter six-cylinder engine, Detective Jackson's Cadillac was no match for Stein's Porsche, except for one important advantage—a police radio.

As Stein topped the 4,144-foot high Tejon Pass, a motley array of vehicles awaited him blocking all four lanes of I-5 at the Frazier Park exit including the shoulder and off-ramp. Seven in all, from left to right—two Caltrans heavy duty trucks, an LA County Sheriff's SUV based out of Lancaster, two Kern County Sheriff's cruisers, and two CHP cruisers out on patrol. Most of the traffic had been diverted off of the roadway at Gorman, or through the far-left lane where a Caltrans truck now sat. An errant Volvo sedan and a Ford minivan that had slipped through the police sieve were quickly directed by deputies onto the far right shoulder.

"I don't believe it!" Stein blurted to himself, slamming hard on the brakes.

Undeterred by the wall of steel erected by law enforcement, Stein swerved to the right, smashed through a fence, shot down the embankment onto Gorman Post Road and continued forward, without missing a beat, albeit at a much slower speed. However, the CHP anticipated this possibility and had positioned their vehicles pointing forward. The cruiser in the shoulder led off, followed by the other down the off-ramp parallel with Stein's Porsche moving just below them on the frontage road. The other police vehicles followed suit. As Stein made a hard left onto Frazier Mountain Park Road two LA County Sheriff's cruisers advancing from the west blocked his path, forcing him to an abrupt stop. The CHP cars showed up seconds later. Stein turned off the car, raised his hands in surrender, as the deputies and patrolmen carefully approached with guns drawn.

"Hands on the wheel! I repeat, hands on the wheel!" screamed a deputy.

"Okay, you got me," Stein complied.

Suddenly, there was a loud rumble, as if a freight train were passing nearby. Everyone's heads turned looking around as the earth began to shake. The policemen reached out their hands in desperation trying to maintain their balance, but the force of the shockwaves knocked them to the ground. Seeing an opportunity for escape, Stein started his Porsche and drove straight through yet another fence and beneath the freeway overpass, circumventing the police cars. Just then the pylons holding up the roadway began to sway.

As Detective Jackson's car passed the exit for State Route 138 it pitched from side to side making it difficult to control. Cracks began to emerge in the roadway.

"What the hell?!"

Jackson pushed hard on his brake pedal bringing the Cadillac to an immediate halt. The sheriff's cruiser that had accompanied them from Santa Clarita followed suit just as the road in front of them began to buckle and split apart.

"Jeezus, look out!" yelled Chin, as his body pitched to the right against the door window. Jackson held tightly to the steering wheel.

The section of the broken pavement ahead of them rapidly shifted to the right, while a fissure, nearly five feet across, opened up nearly swallowing their car in its newly constructed mouth. Then the tremor ceased. Jackson put the car in reverse and gingerly backed it away from the edge.

"Chopper Six?"

"This is Chopper Six."

"You're not going to believe this, but we seem to have had a huge earthquake down here."

"10-4 on the earthquake. We can see quite a bit of dust flying in your area. Are you okay?"

"Uh, yeah, we're okay . . . I think."

"Roger that."

Chin interrupted, "You're not going to believe me when I tell you this."

"What?" Jackson threw up his hands.

"Remember back at the Stover crime scene, when I told you about the 'Bulge' on the San Andreas Fault?"

"Yeah, so."

"I think the tail of it just snapped right here," pointing out the windshield at the tear in the road, "Dude, this is the San Andreas Fault!"

"No shit!"

At that moment an aftershock hit, jarring the car and causing chunks of the road along the new crevasse to drop.

"Detective Jackson, this is Chopper Six."

"Jackson here."

"Deputy Ryan just reported from the roadblock that suspect's vehicle had been stopped, but managed to escape westbound on Frazier Mountain Park Road after the earthquake hit."

"Are the deputies in pursuit?"

"No can do, Detective. The freeway crashed on the road before they could follow."

"You got a 10-20 on him?"

"Negative. The dust clouds are blocking our vision, plus there's a fire at the truck stop on the other side of the exit. We're going lower for a better look."

"Bob, I told you what a slick bastard this Stein was. He probably pushed a special button in that fancy car of his and made all this happen."

"You're nuts!"

"You gotta better explanation?"

Chapter 40

"IT AMAZES ME that these ancient UMB's have survived so many quakes without serious damage, especially that one!"

"It had two exceptional architects."

Alex cocked his head, then shook it, "Where do you come up with that?"

"You are an expert on the Alabama Hills and San Andreas Fault. I know these unreinforced masonry buildings, and their designers, Anthemius and Isidore," said Kiraz pointing to the left.

"Impressive, and that one?" pointing to the right.

"Sedefhar Mehmet Ağa."

Alex reflected on the two houses of worship, his head moving back and forth, "You've got to admit, they look a lot alike, except that one has two more minarets," pointing back to the right.

"I would think that with such a good example of seismically survivable architecture right next to him, it made sense to incorporate those qualities in the new mosque. What worked in the sixth-century should also work in the seventeenth."

Kiraz and Alex stood by the fountain in Sultan Ahmet Park, a green space in old town Istanbul that allowed for an unobstructed view of both Hagia Sophia and the Blue Mosque.

"You know, these buildings would never pass California building codes. After the '33 Long Beach Quake, UMB's were essentially outlawed. I can't even imagine what it would take to do a seismic retrofit. What's their secret?"

"Years ago, ISI performed an in-depth study of Aya Sofya and discovered that Anthemius mixed a special mortar using crushed brick which increased the tensile strength of the structure. The concrete still has active elements in it. Computer models demonstrated that a quake as large as a magnitude 7.5 would not topple it. Then in 1999 it was put to the test."

"Were you a part of that study?"

Kiraz nodded, "Along with many other geologists, some of whom you met this morning."

"How did I get so lucky to have such a smart and cute girlfriend?"

"Cute? Like my car?"

"Okay, pretty."

"That's more like it."

A distinguished looking man in his late forties, a tall attractive brunette in her late thirties, and a teenage girl, came up to the white metal gate fence surrounding the fountain and commenced taking photos of each other.

"Here, let me take your picture together. Do you speak English? Hold on," Alex began to pull his phrasebook out of his pocket, *"İngilizce konuşuyor musunuz?"*

"English works better for me," replied the man.

"For me too. I just started learning Turkish, and I'm not so good at it yet."

"You're American?"

"Yeah. Alex Demurjian."

They shook hands.

"Hank Hudson."

"Good to meet you, Hank and . . . ?"

The woman spoke with a mild accent, "I am Natasha, and this is my daughter, Katerina."

The girl waved.

"Where are you guys from?"

"Ohio."

"I'm from LA, and this is Kiraz, from right here in Istanbul."

Kiraz shook their hands, "It is good to meet you."

"What brings you to Istanbul, if you don't mind my asking?"

"Nah, it's fine. We're both engineers attending a conference at the . . . what's the name of it?"

"Haliç Congress Center."

"Thanks, dear. Anyway, we'd thought we'd make a family vacation out of it, and then we're flying up to Russia to visit with Natasha's family."

"Cool. Engineers, like civil engineers?"

Alex pointed at the nearby attractions standing guard at each end of the park.

"No, we're power engineers, electric power. We're here to learn more about renewables for our company, especially wind power. Tomorrow we're going to a wind farm outside of town. And you?"

"We're both geologists. Isn't it an interesting coincidence that the two of you and the two of us work in each other's fields?"

"Well, Alex, you know what they say, birds of a feather." Kiraz looked to Alex for help.

"People with similar interests are attracted to . . . we were meant for each other."

"Do you have trouble with American expressions too?" Natasha asked Kiraz.

She nodded, "I'm learning fast, almost as fast as Alex is learning Turkish. We met in California last week where I was lecturing."

"That's very nice. Hank and I met at a conference in France a few years ago. We've been together ever since," giving him a squeeze of her hand, "but his Russian needs some work!"

"Hey, it's a difficult language! At least you have the same alphabet to work with," looking at Alex.

"You have a point there."

Alex fulfilled his offer to photograph the Hudson Family, and Hank reciprocated.

"Alex, Kiraz, it was good meeting you. If you're ever in the Midwest, look us up. We're with Ohio Valley Power. Where to next, my dear?"

"The Topkapı Palace. I hope I'm saying that correctly."

"Perfectly. You have a good ear for languages," said Kiraz.

"Thank you."

Once the Hudsons departed Kiraz asked, "Are you hungry now?"

"Yes, I think your awesome breakfast is finally wearing off.

"Good, I know just the place for lunch. We could even make a picnic of it."

"I'm intrigued!"

Kiraz took Alex's hand and they strolled out of the park and down Yerebatan Caddesi in the general direction of Cağaloğlu Square.

"Over there is the Yerebatan Sarnıçi," she pointed to the right.

"Uh-huh."

"Ancient cisterns built by the Byzantines."

"Let me guess, another UMB?"

"Yes, but it's an underground one."

"That's different. It's already in the earth in case a quake takes in down."

"You've seen James Bond movies?"

"Who hasn't?"

"You know the scene in *From Russia With Love* where they go under the city in a boat?"

"Yeah! Don't they look through a secret periscope underneath the Russian Embassy and watch a meeting of KGB guys? And James Bond sees the Russian girl for the first time?"

"It was filmed right there. We love that movie here in Turkey."

"I think it's the best early Bond film. Wasn't there another one filmed in Istanbul, a more recent one? The title escapes me."

"The World Is Not Enough."

"Yeah, that's it!"

The mid-afternoon sun lit up the colorful facades of the buildings along the street, many of them housing restaurants and hotels. They turned the corner at Nuru Osmaniye Caddesi and the streetscape expanded to include shops selling souvenirs of all kinds, everything from postcards to rugs. After another turn they were on Bab-i Ali Caddesi.

"We're almost there."

"Good, I could eat a hor—"

They were now standing in front of a restaurant, its red brick exterior crowned by a dark green sign in white and yellow lettering that read, "SUBWAY."

"I don't believe it! You weren't kidding me back in Mojave when you said you'd been to one."

"Are you hungry enough for a thirty-centimeter, I mean a twelve-inch Spicy Italian sandwich? That is your favorite one, isn't it?"

"You're quite the prankster, aren't you?"

Kiraz's grin filled her cheeks from end to end and she said in her best southern drawl, "Ah jus aim t'pleeze!"

"Where'd you learn to talk like that?"

"Watching *The Dukes of Hazzard.*"

"You are joking!"

"Okay, when I was resetting my automatic e-mail message this morning I looked it up in an online idiom dictionary."

"On how to talk hick?"

"What is hick?"

"Remember my travels in Missouri . . . never mind."

The inviting neon "OPEN" sign was lit, just like in the windows of thousands of restaurants across the US. As Kiraz predicted, Alex ordered a thirty-centimeter *Baharatlı İtalian,* and she a fifteen-centimeter *Tavuk Fileto,* chicken filet. They opted for an open table outside and dug into the sandwiches.

With lettuce hanging out of the edge of his mouth, "You live in a fascinating city. I mean, here we are sitting in an American fast-food restaurant, and right down the street are thousand-year-old buildings. We've got nothing like this back in the US, except for some Spanish missions. We think something is old if it's from a hundred years ago."

Alex noticed Kiraz's long pause before responding, as if she were distracted by something other than their conversation.

"I guess we don't really think about it too much. If you're born here in Turkey, and you see something old, like Aya Sofya or Topkapı, you simply take it for granted. They are the past glory of former civilizations. The city has changed a lot since then."

"And you've had two James Bond movies filmed here!"

"You like Istanbul?"

"I like."

"Let's go to the mall!"

"The mall?"

"Don't you know that women love to shop, and I think you'll like it too."

After finishing their sandwiches, they continued their trek further down Nuru Osmaniye Caddesi. Alex's eyes drank in the architectural and human scene. Kiraz towed him through several back streets of mercantile enterprises until they arrived at a stone gate headed by an inscription, "KAPALIÇARŞI, GRAND BAZAAR."

"The mall?"

Kiraz nodded, "The mall."

"Judging by that sign, it's not a new one either. Let me guess, that '1461' up there on the wall isn't the street number, is it?"

"The founding date."

"Jeezus, that's before Columbus."

"Columbus?"

"The guy who discovered America."

They entered through the Beyazit Kapisi and wandered around the vast covered labyrinth. Over four thousand shops and stalls, grouped together according to merchandise, offered everything anyone could possibly want. Alex noticed metal bars spanning the middle of the arched ceilings and pointed up to them.

"Seismic retrofit?"

Kiraz nodded, "They are taking our photo too," noting the security cameras perched on them.

They browsed through carpets for a while until they came upon the gold jewelry section. A shopkeeper approached Alex and began speaking rapidly in Turkish, mistaking him for an *Istanbulu.*

"Uh," Alex reached for his phrasebook, *"Amerikalıyım."*

"American! How about a nice gold ring for your woman? We have the best deals anywhere!"

Kiraz tugged hard at his arm to go.

"Maybe later."

They continued walking straight-ahead ignoring the repeated entreaties of all the nearby gold merchants who smelled the cash in his wallet. Suddenly the noise around them faded.

She said looking at him, "You really want to buy me a ring?"

"I'd like to very much."

"You want to marry me?"

"Yeah, that's the idea. But, I've got to warn you, I've never been married, and have no idea what I'm—"

"Evet! Seni seviyorum!"

"I know that's Turkish for something good."

"It means, 'Yes! I love you!'"

"And, I love you! Is it appropriate to kiss you right here in front of all of these people?"

"Kiss me!"

Alex leaned down took her in his arms, and gave her a big smooch. The merchants all applauded.

"So, where should we go to buy a ring?"

"I know just the place. It's not far."

"Not far! We've been heading there all this time, haven't we?"

She winked at him, "Follow me."

They walked further along Kuyumcular Caddesi and up Acı Çeşme Sokak. A sign "Zincirli Han" pointed them to the right through a narrow passageway laden with rough paving stones and into a small, intimate courtyard. Sunlight burst through from above adding a luster to the white trimmed pink walls. A few people lingered under a tree growing in the middle of the courtyard. They passed by them and up a stairwell into a small shop on the second floor.

"Ece and I have been here many times. This shop makes custom jewelry at half the cost of those others."

"Show me what you want and it's yours."

Kiraz spoke to a young man who brought out an assortment of gold bands. They both tried on several until they found two to their liking, and an engagement ring for her. Once a price was agreed upon Alex paid for the rings. They would be ready for pick up within the hour, but he was starting to wilt as they walked back down the stairs to the ground floor.

"You look tired, my dear."

"Jetlag is catching up with me, or maybe it's just shopping. It's not my forte."

"Tea time?"

"Why not? We've got some time to kill."

Just across the courtyard was a tiny teahouse, "How about over there?"

"Wow, how perfect is that?"

They both ordered tea and relaxed in the sanctuary of the courtyard.

"Feeling better now?"

"Much better. I can't believe we're doing this, but it feels so right. What are we going to tell our parents, our bosses? Where will we live, work? You're here, I'm there."

She momentarily closed her eyes and then opened them as she spoke, "That couple we met in the park today, Hank and Natasha. If they could make it work, an American and a Russian, why not an American and a Turk? If something is right, the way is always shown. Don't you believe that's true?"

"You've convinced me."

Suddenly an unwanted interruption sprang upon them when Kiraz's mobile phone went off. She immediately responded to the caller in Turkish. Alex watched unable to discern the meaning of the conversation. Her face began to show signs of concern.

"What is it?"

Kiraz finished the call, "It was Dr. Sargut. There has been a 7.9 quake in California."

"Where?"

"Do you know a place called Three Points?"

"I sure do."

Alex reached for his cell phone.

"Where is it?"

"Not far from Cousin Danny."

She let out a deep sigh, "I hope he's all right."

"You knew it had happened, back there at the Subway?"

"You noticed?"

He nodded.

Chapter 41

"A BRIEF RECAP of what's being called, 'The Big One.' the U.S. Geological Survey in Pasadena has downgraded yesterday morning's earthquake from 7.9 to a 7.8 magnitude, according to seismologist, John Lopez. It appears that Greater Los Angeles was spared the brunt of the tremor, with the epicenter located in a sparsely populated section of the San Andreas Fault thirty miles west of the Lancaster-Palmdale area. The hardest hit communities were Frazier Park, Lebec, and Gorman. So far, six fatalities have been reported, all of them from a fire that broke out shortly after the quake struck at a truck stop near the Frazier Mountain Road exit on Interstate 5. The Grapevine over the Tejon Pass between Los Angeles and Bakersfield has been closed indefinitely from Castaic Lake to State Route 166. North-south traffic from Los Angeles is being diverted to I-15 and State Route 58 through San Bernardino, Barstow, and Mojave. The Antelope Valley Freeway, State Route 14, has been closed while Caltrans repairs pavement cracks and checks overpasses for safety. They are hoping to have it reopened for tomorrow morning's commute. Metrolink trains are operational on a limited basis from Lancaster to Union Station. Check their website for scheduling updates."

Jose turned off the TV.

"Joe, I want you to stay home today."

"How come? I can catch a train to work. You heard what the guy said, Honey."

"Look how long it took you to drive home last night! What was it, almost four hours?"

"It was just over three, but what do you expect with everybody freaking out about the quake? It wasn't that bad. Nothing's going to happen."

Jose dug into his breakfast of eggs, chorizo, and toast. Molly, who was patiently observing his every bite of food, suddenly flinched and began barking uncontrollably. Within seconds, the dishes on the table rattled then stopped.

"So, what was that?"

"Shut up, you stupid mutt," Jose shrugged his shoulders as looked at his wife, "A baby quake?"

"Don't listen to him, Molly," Rosa affectionately stroked her head stopping her rant, "You're such a good doggie!"

Molly shared her attention between Rosa's praise and the movement of Jose's fork. He shoveled in another bite, then looked at her holding up a scrap of toast.

"Are you trying to con me out of this?"

Molly's eyes were locked on his hand.

"Joe, don't do that. You're encouraging bad behavior."

Ignoring his wife, he pitched the teensy morsel in the air. Molly snapped, knocking it on the floor. A second later it was gone.

"Awhh, come on, shouldn't we give her a little reward for alerting us to that aftershock?"

Rosa rolled her eyes and shook her head, "You two are a pair. If you won't listen to me, then listen to her. She wants you to stay home and pay attention to her."

Molly looked up at Jose with deep devotion. "Will you stop looking at me like that!" Molly ignored him and kept staring.

"There are plenty of subs down below who could pick up your route. Besides, you've got a gazillion hours of personal time that you haven't used yet, and the girls are off from school today. Let's make it a family day at home."

Jose could see that his dedication to Metrolink was not falling on receptive ears, "Fine. I'll go get my phone."

After breakfast, Jose and his four-legged, redheaded girlfriend went in the backyard to survey the damage from the quake. One of the outside panes of glass from a second story window had broken and was laying in pieces on the lawn. He retrieved the extension ladder from the garage and climbed up to more closely survey the damage. He knocked out the remaining shards with his bare hands while Molly dodged the falling debris. Suddenly, she broke out into another round of incessant barking.

"Didn't I tell you to shut your . . . whoa!"

Jose's ladder began to shudder then sway, scraping the tan stucco surface with its upper edges. He grabbed hold of the window frame and hung on, his feet still planted on the rungs.

"Honey! I need some help here!"

Rosa flew out the back door and ran toward the ladder arriving in time to prevent his fall. After fifteen seconds the tremor ceased.

"Joe, come on down. The window can wait."

Jose carefully dismounted the ladder, one step at a time, until his feet touched terra firma. He pulled Rosa to his side and gave her a big hug.

"Honey, you saved my life."

Rosa hung on to her husband and wouldn't let him go. From an upstairs window two teenaged girls watched and giggled.

Sixty miles to the west a man sat in a wood paneled room looking out at a forest of pines. The polycarbonate floor to ceiling windows remained unbroken in spite of the relentless parade of aftershocks that had shaken the A-frame chalet. A large flat-screen television was on in the living room while a generator whirred outside.

"And this just in to our news room, the USGS has confirmed yet another strong aftershock, this one measuring a magnitude 6.6. The epicenter was located just ten miles west of yesterday's main shock near the intersection of State Route 138 and County Road N2. Many of our viewers may not be familiar with this part of Los Angeles County, but there is a small lake nearby called Quail Lake, which is part of our California Aqueduct system. I can imagine that personnel already onsite will be checking for leaks as they have throughout the Antelope Valley since yesterday morning. It's also interesting to note that this area near Quail Lake is the proposed site for the planned community of Centennial. How this earthquake may impact the future of the project remains to be seen. The San Andreas Fault is certainly flexing its muscles."

"That's true, Tom," a female newscaster followed the male one, "This most recent aftershock comes on the heels of a 5.2 less than an hour ago. A 6.6 quake by itself would be considered a main event. You'll recall that the '94 Northridge quake was a 6.7, and I think we all remember how devastating that quake was, with over seventy people killed. The 5.9 Panorama City quake this past Sunday reminded us all how destructive earthquake faults can be in densely populated urban areas. Many cities in California have been built either directly on or near the San Andreas Fault. San Francisco, San Bernardino, and Palm Springs come to mind. Centennial may be the next. But you're right, it appears that the Fault has awakened from a deep sleep. When it will return to its slumber is anyone's guess."

Michael Stein pushed the mute button, walked into the kitchen, picked up the house phone, and dialed a number he retrieved from his cell phone.

"Dmitri?"

"Mr. Stein. You survived the earthquake?"

"Of course."

"We wondered what happened to you after the tunnel. Our assignment is to protect you 24/7."

"You and Andrei were most helpful in enabling me to elude the police. I must put in a good word for you with your superiors in Moscow."

"*Spasibo*, but where are you now?"

"In a safe place far from the prying eyes of the *ment*, as your countrymen are accustomed to calling them. No doubt their resources are consumed with the latest calamity and not on locating me."

"So, what can we do to help you, Mr. Stein?"

"There is a helicopter company located on the northeast end of the Van Nuys Airport. Ask for Mr. Mansfield, and give him these coordinates: 34.809564, 119.012481. I will be waiting for him at 16:00 today."

"Consider it done."

Stein hung up the phone and returned to the living room. He picked up a well-worn paperback copy of *Californios* and resumed reading while images flashed across the television screen.

Chapter 42

"YOU WERE RIGHT about your mother's cooking. Those little pizza boats were awesome!"

"You mean *pide*."

"Sorry, pide. I'll get it right. I really liked the one with the garlic and onions."

"I know, you're still wearing the scent," waving her hand in front of his mouth.

"Sorry."

"Doesn't your mother make them? I don't know the Armenian word."

"Come to think of it, my grandmother used to make something like it, but, it was round not elongated like a pide."

"Yes, we have that too. It's a very Middle Eastern dish." Alex recognized the sound emanating from his cell phone, but the ring tone seemed out of place.

"David, how's it going?"

"Real busy, as you can well imagine. And, how's your cousin Danny doing? Isn't his orchard near the epicenter?"

"Yeah, I talked to him yesterday. He's doing fine. I guess one of his old outbuildings lurched off its foundation, but nothing catastrophic. I'm sure he's already engineering some kind of repair."

"Are you okay, Lex, where've you been?"

"On vacation."

"Vacation? You mean you missed this last quake too?"

"Yep! I seem to have missed all the action."

"Hey, we need to talk with your friend, Kiraz."

"You mean my fiancé? No problem, she's sitting right next to me."

"Your fiancé! Where the hell are you?"

Alex looked out the left window of Kiraz's car at the sunlight shimmering on the azure waters of the Gulf of Izmit, "Driving along the coast. It's quite a nice view."

"Where, like Pismo Beach? You guys didn't go up to the Madonna Inn, did you?"

"Nope, we're on the O-4 Motorway heading back to her place after visiting her parents."

"You're in Turkey?!"

"That's right."

"Hey, we're on a Skype chat with the big bosses in Menlo. Kiraz's predictions have got them all in a buzz. When can you get back here for a meeting, like yesterday?"

Alex turned to his beloved, "Ready to go back to California? They need us, or at least you."

"I expected they would call."

"Is the day after tomorrow soon enough?"

"I guess we could e-mail you the plane tickets. Hold on a sec . . ."

"Okay."

A couple of minutes went by.

"Lex, how far are you from the Incirlik Air Base in Adana?"

"Let me find out, hold on," he turned to Kiraz, "Are we close to Adana?"

She pointed behind them, "Adana is the other direction."

"Is it far?"

"Uh-huh."

"Real far?"

"Half-way across the country."

"David, Kiraz says it's too far to drive."

"Okay, just a sec . . . I'm told there's a Turkish Airlines flight to Adana leaving Istanbul at nine o'clock tonight. Can you make that?"

"Why don't we just fly straight back from Istanbul?"

"No can do. While we've been talking they've mobilized a special flight for you on an Air Force jet. Flying commercial will take too long, and the regular civilian government jets are booked with congressional junkets."

"Wow, an Air Force jet! This sounds serious."

"You know how we feds are when there's a mission to accomplish. There are nearly infinite resources at their disposal, thanks to the taxpayers."

"Can we get to the airport in time for a nine o'clock flight?"

She looked at her watch that read 4:44, and said, "Sure, but we may need an angel or two to clear away the traffic."

"David, we can do it, provided this freeway we're on isn't the Istanbul version of the 405!"

"Good. The tickets will be waiting for you at the airport. And, by the way, congratulations! Have you guys set a date?"

"Soon, we hope, but with all this government interference, I dunno, but whenever the date comes, I'm gonna need a best man."

"You're on. See you soon, Lex."

"Later."

They drove for a few minutes until Alex spoke.

"Do you ever feel that in spite of your best efforts to choose what you want to do, like have a nice vacation along a sunny coastline with a pretty girl, that there's another force at work taking you somewhere else?"

"Frequently."

"You know the saying, 'go with the flow?'"

"I've heard that before. Perhaps we could go with the flow to a sunny coastline just like the one where I was only a few days ago holding hands with a handsome man."

Alex took her hand in his, "That can be arranged."

"You think so?"

"We've got friends in high places."

Chapter 43

"WHERE THE DEVIL is 34.809 . . . what was all that?"

The wiretap on Dmitri Somov's cell phone, courtesy of the Los Angeles County judicial system, and with the cooperation of Fortress Solutions, had yielded abundant fruit.

"34.809564, 119.012481. Let me punch that in, just a sec . . . it's at the intersection of Lockwood Valley Road and Forest Route 8N04."

"English, please!"

"About ten miles west of where we turned your Caddy around after the quake."

"Thank you, Detective Chin."

"You're welcome, Detective Jackson."

"What's the closest town to that location?"

"Lake of the Woods."

"What county?"

"It gets a little tricky up there. When I used to patrol the Gorman area we would often meet our neighboring county mounties for coffee over at the travel plaza on Frazier Mountain Park Road. Lake of the Woods is Kern County, but this spot looks like it's just into Ventura County."

"That Stein is a crafty son-of-a-bitch, dancing around the county lines."

"And he's ordered a chopper to go somewhere."

"Too bad all of ours are spoken for with the quake, and since the roads all jacked up, we can't exactly drive out there. Hell, it was all we could do to get back here to the station house in one piece. It's a good thing you knew the way around on those aqueduct roads or we'd still be sittin' out there staring at each other."

"What's a partner for other than to contribute to the cause?"

"You got any ideas how we can nab Stein now that we know where he'll be at four this afternoon?"

"I was thinking, how do you feel about employing the private sector?"

"What do you mean?"

"Well, with all the news choppers buzzing around the quake area, a well-placed call to one or more television stations saying there's a dangerous fugitive on the loose who's attempting to leave the country by way of helicopter from those coordinates would certainly evoke a response, don't you think?"

"Yeah, those eager beavers would be there in a flash, and put that video feed on the air for everyone to see."

"Including the fine officers of the Los Angeles County Sheriff's Department!"

"Bob, you actually may be craftier than Stein. You weren't a criminal in a past life, were you?"

"That's what my dear mother always said every time she'd uncover one of my plots to get my older brother in trouble."

"Did she beat your ass for it?"

"When she could catch me."

"You want to be the one to make the calls, since this was your brainchild?"

"You think we might get in trouble?"

"Nobody's tapping our phones."

"Point well taken."

"You call one, I'll call one."

"Like partners?"

"Partners."

The two inventive policemen sat in their office wondering to themselves if they had just joined the ranks of the criminal world, even if it was in the interest of apprehending one of LA's most elusive fugitives.

Chapter 44

Istanbul's ATATURK AIRPORT was crowded with travelers arriving and embarking on evening flights, including the two geologists who had been summoned to the United States. Alex and Kiraz arrived in the nick of time thanks to Ece's expert urban driving skills.

"I need to go the restroom. Back in a sec."

Kiraz nodded her acknowledgment from deep within her laptop. Alex trotted off to do his business, stopping briefly at a gift shop on the way back.

"I promised the guys back at the Bean Head that I'd send them a postcard from my vacation. I think this will get to them quicker if I just deliver it myself."

Kiraz glanced up at the postcard then back to her computer, "Who are these guys you're always talking about?"

"Jack and Hans, my Bean Head buddies."

"Bean Head buddies?"

"We've been drinking coffee together almost every morning for years. You'd like them. I'll introduce you when we get back to LA."

Kiraz rolled her eyes, "Okay."

Alex tucked the image of Hagia Sophia into his shirt pocket and leaned back in his seat taking in the view of his immediate surroundings. The enormity and importance of their mission was sinking in. David's call had an urgency attached to it that intruded like an unfamiliar amphetamine into his laid-back Southern California psyche. This was now serious business with Kiraz in the hot seat. He marveled at her capacity to deal with hyper geo-sensitivity and yet maintain her composure as a scientific professional. There was no denying her ability to discern future seismic events having already proven herself twice in a just a matter of days. Luck or chance certainly had nothing to do with it. It was a gift, a godsend to humanity, but one that was equally as much a curse to her *joie de vivre.*

He thought of his recurring dream of the three quakes and the shattered convenience store. Did he too have an intuitive side? Was this why they had been drawn together? His own past lectures on the unpredictability of earthquakes, and his mother's disdain for the Ottoman Turks, reverberated through the canyon of his mind. Now, these echoes of a former reality naturally dissipated as his attention returned to this gorgeous, brilliant dynamo of a woman sitting next to him, a woman he adored and with whom he wanted to spend the rest of life.

Boarding soon began for their flight from Gate 102. Most of the passengers were businessmen returning home to Adana from the day's work in Istanbul, hence even the U.S. government's best travel agents had not been able to book them seats together in business class. They settled in coach.

"How are you doing?"

"I'm fine."

"You were sure busy back there at the gate."

"I keep a log of my premonitions to track their accuracy. I thought this would be helpful when we meet with the U.S. Geological Survey."

"What, like a spreadsheet?"

"Yes, I chronicle the date, time of day, strength of the feeling in my body, and whatever information that comes to me about the magnitude, hypocenter, and timing."

"And the verdict?"

"Verdict?"

"How accurate are you?"

"So far, 93%."

"I think they'll hire you."

"You think so?"

"I know I would."

He took her hand in his as the Turkish Airlines 737 lifted off over the Sea of Marmara, the sun beginning to drift toward the horizon. Ninety minutes later they touched down in Adana, the sun firmly tucked away for the night. A US Airforce officer and an airwoman greeted them in the terminal.

"I'm Lieutenant Bowers. You must be Dr. Demurjian. Did I say that right?"

"Yeah, pretty good."

"And, Dr. Karahan?"

"Yes."

"Do you have any checked luggage?"

"Two bags."

"Airwoman Thomas will assist with them. Your claim checks?"

Alex handed her the stubs, "I don't mind carrying them."

"Sir, it's my pleasure to serve you."

"Sure, if you insist."

"Folks, we're in kind of a time crunch here. They're holding the plane for you. I'll go fetch the car and hopefully the local baggage handlers will be up to snuff tonight."

They were. The car pulled up to the curb just as Airwoman Thomas wheeled their bags behind her. Alex and Kiraz sat in the back, and Lieutenant Bowers navigated the car past the terminal building, around a traffic circle, and out of the airport. Within minutes they were cruising down Turban Cemal Beriker Boulevard, the main east-west thoroughfare through Adana. Alex's eyes were transfixed out the window.

"Too bad we're not here in the daytime. I kind of wanted to see my family's hometown."

Kiraz whispered in his ear, "We'll come back someday in my cute little car."

"Maybe we could stay there," pointing to the high rise Hotel Seyhan.

"That's a very classy place. I'm sorry to cut your visit to Adana so short. General Black has an appointment tomorrow morning at the Pentagon. You're flying with him to Dulles, then on to LA."

"Awesome, they're making the general wait for us!"

Airwoman Thomas giggled, then quickly stifled herself.

"Coming up ahead on the left is one of the largest mosques in the world."

Sabancı Merkez Camii gradually came into view; its 99-meter tall minarets resembled lit candles towering over the Adana skyline along the Seyhan River. Alex continued his nocturnal urban tour while Kiraz nudged closer to him and let out a long yawn.

"It's amazing how well that mosque has withstood the test of time and seismic activity. I mean, it looks brand new."

"That's because it is new. I was stationed here right after it opened for business in '98."

They crossed the river into the eastern side of Adana, inching closer toward their destination. Within minutes they passed through the security and onto Incirlik Air Base. A C-37B Gulfstream was parked on the tarmac in front of the hangar, an American flag painted on its tail, and the words "UNITED STATES OF AMERICA" across the top.

"Here's where we part, Doctors."

Airwoman Thomas quickly retrieved their bags from the trunk and handed them off to an airman who put them on the plane.

"It looks kind of small, like those puddle jumper regional jets back home," said Alex as he got out of the car.

"Don't let its looks fool you. This is the latest in executive jets. This baby can fly over six thousand miles without refueling.

You'll make it back to the US without a hitch. Heck, the President himself has been known to fly on this one from time to time."

"Like a mini Air Force One. Well, if it's good enough for him, I suppose we can give it a shot," Alex looked at Kiraz.

"You're too funny."

"Thanks for the lift, Lieutenant, and the tour of Adana."

"My pleasure, Doctor. Have a good flight."

Alex took their carry-on bags and motioned Kiraz up the foldout stairs onto the plane while he trailed behind. Seated toward the rear was General Randall H. Black reading a copy of *Air & Space Smithsonian*. Like their driver, the general was wearing a standard issue dark-blue Air Force uniform. His cap lay on a briefcase in the adjoining seat.

"Come on back here, there's plenty of room!"

"You must be General Black?"

"So, you're the two geologists California is depending on to save itself from being swallowed into the bowels of the earth?"

"No, just her," Alex pointed his head at Kiraz.

She extended a hand in greeting, "General, I'm Dr. Karahan, but please call me, Kiraz."

"Kiraz, *memnun oldum!*"

Alex shook his hand as well.

"Alex, Alex Demurjian."

"You're an Armenian?"

"American."

They settled into adjacent seats facing the general. Before long the flight attendant closed the front door and the plane's two engines began to whir indicating that their departure was imminent. The general put down his magazine and continued the cross-examination of his travel guests.

"Your surname is Armenian."

"It's pretty obvious, isn't it?"

"But, your accent is pure American. Glendale? Burbank?"

"Close. Hillhurst, but my parents own a business in Glendale. My mother's family actually came from right around here."

"Full circle then, isn't it?"

"Now that you mention it, you're right. I'm probably the first member of my family to return to Turkey in almost a hundred years . . . ninety-five to be exact."

"An Armenian-American and Turk sitting together in front of me, hand in hand. I never thought I'd see that in my lifetime."

"And, we're engaged too!"

Alex showed off Kiraz's engagement ring.

"Well, allow me to offer my congratulations!"

"We were in Izmit today visiting with my parents to tell them our news."

"Oh, my apologies, I guess we interrupted your holiday didn't we? If you don't mind my prying, how did that go?"

"They are very happy for us."

"That's good. Family support is so important to success in life and marriage."

"Alex, what about your folks?"

"We'll be talking with them when we get back, but I think they'll warm to the idea. They're both quite fond of Kiraz."

"By the way, I've been fully briefed on the reason for your trip," looking at Kiraz, "You really can predict when a quake will happen?"

"She's got a 93% rating."

"Then we better get you two to LA, ASAP!"

Chapter 45

"BREAKING NEWS OUT of the Tejon Pass! We've just received word that a fugitive wanted by police in connection with a murder investigation is attempting to flee capture using a helicopter. Our 'Eyes In The Skies' chopper covering the earthquake rescue effort is now in position over the area in question."

Detectives Julius Jackson and Robert Chin sat by the TV in the Palmdale Sheriff's Station break room tuned to a local news channel.

"Bingo, we got 'em!" Jackson pointed at the screen.

"I knew somebody would take the bait. Now all we have to do is see where he goes."

"Like shooting ducks in a barrel."

"Doesn't seem fair, does it? Stein's the sitting duck, pardon my pun."

"Bob, I think I'm going to like being partnered with you, until my retirement."

"Who knows, maybe you'll stay on longer and hang out with this upstart Chinese guy," pointing his thumbs back at himself.

"Maybe so, maybe so."

The clandestine surveillance ratcheted itself up as video of the spectacle was displayed on the screen for the first time.

"We can clearly see a helicopter sitting in a field near a ranch. Now there's someone riding on horseback across the field toward the helicopter. Let's see if we can zoom in closer . . . it appears to be a man wearing a black jacket and blue jeans."

Chin couldn't control himself, "Check it out, Stein's riding a horse!"

The reporter continued, "The man is dismounting, tying the horse to a fence. Now he's climbing aboard the helicopter."

"I see that. Who does he think he is, John Wayne?"

"John Wayne?"

Stein's helicopter took off and zoomed over Frazier Mountain heading southeast. Within minutes the two aerial vehicles, one shadowing the other from a thousand feet above, flew directly over Interstate 5.

"Whaddya think, Bob, is he heading back to LA?"

"I'm not so sure. He's gotta know that we're watching his plane in Van Nuys and his Russian goons."

The tandem of choppers continued to follow the freeway for another minute and then suddenly abandoned that route after passing by Gorman, maintaining a southeasterly bearing directly above the San Andreas Fault.

"That's not the way to LA, he's going to the mine!"

"I think you're right. Come on, Tonto, let's saddle up and bust this perp."

"Yeah, as long as I don't have to call you, Kemosabe."

"You're on!"

The two detectives gathered their jackets and firearms and beat it out of the station house into Jackson's white Cadillac. A sheriff's patrol car tagged along behind them southbound on the Sierra Highway, and then took a turn at Avenue R in the general direction of Stein Mining, Inc.

Jackson got on the radio, "Unit 36, approach Code 3."

"Roger that, Detective."

"I know we want to catch this asshole, but may I suggest we avoid arriving in a blaze of glory. What if we casually slipped into visitor's parking, and hold the cruiser in reserve in case things go awry?"

He looked appreciatively at his new partner then returned to the radio, "Cancel that Code 3. Pull into the landfill just ahead and await further instructions."

After navigating the twists and turns of City Ranch Road, they arrived at the entrance gate of the mine. When a uniformed security guard approached the car he rolled down the window.

"Gentlemen, how can we help you today?"

"We're state mining inspectors making an unscheduled visit to the mine. Please admit us promptly, we're on a tight schedule."

Jackson flashed his badge and quickly returned it to his jacket pocket.

The guard looked at his watch that read 4:17, "No one told us you were coming."

"That's why it's unscheduled."

"Oh, okay. I get it now. Go ahead, Inspector."

"Thank you."

He rolled up the window he eased the car through the gate across the compound and over to the visitor's parking area.

You call me, crafty. Mining inspectors? I don't think we even remotely look the part, especially driving this car?"

"He bought it."

"Yeah, but by now he's called the office announcing our arrival."

"Then let's not disappoint them. Shall we?"

They calmly exited the car and walked into the mine's main office. A blonde female receptionist nervously greeted them.

"Inspectors?"

"Jackson and Chin, California State Mining & Geology Board. How are you today?" looking at the name plate on her desk and the ring on her left hand, "Mrs. Ramos?"

"I'm fine."

"Could you call your manager? We need to check out some minor irregularities in his last report. It's just a formality."

"I'm sorry, but he's gone for the day. May I help you, or perhaps you could return tomorrow. I could set up an appointment?"

Chin laid into Jackson, "I told you we should've called ahead! Now we're going to be stuck in this crap hole of a town for another day. I don't think I can handle any more of your snoring!"

"Please forgive my partner's outburst. State budget cuts now require that we have to share a room together in budget motels. No offence about your wonderful city."

"Oh, that's quite all right. May I recommend the Super 8 on Palmdale Boulevard? My son, Ramon, is the night clerk. Perhaps he can put you in a room with the best beds. I'll give him a call if you'd like."

Jackson nodded, "That's very thoughtful of you. What do you think, Bob?"

"Is that the one near the In-N-Out? I think we passed it driving over here from Victorville."

"Yes, it's just a block over."

"Cool, I can do that."

Suddenly, the familiar sound of helicopter blades fanning the air could be heard through the windows. Jackson and Chin looked at each other and grinned. Julie Ramos was perplexed until she saw the face of the man exiting the aircraft. Stein assertively walked through the front door and immediately froze in his tracks upon seeing three familiar faces.

"Mr. Stein, we weren't expecting you today."

"Ahh, but we were!"

Detective Chin pulled out handcuffs and clamped them on his wrists, "It's the end of the road for you!"

"Michael Stein, you are under arrest for conspiracy, obstruction of justice, and evading arrest, not to mention several violations of the California Vehicle Code."

"You mean you're not mining inspectors?" she asked.

"Nope, not even amateur geologists."

"Julie, allow me to introduce Detective Jackson and Deputy . . . ?"

"Excuse me, that's Detective Chin."

"Hmm, Detective? I didn't recognize you in that new suit. I demand to see my lawyer."

"As is your right. Tonto, call the cruiser and have them pick up the prisoner. I don't want him stinking up the back seat of my Caddy."

"As you wish, Kemosabe," Chin pulled out his radio.

Flustered, Stein glared at Jackson's face, "I've got one question for you. How could you possibly have known I was coming here?"

"Let's just say, we had a little help from our friends. In fact, here come some of them right now."

Everyone looked out the windows as a second helicopter began to set down in the parking lot stirring up such a thick cloud of dust that it obscured its markings.

"Oh, some of your sheriff friends, I gather."

"Actually, no."

"CHP?"

"Nope."

Just then a reporter and cameraman came through the front door. Stein's eyes leapt out of their sockets.

Detective Jackson walked up to the reporter and shook his hand, "Thanks for the help."

Mystified by the appreciation, he said, "Sure, anytime."

Chapter 46

A SELECT TEAM of federal and state emergency management big wigs had been assembled in the California Emergency Management Agency's Southern Regional office in Los Alamitos, a stone's throw from Los Alamitos Army Airfield, the final destination of Alex and Kiraz's flight from Turkey. After bidding farewell to General Black at Dulles Airport, another six hours of flying time had awaited them. Although the creature comforts of the luxury jet had made the long flights quite bearable, the lack of sleep was beginning to take its toll on both of them. Alex sat quietly next to her while she fielded questions from her curious bureaucratic inquisitors.

"Dr. Karahan, do you continue to stand behind your prediction that a magnitude 9-plus earthquake is imminent along the southern San Andreas Fault, even in light of the recent Three Points quake?" asked Dr. Raymond Walker, Region IX Director of FEMA.

"That is correct. It will happen within the next week to ten days. The quake you mentioned was a foreshock."

"And, you have suggested that a subsequent tremor will occur along the Garlock fault?" added Leah Muñoz, Assistant Secretary of Planning, Protection and Preparedness for CAL-EMA.

"I am aware that the geological record of this fault shows little activity in modern history, but I must include it in this current premonition. I see the event happening within hours of the main shock. You might call it a double . . ."

"Whammy! We call that a double whammy," said Dr. Walker.

Dr. Lassandra Jeffries of the USGS pushed a topographical map of Southern California laid out across the table in Kiraz's direction.

"Can you pinpoint the epicenter of each quake?"

She rested her eyes momentarily.

"Dr. Karahan, are you all right?"

"We're both pretty blitzed from the flights we took to get here," Alex put his hand on her arm.

Kiraz opened her eyes and smiled at him, then turned her professional face toward her fellow seismologist.

"The stress on the Fort Tejon section of San Andreas Fault has been relieved somewhat by the 7.8 tremor, but this has consequently increased the stress on the Garlock fault. Look to this place for the epicenter," pointing to a virtually uninhabited spot in the Tehachapi Mountains roughly equidistant between Mojave and Frazier Park.

Dr. Jeffries nodded, "Very interesting. We've been monitoring several swarms of mirco-shocks along that fault since Three Points happened. You didn't know that, did you?"

"Not in a conventional manner."

David Horita joined in the conversation, "That's what I've been talking about! She can feel the faults creak. How? I haven't a clue."

"Have you assigned a magnitude to this event?"

"8.2, plus or minus 0.3."

"This mega-quake on the San Andreas Fault, what information can you provide about its location and magnitude?"

"This earthquake concerns me the most because it will happen in a populated area, and is the impetus for my agreeing to consult with you on such short notice. All of my life I have been reluctant to speak about my insights regarding future seismic activity for the obvious reason, it's not scientific, only 'intuition.' I could go about my life, do my job, and keep my insights to myself, but I overcame my reluctance in the company of some of you this past week. My own scientific self-observation and assessment of my past predictions demonstrates to me that I can no longer distrust what I am sensing. I must share it with those who can put the knowledge to constructive use. This quake can and will cause immense destruction beyond anything we've experienced in Turkey, possibly exceeding your 1906 quake. But, I know that many lives can be saved if preparations are made in advance of its coming."

The room became quiet as everyone's eyes and ears were trained on her next words, "Look to here for the epicenter," the tip of her finger landed atop Stein's mine in Palmdale.

"And the magnitude?"

"9.2, possibly higher."

"Jeezus Christ, that would make Hurricane Katrina look like a walk in the park!" Dr. Walker couldn't contain himself.

Mrs. Muñoz looked at her, "You're sure about this?"

"I wish I wasn't, but I must reaffirm what I have said," pointing back to the Antelope Valley, "this place is in great peril, as is all of Greater Los Angeles."

Alex made a mental note to warn Cousin Danny to take a vacation from the farm, even if the cherries were all ripening about now.

"I'm going to have to call the Secretary and discuss your prognostication further. We've never dealt with anything on a scale like this before. Do you realize that there are nearly a half-million people living around there? We can't exactly have all of them evacuated on a hunch, even a good one!"

"I have been thinking about this problem for many years, whether it's my country or yours, it makes no difference. The logistics of moving thousands of people away from a seismically active area is impractical. If I may make this suggestion: Alert the public that an impromptu earthquake safety drill will be held over the next two weeks for everyone living in the southern half of California. Ask people to assemble emergency preparedness kits including potable water, non-perishable food, portable lighting, and develop their own communication contingency plan in the event of a quake. Encourage the securing of all items that when hit by a shockwave would cause fire, flood, or injury."

"Water heaters!"

"Yes! And, strategically place relief workers in position near hazards like dams, rivers, and electrical lines that may fail so that people near them can be quickly moved out of danger. Creating a heightened awareness around earthquake safety will minimize casualties."

Kiraz thought of how she had failed the people of Kocaeli, Mehmet among them.

Dr. Walker assumed control of the meeting, "What a great idea! We can quickly mobilize and start moving emergency supplies in position as a part of this proposed drill. We already started bringing them in right after the Three Points hit. I'll call Edwards Air Force Base and get the ball rolling—that would make a good base of operations to work from. Hell, if nothing happens we're not out anything. If it does, we're one step ahead of the game."

"I have given you the specifics about these premonitions, and I am truly heartened by your response, but I implore you to avoid publicly announcing them. People will act out of fear and make the outcome much worse."

"You make another excellent point. There's no good that can come from inciting panic. Are we all agreed?"

"Yes."

"Dr. Karahan, we appreciate your coming all the way from Turkey. Would you be willing to remain in contact with us over the next couple weeks as a paid consultant? After all, you kind of started this business."

"Yes, I have time off from the Institute, and plan to be here in California for a while."

"The Institute?" Dr. Jeffries was puzzled.

"She means the Istanbul Seismological Institute, not Cal Tech. You ought to visit there some day," said Alex.

"Oh, okay."

Dr. Walker wrestled back the discussion, "That's quite a gesture on your part sticking around for all the action, Doctor. Naturally, the U.S. government will cover your expenses. We'll arrange for someone to handle your accommodations, transportation, and whatever else you need."

"That would be me."

"And, what was your name again?"

"Professor Alex Demurjian, from Cal State Northridge. I'm Dr. Karahan's—"

"Future husband!" Kiraz beamed as she completed in his sentence.

"Well, as soon as we can arrange for a wedding," looking at her with a gleam in his eye.

"Professor, you're hired to be her handler . . . and husband too. I'll need both of your cell numbers."

The meeting broke up into a flurry of phone activity, both the exchange and calling of numbers.

David asked them, "You guys need a ride somewhere?"

"My car is sitting over at LAX."

They walked out of the building to David's bright blue Subaru WRX, loaded their luggage, and sped out of the parking lot onto Lexington Drive. Soon they were westbound on Katella. The familiar landscape of urban LA quietly passed by until David spoke up.

"You want to get some breakfast? I'm starving. The seven o'clock meeting didn't give me much time to eat this morning. Besides, we might as well wait out the traffic. The freeways will be parking lots for a while."

Alex lazily stuck his arm forward from the back seat revealing his wristwatch. David noted the time, 6:35.

"That would be p.m., right?"

"Right."

"Dinnertime?"

"Correct."

David spotted a sign for a small strip mall. Among the listings was a Café del Sol, "How about this place? This isn't my neighborhood, but it might be worth a shot."

Alex retrieved his cell from his shirt pocket and scrolled through a few windows while David found a parking spot, "Yeah, this'll work fine."

Kiraz was nearly asleep from the twenty plus hours of traveling not to mention the government interrogation she'd just endured. Alex helped her out of the front seat and they walked hand in hand into the restaurant. Two uniformed policemen from the station house across the street were seated on the left. They found seats near them next to a bright yellow wall.

"Hey, Lex, I think this place was made for you. Look at all the photos of burgers," David pointed at the pictures hanging around the restaurant.

"Do you think they serve lunch now?"

Just then a waitress showed up at their table, "Coffees all around?"

"I'll have some."

"Not for me," Alex looked at her name badge, "Paola, could you bring me a Coke?"

She looked at her watch, "Sure, one coffee, one Coke, and for you, ma'am?"

"I would like a cup of tea, please."

"And one hot tea."

She handed them menus. After perusing Café del Sol's eclectic offerings, one that accentuated a distinct Mexican flavor, she returned with their drinks.

"And, what would you like to order?"

David was first, "I'll have two eggs scrambled, an order of chorizo, and sourdough toast."

"We'd like to split one of your bacon avocado cheeseburgers, if that's possible."

"For breakfast?"

"They just flew in from Turkey this morning."

"I'll see what the cook can do for you. How do you want it done?"

"Medium-well."

Kiraz closed her eyes and leaned against Alex's shoulder while he intensely surfed the Web on his phone.

"What are you looking for?"

"Marriage licenses. Would you believe they have an office on La Cienega right next to LAX?"

"No joke!"

"Yeah, and you can apply for one online and pick it up at the office. How convenient."

Kiraz opened her eyes and looked on while Alex navigated through the website.

"What do you think, my dear?"

Kiraz nodded her approval, "Yes, it sounds perfect."

For the next ten minutes they filled out the online application, Alex pausing to ask Kiraz pertinent questions about her date of birth, birthplace, parents' names, passport ID number, as dictated by the form.

"Now, that was pretty slick."

"I didn't realize it was so easy to get a license. Don't you two have to get a blood test?"

"Apparently not."

"Will we have our ceremony at the marriage office?"

"We can if we want to. It says here that it's only twenty-five dollars, but we can be married anywhere as long as the person performing the wedding is certified."

"Hamit and I were married in a civil ceremony at the marriage office. That's how it's done in Turkey."

David asked, "Really? You didn't have a religious ceremony?"

"No, our families were secular in their thinking, but most people observe Muslim traditions. Weddings can go on for days."

"So, what do your parents think of a Muslim marrying a Christian, and what about yours, Lex?"

"I haven't told my parents yet, but my father was very encouraging the last time I saw him. My mother, well . . . it depends what side of bed she got out on."

"In Turkey, Muslim women would rarely if ever marry a Christian, but since I'm divorced, some men would consider me less attractive."

"You've got to be joking. That's so medieval!"

"Not everyone in Turkey is backward. Yesterday, my parents gave us their blessing. My mother thinks Alex is quite charming."

"Wow! How cool is that? So, where do a Christian and Muslim get married in LA?"

Alex began searching the Web for ecumenical wedding ceremonies and then his face lit up.

"Did you know Cal's church does non-denominational weddings? It says here that Reverend Tucker has performed numerous interfaith ceremonies, Muslim-Hindu, Muslim-Christian, Muslim-Jewish, everyone."

"I liked Reverend Tucker. Why don't we call him?" Their food arrived almost as ordered.

"Sorry, we're out of fries. There's a shipment coming in later in the morning. Are hash browns okay?"

"Sure. They're like very, very thin french fries."

"Here's an extra plate."

Alex cut the burger right down the middle and put half of it on Kiraz's plate. As he began to divvy up the hash browns she stopped him.

"That's okay, you can have them all."

"Are you sure?"

"I'm sure."

"I just love watching you two interact. It's like you've been married for twenty years."

Alex and Kiraz looked at each other and laughed. Alex explained.

"That's exactly what General Black said before he got off the plane in Washington."

Everyone dove into their food like hungry lions devouring a freshly slain wildebeest. Soon the carnage was over.

"I could eat another one."

"Dude, you slayed that burger!"

Kiraz looked back and forth between them attempting to interpret the meaning of the last statement, and then joined in the discussion, "It was almost as good as a Double-Double."

Chapter 47

"MR. AND MRS. DEMURJIAN, over here!" a hand waved from across the room.

Alex and Kiraz approached the unofficial "herald" of the Bean Head carrying their freshly minted mochas and blueberry bagels.

"Hans, Jack, I hoped you'd be here this morning."

"Where else would we be this early on a Monday morning? You know I can't get through the day without a double-shot latte."

"Thanks for coming to our wedding, especially on such short notice. It meant a lot to me."

"We wouldn't have missed it for anything, kid," Jack stood up and offered Kiraz a chair, "Mrs. Demurjian."

"Thank you, Jack."

"Lex, we loved the reception food. In-N-Out burgers cut up into quarters and those garlic pizza boats were scrumptious. I can feel my arteries clogging just thinking about it."

"We wanted the occasion to be memorable. A little bit of Southern Californian and Turkish cuisine," Alex pulled up a chair.

"And the ceremony was a nice blending too, especially the way the pastor read verses from both the Bible and the Qu'ran. What was that other reading, the one that your best man read?"

"It was from *The Prophet,* by Kahlil Gibran."

"That name sounds Arabic. Is he a Muslim?"

"I'm not sure."

"Back in the 60s everybody had a copy of his book. I've heard that poem read at dozens of weddings," said Jack.

Alex looked at his phone, "Says here he was a Lebanese Maronite Christian poet and artist who lived in the US during the early 1900's. He was fluent in Arabic and English."

"He's the best known poet in the world."

"You're right, dear. It says that he's ranked only behind Shakespeare and Lao-tsu. Reverend Tucker told us before the ceremony that his writings are recognized by many religious faiths. Oh, I almost forgot," he took a postcard out of his shirt pocket and tossed it on the table, "as promised."

Hans picked up the card, "But, you didn't write anything on it."

"Sorry, I didn't have time. We were in a big hurry."

He handed it to Jack who looked at it more carefully.

"Very impressive architecture, but why the rush to get back here to LA? If I were you, I'd have spent at least a whole day looking around a place like this. It'd make a hell of a movie set. What is it, a mosque?"

Kiraz answered, "It once was, and before that a Christian church, but now it's a museum."

"What's it called? I can't read the fine print."

"Aya Sofya."

"Meaning?"

"I think it would translate into English as 'divine wisdom.'"

"Jack, you've seen it in the movies before. Think early James Bond."

"Okay, got it, *From Russia With Love,* the scene with Bond, the blonde, and the Bob Shaw character who kills the Russki agent."

"So, Lex, are you two going anywhere special for your honeymoon? I can't believe you'd spend it sitting around here drinking coffee with us."

"Maybe in a few weeks we might go to Hawaii, but for now we're sticking close to home. It's a work related issue."

"Come on, nobody works on their honeymoon! I thought you had the summer off. You two need a least a couple of romantic nights together, other than camping out in your little condo. What is it, some kind of geological crisis that keeps you here?"

"You could say that."

"Well, it couldn't be all that important. Why don't you get away somewhere nearby? I have a dear friend who's the manager of the Dreamer's Inn in Ventura. They've got some fantastic weekday rates. Let me give her a call."

"Ventura. Isn't that where we walked on the beach?"

"You've been there with Lex before? My, you two do get around. Istanbul, Ventura, I'm impressed."

"Yeah, we've been there, done that, got the —"

Kiraz stopped her husband in his verbal tracks, "It isn't too far away?"

"About an hour or so."

"That settles it!" Hans retrieved his cell phone, found the right number, and dialed, "Yes, may I speak with Deborah. Yes, I'll wait . . . Deb, it's Hans . . ."

"Let this be our little wedding gift, a couple of nights at the Dreamer's Inn. It's the least we can do for you."

"Jack, that's quite a generous gift. I don't know how I feel about accepting it."

"Lex, you're always doing things for your students, your parents, everyone. We love that about you. You're one of the nicest people we know. Trust me, after my years in the business, I can spot a phony from a mile away. So, let us donate this one little trifle."

"I don't know, Jack."

"Look, just say, thank you."

"Thank you, Jack," came the right words from Lex's wife.

"There you go!"

"Thanks, Deb, you're such a dear. Bye," Hans clicked off his phone, "Lex, you're booked in an oceanview jacuzzi room for the next two nights. Jack, did you tell him it's on us?"

"He's been a little resistant, but Kiraz convinced him to give in."

"Good. Lex, she's absolutely perfect for you. I don't know how it all happened, but he needs you, Kiraz. We've been badgering him for years to find a good mate, someone who could understand his unusual geological predisposition. We were about to give up until you came along. If you could've seen the look on his face when he mentioned you for the first time."

"Aren't you laying it on a little thick, Hans?"

"Hardly. Do you have any idea what a hardship case you are? How old are you, Lex?"

"Thirty-six . . . almost thirty-seven."

"Aeons in geological time!"

"Speaking of which, what's this situation you're monitoring?"

"Jack, there's going to be a huge earthquake."

"What, bigger than the last one?"

"Way bigger, and soon."

"How do you know when it's coming? Nobody can do that."

"Trust me, we know. We're experts."

"Hey, I believe you, I believe you!"

After breakfast, Alex and Kiraz walked back to their condo, holding hands the last block and a half. The morning fog was retreating toward the coast—birds were chirping in the trees that lined Finley Avenue. The idyllic nature of their stroll obscured the impending danger that lay beneath the earth's surface a mere fifty miles away. The Palmdale Bulge was ready to bust loose and there was no stopping it.

"I hope you didn't mind my telling them. My parents and Danny already know."

"At least it will not be a surprise to them when it does happen. My warning to the government was to not scare people. I don't think you frightened them."

"Hans can be a little jittery, but nothing fazes Jack. He's as solid as a block of granite."

"I like your friends. They really care about you."

"I appreciate your accepting their wedding gift. I didn't know what to say."

"That's what partners are for," she winked.

"I know Ventura isn't as exotic a honeymoon spot as Hawaii or Paris, or one of those swanky resorts we drove by along the Turkish coast, but it does have the beach and the Pacific Ocean going for it."

"It also has something else going for it."

"What's that?"

"You."

Chapter 48

NATURE KNOWS NO prejudice; plays no favorites, or as Jesus suggested, "for He makes His sun rise on the evil and on the good, and sends rain on the just and on the unjust." The Big One came as a shock to the oblivious, a confirmation to the alarmists, and sent those in the middle scrambling for safety.

Thursday morning in the Antelope Valley began in the usual fashion with the first wave of commuters up before dawn's light hurtling down the 14 Freeway toward their jobs "down below," as natives would say. Detective Jackson passed by thousands of them before he exited at Palmdale Boulevard on his way to the sheriff's station. His early morning caffeine fix was wearing off, a condition quickly remedied by a stop at Starbucks. As he walked back to his car, black coffee and muffin in hand, he suddenly lost his balance, nearly dropping his purchases on the parking lot. He wondered for a moment if his blood sugar had fallen too low, as had happened before. He continued to have trouble steadying himself. Then it hit him what was really happening. Across the street the windows of Sterlings Furniture began to rattle, fall, and shatter on the sidewalk. A second later he was knocked squarely on his butt, his coffee and muffin now decorating the blacktop.

Customers began spilling out of the coffee shop in full flight, many of them landing on the pavement in similar fashion. Tiles shot off of the roof like exploding shrapnel, knocking a fleeing woman unconscious. Jackson tried to pick himself up to render aid, but the unrelenting rippling of the earth's surface prevented his efforts. Helplessness was not a feeling he often experienced.

Like everyone else, all he could do was surrender to the seismic rollercoaster until the end of the ride. And, it was a long ride.

At no other time in the recorded history of the Golden State had the earth shaken with such ferocity and long duration. The San Andreas Fault ground together for over two minutes pitching most of the fifteen plus million inhabitants of Greater Los Angeles against their bedroom walls, including a couple of newlyweds tucked away in their hotel room eighty miles to the west. The second story of the Dreamer's Inn shook like a wet dog after a swim in a lake, its wooden frame groaning with each wave of energy. The initial force of the quake tossed Kiraz across the king size bed toward Alex.

"It's happening, isn't it?"

"Yes, hold me!"

He did until the tremors finally ceased. Shaking, they both let out of a deep sigh of relief. They were alive.

"Don't let go!"

"I won't, I promise, but at some point today could we go to the bathroom before the next fault cuts loose? Maybe get some breakfast?"

"Yes, my dear."

"At least we didn't miss this quake. I was beginning to wonder after the last two. I don't think I could've handled any more of David's ridicule. I mean, it's just not right for a geologist to be gone for major seismic events, now is it?"

"I can't think of anyone I'd rather spend an earthquake with than you."

He pulled her even closer, "Me either, now how about some breakfast, Doctor?"

"Yes, Professor."

Meanwhile, back in the Antelope Valley, the Martinez family had survived the devastation, and was now bivouacked in their backyard. Martha and Maria sat on plastic chairs attempting to text their friends. Rosa was cooking breakfast on a portable camp stove, while Jose had perched himself on an upside down five-gallon paint bucket examining the damage to his house. Significant cracks in the stucco were obvious, as were several broken windows, but the house remained standing in spite of the force exerted on it by the 9.3 magnitude quake, its epicenter a mere mile away.

A piece of fence, loosened by the quake, suddenly began to rattle back and forth as the Garlock Fault answered its big sister, the San Andreas. The girls screamed. Rosa ran to Jose. This time the earth shook for nearly a minute until the fence crashed to the ground exposing the greater outdoors.

Jose looked at Molly, "Go on, run, that's what you want!" Molly walked over to him and began to whimper, first licking his hands, then his face. They embraced.

"You stupid mutt, you missed your chance."

Then, unexpectedly, she jumped back and looked him in the eyes. Hers twitched.

"Now what?"

Off she bolted.

Somewhere in the Mojave Desert there's a lost Irish Setter running loose through no fault of its own.

Author's Notes

I'VE HAD A FASCINATION with geology since I threw my first skipping stone atop the surface of Lake Michigan near my early childhood home of Dune Acres, Indiana. At age ten we moved to Honolulu, Hawai'i, a dynamic location for any fledgling geology buff given its volcanic heritage. Over the years I've gobbled up books on the subject, and like many people, frequently brought home rocks from places I've visited. The rock garden near my writer's studio can testify to this obsession—basalt from eastern Washington, white granite from California's Sierra Nevada mountains, red sandstone from the Alsace region of France, dark gray shale from the wooded hills of Luxembourg, and skipping stones from the beach of my childhood. They're all there with other displaced geo-orphans, arranged directionally in a circle.

From 1986–92 I served as a minister in the Los Angeles area, specifically, Unity Church of the Valley in La Crescenta. It was here that I became directly familiar with seismology. Up to that point my only experience of an earthquake was in 1973 when a 6.5 magnitude tremor hit the Big Island of Hawai'i. I recall it rocked the lockers on each side of the main hallway in Cooke Hall on the Punahou School campus rather vigorously.

In LA, I continued my earthquake experience with the 1987 Whittier Narrows Quake, or didn't. While driving my wife to work at Occidental College the quake struck. We were probably somewhere around Lake View Terrace when it hit, but it's hard to feel a quake when you're sailing down the freeway at seventy miles per hour. I dropped her off at the college and drove back up to the church. When I arrived, there were people standing in the parking lot acting rather strangely outside their cars. I went into my office, sat down, and the phone rang. It was Donna saying, "Guess, what just happened?" Right then my desk jumped like somebody was shaking it. I replied, "An earthquake?"

My most memorable seismic event was the 1992 Landers quake. We were living in Palmdale when it hit at around five o'clock on a Sunday morning. I normally got up early on Sundays to polish my sermon, and prepare for the big commute down below to the church. This wakeup call lasted over a minute. I remember the house creaking a lot. And, to make sure I hadn't hit the snooze button, there was another quake in Big Bear three hours later that felt nearly as strong, but thankfully was not as long.

The morning news said that people would certainly be going to church that morning. They couldn't have been more wrong. It was the worst church attendance I had seen in my nearly six years as the minister. People had been warned to stay off the freeways, which gave them a valid reason to stay home from services. Upon learning of this alert, we drove the nearly sixty miles home avoiding the freeways—down Foothill Boulevard and up the Sierra Highway back to the Antelope Valley. It was definitely one of those slow Sunday country drives we all talk about taking sometime.

It was also during my time in LA that I became acquainted with a people with whom I had little familiarity, Armenians. Growing up in multicultural Hawai'i gave me an appreciation for the variety of cultures that make up the United States, but Armenians were a mystery to me. At that point the only ones that I'd heard of were the former California governor, George Deukmejian, and Dr. Jack Kevorkian, but that was about to change.

The church is located in the part of La Crescenta encompassed by the City of Glendale. I eventually discovered that the greater Burbank-Glendale area was home to thousands of Armenians, many of them recent arrivals from the former Soviet Union. One day, I asked our church's board president, who was also the president of the

Glendale Chamber of Commerce, what the chamber had in mind with regard to the growing Armenian business community. His response, "We've invited them to come to one of our meetings and tell us what they plan to do." I recall praying for a way to reach Armenians with the services of our church knowing that it was highly unlikely that they would simply walk through the front doors on a Sunday morning. Most Armenians belong to the Armenian Apostolic Church, one of the first in Christendom. Soon my prayers were answered.

Two men came to our door and explained to me that their Armenian-language AA meeting had outgrown their current location and that they were looking for a larger hall to rent. They had heard about a big multi-purpose room that we rented to other 12-step groups. Within a week they began holding their meetings in this room. These men educated me about the complexity of Armenians. I learned that not all had immigrated to the US from the Republic of Armenia. Many had come from diasporic communities located in Iraq, Iran, and Lebanon. Understanding this heritage not only helped explain their use of many languages (in addition to Armenian, namely, Arabic, Farsi, and Russian), but also subtle cultural nuances.

One day, a young Armenian couple showed up at the church responding to our advertisement for non-denominational weddings. I agreed to perform their ceremony, but asked them why they had come to our church instead of the large Armenian church in Glendale. They said that their respective families were not getting along and they had decided, "the heck with it, let's elope!" One family was from Iran, and the other from Iraq. I said to them, "How American of you to just go off and get married!"

My last encounter with Armenians was less pleasant. I was preparing to teach a mid-week class on meditation when two members of the church came rushing into my office telling me that teenage gang members were tagging the outside wall of the church. I walked around to investigate and came upon several young men admiring their "artwork." After an exchange of words I left them and went inside to call the police. I went back outside on the opposite side of the church to wait for the police to arrive when five of them walked up to confront me. The tall one leading the pack, and wearing a San Francisco Giants baseball cap, began pointing in my face and saying words that I can't repeat here. I was beside myself. Then out of nowhere an idea popped in my head, and I responded with my best Austrian accent, "You don't want to find out what I'm about tonight!"

I don't know what Arnold Schwarzennegger would've thought of my mimicking him, but it worked. The kid backed off. Seconds later, two Glendale police cars came flying up the driveway. There was no escape for these guys. They actually wanted to be caught! Apparently a police record was a rite of passage for these aspiring gang wannabes. I also found out that the tall one who challenged me was Armenian, as were most of his friends. Two weeks later I heard that he was beat up in front of the nearby convenience store for harassing someone else's girlfriend. That was my introduction to AP = Armenian Power.

I share these stories to help explain some of the impetus for this book. I'm not Armenian, nor Turkish. I'm an American of Swedish, German, and British descent. When I mentioned to someone that I was writing a book that included Armenian and Turkish characters, they commented that I was taking on a rather daunting task. I realize that there are still strong feelings and perspectives among both groups with regard to their shared history, and I sincerely hope that I've done my best to treat each of these with respect in this book.

My intention in telling this story is to suggest that reconciliation, healing, and transcendence of history is not only possible, but also absolutely crucial to humanity's spiritual progress. This is true of all individuals, groups, and nations. No one is exempt. The grudges and perceived injustices of the past must be overcome. This doesn't mean sweeping them under the rug, but getting the issues out in the open, and then having the maturity and sense to refrain from perpetuating their continuance. Mahatma Gandhi is known to have said, "We must become the change we wish to see in the world." As a fiction writer, especially if we're advocating significant change, then our characters must demonstrate such a transformation of consciousness. My prayer is that Alex Demurjian and Kiraz Karahan have done that for you.

About The Author

ALDEN STUDEBAKER IS an author and minister. He is the author of *Wisdom for a Lifetime in the 21st Century*—How to Get the Bible Off the Shelf and Into Your Hands, a Bible handbook for progressive minded Christians. He is also the author of *The Grid,* a novel set in the electric power business, and the comedic book, *Hoosieritis – The Contagious Condition That Is Indiana.* He has a degree in religion from Western Michigan University.

For further information log onto:
www.aldenstudebaker.com.

Molly and me on "The Bulge" circa 1987.

.